Levi began to twist alarmingly in his ropes

Annja reached up and grabbed his right boot to stabilize him. Whether the experience unnerved him or not, he didn't continue the conversation. That suited Annja fine.

In the early afternoon the storm clouds returned with a suddenness that halfway tempted Annja to believe in Levi's dueling mountain deities. At almost the same moment a soft cry came from above and Annja looked up to see Larry's head silhouetted against the ominous boiling clouds. She could tell he was grinning.

Less than five minutes later Levi and Larry were helping her scramble onto the top of a gently sloping plain of ice, pierced by snow-mounded juts of rock. A mile and a half ahead of her rose the snow-covered peak of Ararat. And there, a quarter mile away to the south and west of them, the long, dark mound of the Ararat Anomaly seemed to hang over the edge of the abyss.

Titles in this series:

ROGUE Angel

Alex Archer

PARADOX

A GOLD EAGLE BOOK FROM

W RLDWIDE®

TORONTO • NEW YORK • LONDON
AMSTERDAM • PARIS • SYDNEY • HAMBURG
STOCKHOLM • ATHENS • TOKYO • MILAN
MADRID • WARSAW • BUDAPEST • AUCKLAND

Recycling programs
for this product may
not exist in your area.

First edition November 2009

ISBN-13: 978-0-373-62139-2

PARADOX

Special thanks and acknowledgment to
Victor Milán for his contribution to this work.

Printed in U.S.A.

The
LEGEND

...THE ENGLISH COMMANDER TOOK
JOAN'S SWORD AND RAISED IT HIGH.

The broadsword, plain and unadorned,
gleamed in the firelight. He put the tip against
the ground and his foot at the center of the blade.
The broadsword shattered, fragments falling
into the mud. The crowd surged forward,
peasant and soldier, and snatched the shards
from the trampled mud. The commander tossed
the hilt deep into the crowd.
Smoke almost obscured Joan, but she continued
praying till the end, until finally the flames climbed
her body and she sagged against the restraints.

Joan of Arc died that fateful day in France,
but her legend and sword are reborn....

1

"Such exquisite form," Roux said. He glided to a stop easily on the ice of the outdoor skating rink. "You make falling upon your wonderfully sculpted posterior a balletic act. Pure poetry." He kissed his kid-gloved fingertips.

"How about a hand, here?" Annja Creed asked. She sat like an abandoned rag doll with her mittened hands on the ice and her legs stuck out in front of her.

She regretted the request at once. The slim old man with the bright blue eyes and the carefully trimmed white beard began to clap slowly.

Seeing her expression start to resemble gathering thunderheads he desisted and extended an arm. All around them cheerful skaters passed by emitting dragon puffs of condensed breath against a black night sky from which the bright multicolored rink lights banished stars. She fought the impression they were laughing at her.

With the help of Roux's strength, surprising in a man his apparent age, she found herself back upright with her feet beneath her. Temporarily, anyway. She teetered, the blades of the rental skates strapped none too comfortably to her feet that slipped back and forth over the ice. Roux held her by the arm, steadying her.

"Where is your vaunted sense of balance, which you have supposedly gained through rigorous study of your black arts?" he asked.

"Martial arts," she said. " And the problem isn't lack of balance. It's lack of *friction*."

"If you say so. Now, pay attention. The principle is simplicity itself. When you go with the direction of the blades, you move without effort. If you press at an angle to the blade, you push. You see?"

Annja did. She was starting to. Sort of. She made herself draw deep breaths to the diaphragm, calming, centering herself. You can keep your head while people are shooting at you, she reminded herself sternly. So you can keep your head while doing something little children do effortlessly.

The fact was, she was determined not to let this get the better of her. She wasn't in the habit of backing away from challenges. It made her curse Roux all the more for talking her into this despite her reservations.

As she propelled herself forward a skinny septuagenarian a head shorter than Annja easily passed her by. Not a yard ahead of her a tiny girl, elfin face bracketed by enormous white puffy earmuffs, skated fearlessly backward.

Annja sighed. "I thought the Quays of the Old Port Skating Rink didn't open until December."

The outdoor rink was in the old St. Lawrence River dockside district appended to Montreal's downtown. Like every other run-down waterfront in every other major North

American city, it had been renovated and gentrified at enormous expense sometime in the last quarter-century. Now the skaters glided and chattered to saucy French techno-pop before the broad, benign domed edifice of the Marché Bonsecours, the old market that once housed City Hall.

"Customarily it does not open so early," Roux said, tipping his hat to a passing pair of handsome middle-aged women. "But the winter has come early to Montreal, as you can see. This global warming, it fails again to materialize, it seems."

He shook his head. "I do not understand you moderns and your superstitions. Even should the good Earth be warming, why is that bad? I lived through five centuries of what your scientists now call the Little Ice Age. Including times in which it lessened. In the times it grew cooler again, the people suffered, grew sicker and poorer. Crops failed. And whenever the weather grew warmer, prosperity and happiness returned."

She said nothing. From her own detailed knowledge of history, especially European history, she knew her mentor was right about the previous effects of climate warming.

She also knew he wasn't kidding about having experienced it for himself. What was worse, he wasn't even delusional.

"All right," she said to her companion as they picked up speed. She was finding a certain degree of control. She learned things quickly, physical or mental. "You've brought me here. You've established your dominance by ritually humiliating me. What's so urgent that you had to see me?"

"What else but the offer of a job? At a fee most welcome, given the sadly depleted state of our exchequer," Roux said.

Annja knew Roux was fabulously wealthy but he loved to cry poor. However, she also knew for a fact that their occasional joint covert enterprises, while tending to command high fees, were phenomenally expensive. For one thing she burned through all-but-bulletproof fake identities, with attendant documentation, the way some people smoked cigarettes. Even with volume discounts, the requisite quality was costly.

"Then give," she said. The old man loved to hear himself speak and would ramble all night, or possibly for days, if she didn't occasionally boot him back in the general direction of the subject at hand. The trouble was, he was highly entertaining to listen to. Being a raconteur was another skill he'd had a long, long time to develop.

He clucked and shook his head. "You moderns have no sensibility of the rhythms of life. Everything is always 'hurry-hurry-hurry.'"

"You got that right, old man," Annja said with a grin.

Roux sighed. "A consortium of wealthy American Protestant fundamentalists are organizing an expedition to examine the so-called Ararat Anomaly, believed by many to be Noah's Ark. They wish you to come along and direct excavation and preservation."

"No," Annja said without hesitation.

His fine brow creased in a frown. "Why must you always make things so difficult, child?"

" You're trying to hook me up with a bunch of Biblical literalists? They're like the archenemies of anthropologists and archaeologists."

"Why must you be so dogmatic? You really should be more open-minded."

"The Ararat Anomaly is a total crock. The mountain's

sixteen thousand feet high, for God's sake! How does a flood plant something up there?"

"It is, in fact, Turkey's highest mountain at 5,137 meters. Or 16,854 feet, as you Americans would say. I'm with you, by the way—the metric system was another unlovely conceit of the French Revolution. We might as well have kept their ridiculous calendar, with its ten-day weeks and its months with names like Heat and Fog!"

"Okay. Almost seventeen thousand feet, then. Thanks for making my point for me."

"But what of the photographic evidence? The Ararat Anomaly has repeatedly been photographed by surveillance aircraft and satellites. Some analysts claim it resembles the Biblical description of Noah's Ark."

"It's just a natural formation."

"Ah, but do you know that for a fact? How? Is this your science, to determine truth by decree like His Holiness the Pope? You've not been there. No one has, for very long. No expedition has ever succeeded in examining it in detail."

"Of course they haven't," Annja said. "The Turkish government won't let anyone in because of trouble with the Kurds. And with the fighting between the Turks and the Kurds continuing the way it is, the Turks are especially unlikely to let anyone in now."

"Just so. Yet the expedition sponsors and organizers, who I assure you are serious men who are not to be taken lightly, believe they have a way to get to the mountain and climb it with ample time to perform at least a site survey and preliminary excavation."

"You mean go in illegally, don't you?" she asked.

"It's not as if you are a stranger to that sort of thing, Annja dear."

She shrugged. The motion momentarily unbalanced her. She felt proud that she managed to right herself without clutching at Roux. He had them skating in a circuit about the rink's long oval now. She noticed he also kept them clear of the rail, most likely to prevent her grabbing it and vaulting to solid ground. Or ground with friction, anyway.

Roux had declared himself her mentor when she first came into possession of Joan of Arc's sword through some kind of power she did not fully comprehend. Even now she didn't really know what that meant. The sword traveled with her in another plane and was usually available to her in times of trouble. She could call it to her hands by willing it there if conditions warranted it. It was a privilege and a burden at the same time and Roux, who claimed to have been Joan's one-time protector, came along as part of the deal. He was always pressing her, pushing her to extend her boundaries, challenge herself.

For the most part Roux seemed content to play business manager for her unorthodox archaeological services. She knew, though, that he had an agenda entirely his own. And she had no real clue as to what it was.

"Where is your dedication to the scientific method?" he asked. "Where's the spirit of scientific inquiry? Where, even, simple human curiosity? Absent investigation, child, how can you be so sure what it is or is not?"

"Well," she said, "I mean, how likely is it?"

"My principals claim to have in their possession relics recovered from the site. Allegedly these substantiate that it is, at the very least, artificial in origin."

His gloved hands gestured grandiosely. Other skaters glanced their way and giggled. But it didn't disturb his balance in the slightest. In fact he skated with the same ease with which a dolphin swam. He's had a lot of time to practice this, too, Annja reminded herself

"Think, Annja!" he exclaimed. "Even if it doesn't happen to be the Ark, would not a man-made structure atop the mountain be a magnificent archaeological find? Would it not also be in dire need of professional preservation? And also, the Americans offer quite a handsome fee."

"There's that."

"You won't even have to organize matters, nor run the expedition. That burden is borne by others. You'll be there purely as chief archaeologist."

She sighed. Roux could be devilishly persuasive.

He was right about one weakness of hers in particular. Science and the scientific method were very important to her, as was the spirit of scientific inquiry. But mostly, she was as curious as the proverbial cat.

"All right, you old renegade," she said. "You've got me wondering just what is on top of that stupid mountain. I'll agree to hear them out."

"Splendid."

"I'm not promising anything else," she said, shaking her head so emphatically she blew her balance again and had to windmill her arms frantically. Her legs in their black tights slid right out in front if her. She landed on her tailbone with an impact that shot sparks up her spine to explode like fireworks in her brain.

Roux blinked down at her. "Try to contain your excitement, child. People stare."

Grumbling, she allowed him to help her up once more with his surprising strength of grip and arm.

"Besides," Roux said as she came back onto her skates,

a little tentatively. "I can't dally here with you forever, delightful as your company always is. I've got other projects to attend to. I'll set up a meeting and will be in touch." He skated away from her with great speed.

"Roux!" Annja called out to him as he disappeared. Once again she was left wondering what she was getting herself into.

2

"If you'd please follow me, miss?" The maître d' was a soft-spoken, light-skinned black man, tall and slender in his white shirt and black trousers, with hair cut short.

The establishment was called, simply, the Penthouse. Its decor was as spare as its name: dark stained oak wainscoting beneath ivory wallpaper, muted chrome accents and crystal lighting. The tablecloths gleamed immaculate white; the only touches of color in the room were the long-stemmed roses—the color of fresh-spilled blood—set on each table in narrow vases.

The real interior decoration was all *exterior*—the glory of midtown Manhattan by night.

Four men sat at a table with an empty chair, right by one window-wall with lights glimmering in it like a galaxy's worth of stars. The oldest man, and largest in every dimension, pushed back his chair as Annja approached behind the quietly respectful maître d'.

"Ms. Creed," he said in a voice that boomed above the

discreet murmur of conversation, the tinkle of silver on porcelain and ice in crystal. "How good of you to join us. I'm Charles Bostitch. Please call me Charlie."

He wore an obviously expensive but somewhat rumpled brown suit with a brown string tie and an expression of jovial indifference to the stares of the other diners on his big, florid fleshy face. His hair was brown and graying at the temples; it looked natural to Annja, not that she was any judge. Seams of his well-rumpled face, exaggerated by his big grin, almost concealed his brown eyes.

As she approached she realized he was very tall. He towered over her, which was rare: he had to be six-four or thereabouts, probably crowding three hundred pounds. He had the look of a former star college quarterback who hadn't quite had the NFL stuff, and whose career and physique had begun their downhill slide about the same time as graduation and continued until his fifties.

He was a billionaire who had made his money the old-fashioned way—inherited it from his Oklahoma oilman daddy. But, according to the information Roux had given to Annja, he had more than doubled the family fortune despite frequent bouts with expensive bad habits. He'd supposedly cleaned himself up and was now a vigorous proponent of muscular right-wing Christianity.

Bostitch's handshake was firm and dry and all-enveloping. Annja could feel at once how he could over-power most people without consciously trying. But Annja was not most people and she was hard to intimidate.

"It's an honor to meet you at last, Ms. Creed," he boomed. Two of the other men at the table had risen politely. The third sat hunched over and peered myopically at an electronic reader.

"Please allow me to introduce my good friend and associate, Leif Baron."

"A pleasure." Baron smiled and nodded. The smile didn't reach his gray eyes. He was Annja's height. He had the broad shoulders that tapered through well-developed trapezoid muscles and thick neck to the almost pointed-looking crown of his shaven head of an aging but still formidable mixed martial arts prizefighter. His suit was expensively tailored to a form as compulsively fit as Bostitch's was sloppy, his tie muted. She could feel the callus on his trigger finger when she shook his hand. The guy was ex-military, she had no doubt.

"And this is my aide-de-camp, if you'll pardon my French, Larry Taitt."

This was a jockish bunch, Annja thought. Taitt was a gangly brown-haired man who was not quite tall enough for basketball and not quite burly enough for football. Maybe baseball was his game in college. Or, she couldn't help thinking, high school; he *looked* seventeen, despite the ultraconservative dark suit and tie, even though he must have been in his early twenties at least.

"It's great to meet you, ma'am," he said, big floppy-dog amiability warring with painfully proper upbringing.

He worked her hand like a pump handle until his boss dryly said, "You can let go anytime now, Larry." He dropped her hand and blushed.

"And you'll have to excuse the rabbi," Bostitch said pointedly. "He couldn't bring any real books to bury his nose in, so he's settling for second best."

"Oh," the fourth man said. "Please forgive me. I was just catching up on the latest digest from *Biblical Archaeology Online*. I got engrossed and forgot my manners."

Momentarily he got crossed up as to which hand he was going to shake Annja's with, and which he was going to use to straighten his yarmulke, which had begun to stray from the crown of his head of curly brown, somewhat scraggly hair. He had an ascetic's face, bone-thin and pale olive, a disorderly beard and brown eyes that looked enormous behind round lenses so thick he should have been able to see the rings of Saturn with them. He looked to be in his early to mid-thirties. Finally sorting the unfamiliar mundane details out, he shook Annja's hand as eagerly as Taitt had, if with a far less authoritative grip.

"I'm Rabbi Leibowitz," he said. "It's wonderful to meet you. I'm a big fan."

"Thanks," Annja said with a thin smile as Bostitch pulled out her chair. She sat. She was secure enough in her own strength of character not to resent what others would probably take as a male-chauvinist gesture. Even if, considering the source, it probably was one.

"You may or may not have heard of me before," Bostitch said, seating himself. "What really matters is that I'm a rich guy who finally got serious and accepted Jesus Christ as his personal Lord and Savior kinda late in the game. And I'm dedicated to proving the exact, literal truth of the Bible to help save a skeptical world."

Annja looked at him over the top of the menu. "Not just *the truth,* then."

He laughed. He seemed to do that easily. "Of course I'm interested in the truth, Ms. Creed. I say we go take a look and let the chips fall where they may."

He leaned forward. "In this case, though, I'm pretty confident what we're going to find will confirm the Book of Genesis. And blow the world away."

Annja glanced at the rabbi. He was lost in his reading again. Annja wondered what his role was in the expedition.

"We'll see," she said.

"Let me tell you a little bit about myself and my associates," Bostitch said. "I inherited a bit of money from my dear old daddy. I did the college thing, majored in partying. Got serious enough to get my MBA and come back to the family business, which was mostly oil. We expanded into agribusiness and, eventually, into defense.

"I was a pretty wild colt as a young man, Ms. Creed. Until, as I said, I was saved. Since then I've been mindful of giving back. I founded and fund the Rehoboam Christian Leadership Academy for young men in Virginia, near Quantico."

He nodded to Baron, who sat to his right. "Mr. Baron here came through that program. That's how we met. After he went through he consented to become a volunteer instructor. Leif was quite a bit older than our usual students, actually—he'd served as a Navy SEAL and then built his own security firm into quite a successful operation."

"Security?" Annja asked.

"Private security contracting, Ms. Creed," Baron said. "I own China Grove Consultants."

"Oh. Mercenaries," Annja said, nodding.

He smiled humorlessly. "That's not a term we're particularly fond of. In fact we've devoted a substantial amount of money to lobbying the UN to closely regulate the international private security and private defense contracting business. We'd like to see the UN move away from their conventional Blue Helmet peacekeepers, who tend to be brave but ineffectual, to contracting with private agencies to conduct peacekeeping operations."

"And you'd be the contractor, I'm guessing?" Annja asked.

He shrugged his massive shoulders. "We'd be there bidding along with the others. And we do a good job. At a lower cost to our principals than conventional military forces."

"Leif's taken a leave of absence in order to help with our expedition," Bostitch said. "He's our organizer and expediter. He'll run the show on the expedition. And Larry, here, went through the academy. He was a star pupil and I decided to take him under my wing, once he got his law degree."

Larry grinned and bobbed his head. "It's a real honor," his said, "getting to work with such great men and great Christians as Mr. Bostitch and Mr. Baron."

Annja couldn't help but like the enthusiastic young man.

"And Rabbi Leibowitz is a rising star at the Israeli Archaeological Institute," Bostitch added. The man in question looked up, blinked, grinned shyly and promptly went back to his reading. Annja had known some compulsive readers in her life—she came close at times—but the rabbi definitely took best in show.

Their waiter arrived and asked her for her order first.

"How rare is your prime rib?" she asked.

"Almost bleeding, ma'am."

"Great. I'll take the sixteen-ounce cut with the rice pilaf and steamed broccoli. Tossed salad with vinaigrette, no croutons. And iced tea and ice water, please." She thought about ordering wine to see if it put her hosts off balance. But she was no wine connoisseur, any more than she was a consistent drinker of any sort.

Nor did she want to risk diminishing her capacity even a little bit. It was definitely a temptation to a person of her scientific background to dismiss them all as religion-addled halfwits, especially Bostitch with his slathered-on hick accent and goofy good-old-boy manner. But Bostitch was an extremely successful businessman.

And although she had known some Navy SEALs who, while good-natured and in certain ways frighteningly competent, were not too bright, she didn't have Baron sized up that way, either. While a lot of fairly random and even wacky types had prospered in the general rain of soup that had fallen on the defense and security industries after 9/11, she knew the mercenary business, whatever euphemism it operated under, was literally a cutthroat business. She'd heard of China Grove, as it happened; their reputation wasn't too savory. If anything, they tended to be a bit too good at what they did. Leif Baron was not a man to be taken lightly.

"I guess you don't worry about your weight much, Ms. Creed," Baron said as the waiter left, having taken all the food orders.

"Constantly," she said. "I really have to work to keep it up enough that I don't start burning muscle mass."

He sat back. She got a flat shark stare from those gray eyes. Then Charlie Bostitch guffawed and slapped his thigh with a beefy hand. "Good one!" he said. "Our Ms. Creed's a woman with spirit."

She wondered if there was more to this group than she was being told. Despite Charlie's boisterous good nature Annja was starting to fear working with them would be a mistake. The way Baron joined in the laughter a beat late didn't greatly reassure her.

Their food arrived. It was excellent and excellently prepared; Bostitch had decent taste in restaurants.

Annja's prime rib was rare, as advertised, which made her happy. It could be hard getting a really rare piece of meat these days.

As they ate Bostitch gave her his pitch, with occasional comments from Baron. They were brief and to the point, Annja had to admit. The former SEAL might not be likable and might be a touch too tightly wired. But he seemed to know his stuff.

"The Ararat Anomaly," Bostitch said, "was first spotted by an American recon flight along the Turkish-Soviet border in 1949. Since then it's been photographed on several occasions both by surveillance aircraft and satellites."

"Most recently by the space shuttle, in 1994," Taitt said.

"But no one's been allowed to examine it firsthand," Annja said.

Bostitch looked to Baron. "Not *allowed* to, no," the shaven-headed man said. "But last year an expedition did manage to reach the Anomaly. Briefly."

"And you had something to do with this?" Annja asked.

Again the unpleasant smile. "Not directly. At the time I was deployed to Kirkuk with my boys." Annja knew he was referring to northern Iraq—the part claimed by the Kurds, as it happened.

"Let's just say I had a hand in expediting the process," he said.

"So what did they find?"

Under the table Charlie evidently had his hand in his coat pocket. "This," he said, producing a plastic bag with a showman's flourish. It contained an irregular dark brown object about five inches long and maybe an inch wide.

"What's this?" Annja asked. He passed the bag to her. She turned it over in her hands. "It looks like a piece of old wood."

"Very old wood," Bostitch said. "It's been carbon dated as just under 3,500 years old."

"We believe the Flood happened in 1447 BC," Taitt said.

"Interesting," she said in a neutral tone. She passed the bag back to Bostitch. Taitt handed her several sealed plastic bags containing shards of pottery he'd taken from an attaché case.

"And here," Bostitch said, shoving a thick manila folder toward her, "we've got the documentation on the artifacts. All done up proper."

Except for the little detail about lack of official permission, she thought. Ah, well, stones and glass houses, as it would gratify Roux way too much to remind her.

She flipped through the papers inside the folder. "All right," she admitted. "Whoever did this appropriately documented the discovery and extraction of the artifacts, and didn't record the use of any kind of destructive practices. But these artifacts were basically found lying around in the snow. There's nothing about the structure itself. If any."

"Oh, it's there, all right," Bostitch said. His eyes shone with fervor. "The expedition members saw it plain as day, rising before them—a great ship shape, dark, covered with snow and ice."

"And they didn't document that?" Annja said.

"They had some…equipment malfunctions," Baron said. "Only a few shots one of them took on his cell phone actually came out."

Annja raised an eyebrow at him. Taitt pushed a sheet of paper at her. On it were printed several blurry photographs.

Her frown deepened as she studied them. "This could be anything." It looked big. It even looked vaguely ship-shaped.

She shoved the printout back at Taitt. "Then again, so do a lot of things. If I understand correctly the usual scientific explanation for the Anomaly is either a basalt extrusion or some kind of naturally occurring structure in the glacier itself. I don't see anything here to make me think differently."

"Ah, but the men who were there, Ms. Creed," Bostitch said, "they saw. And they *know.*"

"None of you was on this expedition?" she asked.

"Unfortunately, no," Bostitch said.

"And can I talk with anybody who was?"

"Unfortunately," Taitt said, the young lawyer coming out, "it would be inadvisable at this time."

Meaning, somewhere along the way they had stepped on serious toes, she figured. And they were hiding out. Or…worse? They played for keeps in that part of the world. They always had. It was something she suspected U.S. policymakers, even many of their grunts on the ground, failed to really appreciate.

It was a game Annja was far too familiar with. She'd played for such stakes before. She didn't doubt she would again.

But not for a wild-goose chase like this.

"Gentlemen," she said, "thank you for a wonderful dinner. And now, if you'll excuse me, I have to get home. I got an early start this morning."

That was true. And while the flight from Montreal to New York had been anything but lengthy the attendant hassles and stresses of air travel constituted a sort of irreducible minimum. She always thought so-called "security" measures—which would make any serious-minded terrorist bust out laughing—couldn't get more intrusive or obnoxious. Any kind of air travel these days was exhausting.

She rose. Larry Taitt stood up hastily, knocking his chair over. "You mean you won't do it?" he said in alarm, turning and fumbling to set the chair back up.

"That's exactly what she means," Baron said evenly.

"Are you sure you won't consider it, Ms. Creed?" Bostitch said, also standing up politely, if with less attendant melodrama. "It's the opportunity of a lifetime."

"That's what I'm afraid of," she said.

3

Annja's cell phone started ringing as she closed the door to her loft apartment behind her. As she fastened the various bolts, safety bars and locks with one hand she took the phone out with the other and checked who was calling.

"Doug Morrell," she said aloud. "*That* can't be good." Morrell was the boy wonder producer of the television show she worked for. Although she genuinely liked Doug, he could be trying at the best of times.

Despite her better judgment she held the phone to her ear.

"Hello?" Once again, her curiosity had the better of her. Damn it anyway.

"Annja?"

"Did you forget who you were calling, Doug? Or did you hit the wrong speed-dial button again?"

"Huh? What?"

"Never mind. What do you want, Doug? It's late."

"If you had any kind of social life the evening would just be starting."

"You're starting to sound like a nagging mother, Doug. What is it?"

"I'm doing you a favor here, sweetheart. You should thank me."

"Maybe if I knew what it was."

"Something's come down from Corporate. Something hot."

"You know what they say rolls downhill, Doug. It's pretty hot sometimes, too."

"Annja, just, like, listen for a change." This from Doug, who had the attention span of one of those little midges that live for six hours. "This is actually a *good* idea. Not like those other ones. Have you ever heard of Mount Ararat?"

She suddenly teetered over to her sofa. The end nearer the door was stacked with archaeological journals and printouts of recently submitted papers. Her legs were suddenly so shaky she sat right on top of the foot-high pile.

"Yes. I've heard of Ararat."

"So, like, it turns out Noah's Ark is on top of the freaking mountain. Who knew?"

Anyone who watches our rival cable networks, for starters, she thought. "Doug, we don't know it's Noah's Ark. For one thing, the mountain's seventeen thousand feet high."

"Really? That's a lot of rain. Anyway, there's an expedition headed up it. Nothing to worry about, it's an American operation all the way, not run by any people from Madagascar or wherever. You'd be their pet archaeologist. You'd also have a team from the show along to shoot everything. Do you hear what I'm saying, here, Annja? You're working for them and us. You're double-dipping, all open and aboveboard."

"Wow," Annja said.

"Try to muster some excitement, here. Because wait, there's more. If the suits decide to run with this you will be talent and producer for that episode. You, in person. Annja Creed."

That actually penetrated her fog of dismay and incipient paranoia. "You're kidding!" It meant that the show's coverage might actually feature her real archaeology instead of the entertainment bits that usually won out.

"Not at all, kiddo. Not at all. Focus groups say America's getting tired of the superficial. They want their infotainment shows to be more serious."

"Do they, now?"

"So what do you say? Yes?"

"I say I'm tired, Doug. This is a lot to heap on my plate. Let me sleep on it, at least."

"What's to think about?"

"Plenty," she said grimly. "Look, Doug. Thank you. I really, really appreciate that you're looking out for me. But I need to think about it."

"Don't think about it too long, babe. You know network. It's got the attention span of a hyperthyroid weasel."

She broke the connection, in case he had any further blandishments to offer. He really did mean well, in his air-headed way.

Her shoulders slumped. She tossed the phone on the sofa and rubbed her face with her hands.

"Is something else going on here?" she said to the half-lit room. "Am I getting paranoid?"

And the little voice in her head answered, Is it paranoid when they really are out to get you?

ANNJA HEADED OUT OF the television studio building into warm autumn sunlight. Some dried leaves skittered along the steps.

It was a little after one. She had two full hours for lunch before she was due back for a script conference for *Chasing History's Monsters* on star-children—hybrids between creatures from the stars, which was an old-time way of saying aliens, and men. Some people claimed they were spoken of in legends from all over the world. Annja was almost as skeptical of that claim as she was of the alien-human hybrid thing itself. She knew that her show was fluff but it paid well and allowed her to do a lot of real archaeology that she'd never have the time or money for otherwise. And now Doug was promising to let her shape an episode entirely her way. He'd been hounding her all morning to accept the Noah's Ark expedition. It seemed Charlie Bostitch was throwing his weight and his money around and he really wanted Annja on his team.

Annja had no idea what she was going to do for lunch. But after a morning of Doug and his antics she just had to get away from the show and everything connected to it for a while. Even if she just walked aimlessly the whole time. Actually, even if she stood banging her forehead against the corner of a building.

Her phone rang. She pulled it from its carrier. The number was unfamiliar. She thumbed Answer anyway. What the hey? She was an adventuress, wasn't she?

"Ms. Creed?" asked a man in a slightly Middle Eastern accent.

"Yes," she said in a neutral tone. Irrationally she started flicking her eyes all around, studying the slow-moving tourist swarms and the busy locals bustling past them with

their usual welcoming snarls and occasional shouted ob-
scenities. If anyone was stalking her they probably
wouldn't need to resort to a trick like dialing her number
and seeing who answered. But she also had a well-honed
aversion to taking things for granted.

"I hope you will forgive me bothering you. This is
Levi."

"Levi?"

"Rabbi Leibowitz. I met you last night at dinner at the
Penthouse."

"Oh. Yes. Rabbi. How are you?" Politeness, her default
mode, took over. Very few people, herself definitely
included, thought of her as a Southerner, although to all
practical purposes she was, having been raised in New
Orleans. She was a New Yorker through and through. She
was most particularly not a Southern belle. But the sisters
at the orphanage had brought her up to be polite, and on
the whole, she was pleased with that. Unlike a great many
other elements of her upbringing.

"Oh, I'm fine, fine, Ms. Creed. And I'm terribly sorry
if I or my associates offended you last night."

"No. I wouldn't say *offended* is the word." She could
think of plenty others. But gratuitous meanness didn't
form a major component of her personality. She liked to
think, anyway. Besides, there was something about the
rabbi's halting voice that struck a chord inside her. A
quality of vulnerability. Of innocence.

"But not too favorably impressed."

"Well…not with your associates. To be perfectly candid
with you, Rabbi Leibowitz, I hate to think of myself as
giving in to guilt by association. That said—given that
you chose to surround yourself with such associates, and

their project—I formed a certain impression of you. I apologize if I judged you unfairly. I guess I'm as subject to human frailties as anybody."

He laughed. "Oh, don't say that, Ms. Creed. And please don't judge the men you met with me last night too harshly. They are good men, whatever their enthusiasms."

"It's good men I've learned to fear most in the world, Rabbi. Especially the enthusiastic ones. Look, I'm willing to admit I may have judged you too hastily. I apologize for that. Now, if you'll excuse me—"

"Please, Ms. Creed." His voice pulsed with urgency. "Hear me out. I'm not really concerned…with your opinion of me. But I think it would be a great tragedy if you passed on participating in this project without hearing certain aspects of it that, that maybe got glossed over last night. And I'd like to ask you, as a favor to me, even though you certainly don't owe me anything, if you would at least examine my credentials online. I'm not in fact a colleague of yours, strictly speaking—I'm no archaeologist, naked or otherwise."

She had to laugh at that.

"I am an antiquarian, a historian, a scholar of ancient languages. I believe this expedition could add significantly to the sum of human historical and cultural knowledge."

"Let me ask you flat out," she said. "Do you believe in the literal truth of Genesis?"

His laugh sounded incredulous. A lot like she figured hers would have sounded if faced with the same question. "Oh, certainly not, Ms. Creed. Very few educated Jews today believe any such thing. Certainly few serious scholars, of which I flatter myself I'm one. But I ask, does that mean there cannot be something there, on that frightening mountain surrounded by very frightening people, that could still be worth unearthing?"

She felt her pulse quickening. The old atavistic joy of the hunt. Sneaking into eastern Turkey, in the heart of a war zone, and climbing to a mountain height where no official expedition had been allowed—it was hard to resist a challenge like that.

"All right, Rabbi," she said. "I haven't bought into this yet. But I gather you have a pitch for me. I'm willing to hear it. All right?"

"Oh, that's wonderful, Ms. Creed. Thank you so much. Are you free for lunch?"

RIGHT AROUND A CORNER FROM the television studio was a fancy coffee shop of a sort she usually avoided, mostly because they exuded a self-satisfied smugness that just scraped right up her spine. She bought a cup of coffee for a price outrageous even in the Big Apple, she thought as she walked away from the counter.

No seats were available in the crowded shop but there was some counter space by the window where she could unlimber her notebook computer and avail herself of their "free" Wi-Fi—although to her mind that was what she paid the steep coffee tariff for.

She ran *Leibowitz, Rabbi Levi* through Google. She would have done it the night before if she'd thought she'd ever have any more dealings with him. But when she took her leave of him and his companions nothing had been farther from her intent.

As soon as the search results began to pop up she wondered if maybe she should have checked after all. Interesting, he looks legit, she thought.

She had been inclined to dismiss him as some kind of right-wing Israeli nut of the sort who tended to run with a certain breed of U.S. militarists—ones like Baron and Bostitch. Instead, she found, he was a homeboy of hers, Brooklyn-based, a high-level genius making his name in the world as a leading authority on ancient Middle Eastern languages and cultures. If not, as he confessed, precisely a colleague of hers, he was a heavyweight in a closely related discipline. Because their areas of specialization—his the ancient Middle East, hers Renaissance Europe—lay so far apart, she'd never come across his name before.

It did surprise her that she hadn't seen his name on any of the fringe archaeology newsgroups she followed when time and energy allowed. The possible existence of Noah's Ark, or really *any* significant artifacts on the perpetually frozen top of a mountain, was right in the zone for discussion in those groups.

"I HOPE I'M NOT LATE," Levi said, sliding into a chair across from her.

They were in a Cantonese restaurant tucked away on Mott Street above Canal, in a part of Chinatown where the locals still seemed successfully to be resisting the inroads of the hipsters. The lunch crush had mostly eased. The restaurant smelled of hot oil and a touch of spice. The soft gurgle of a fountain mostly drowned out the conversations around them.

"Not at all, Rabbi," she told him. "I just like to get to a place early."

So I can get a look at the party I'm meeting as he approaches, see if he's acting strangely or has unexpected company, she thought. And so I have the best possible chance of getting a seat away from the windows and doors, so I'm harder to spot from the street. She'd made a practice of all of those things long since inheriting the sword had put her in almost constant danger.

He smiled cheerfully at her. "Try the wonton soup," he said. "It's to die for."

"Sounds good. I haven't been here before. It smells good, though. I'm always looking for a good new Chinese place."

A tall, young waiter took their orders. They ordered the soup; Leibowitz specified "no noodles," but she let it go. He ordered duck braised in soy sauce. Annja went for the crispy bean curd stuffed with chopped shrimp.

When the waiter left he smiled shyly at her. "I always order it without noodles," he said. "You get lots more wontons that way."

"Good thinking," Annja said.

"Are you sure you're not Jewish, Ms. Creed?" Leibowitz asked. The waiter returned and poured them each a cup of steaming green tea. "After all, if there's one characteristic the Chosen People have in common, it's love of Chinese food."

"Not that I know of. In my case it's more just a New York thing."

She sipped tea. The warmth felt welcome after the day's chill. And green tea always felt nourishing to her somehow. Although in this case that mainly served to remind her how famished she was.

"Although I guess I could be part Jewish," she added.

The truth was, she didn't know much about her lineage. Her parents had died when she was very young, leaving her with no surviving family and little by way of family records or possessions. None that had ever come Annja's way, in any case.

"Please don't be put off by Charlie and Leif and their naive enthusiasms," Leibowitz said. "They mean well, but—" He shrugged. "I don't think they really understand the concept of intellectual rigor."

"Probably not," Annja said. "It gets pretty annoying, sometimes, when amateurs get out of their depth with the science, and start talking about things they don't really understand."

He nodded vigorously. "That's so true. It's the same with scholarship—especially ancient languages. And this whole Biblical-literalness thing—" He had got himself worked up enough to be so flustered he couldn't continue, but could only wag his head like a dog in denial.

He's definitely a nerd, she thought. Also a bit of a fanatic. But not the sort of fanatic she'd been afraid he was at first. He was clearly fanatical on his subject: ancient languages and cultures.

Not like that's a bad thing, she thought.

"So you were saying you don't believe in Biblical inerrancy."

"Oh, of course not, Ms. Creed. Stories such as the Garden of Eden and the Flood are *allegories.* They were written by ancient mystics who never intended for them to be taken as factual accounts. They convey profound truths about humanity and its relationship to the Creator. And haven't fables always been a powerful tool for teaching?"

"True enough."

"In any event, to talk about any kind of 'inerrancy' in the Bible, what you call the Old Testament or New, or any ancient writings really, is just absurd. Leaving aside the doubtful provenance of whole sections of the holy books, they're filled with errors. I mean, what we'd call simple typos. Remember they were copied out time and again by hand, not always by people who were particularly literate in the character set they were using. Not always literate at all, so far as we can tell—sometimes religious communities found themselves so sorely pressed for one reason or another texts had to be copied by artisans who basically reproduced the characters as images. Pictures, not units of meaning. It's one reason the whole Bible Code concept is so unworkable as well."

Annja nodded. Their soup arrived. It was topped with chopped cilantro and finely sliced pickles. She tasted hers. The broth was hearty and cleverly flavored with herbs.

"This is delicious."

He smiled. It obviously pleased him to please her. That could get to be a problem, although he didn't seem the sort to push a schoolboy crush anyplace unpleasant.

"Yet, despite all that you tell me, you still think it's worthwhile going up that mountain?" she asked him.

"Oh, absolutely. You saw the artifacts they had?"

"Sure. And the documentation was in order. I'm not a carbon-14 dating expert, but I know enough to recognize the numbers were all in the right column. I don't have any reason to doubt the wood is as old as they say."

"So how did it get there, Ms. Creed?"

She tipped her head to the side. "Not by any flood, I'm pretty sure."

"Me, too."

"How, then?"

He laughed. "I don't know! But I want to find out."

Their food arrived. In his enthusiasm the rabbi fidgeted in his seat while the waiter set down their dishes. Then he leaned forward over the table, oblivious to the way the steam rising from his duck fogged his glasses.

"What I am sure of is that whatever's on top of the mountain—this so-called Ararat Anomaly—is a human construct. It must be of inestimable historical value."

She drew a deep breath, heavy with the fragrant steam. "You make a compelling case, Rabbi," she said.

"Levi. Please."

"Levi. Okay. I just—I'm not sure about the kind of people we'd be going with."

He shrugged. "I've led a sedentary life, Ms. Creed. I am a scholar, a man of books, of knowledge, of contemplation. But I am willing to undergo whatever hardships, do whatever it takes, to uncover this secret." He gave the impression he'd be willing to take his chances with almost anyone, if that would get him at whatever knowledge lay buried in the eternal snows of Ararat.

She wondered if it were some kind of twisted prejudice of hers, to find his scholar's zealotry so laudable, and that of Bostitch and his Rehoboam boys so scary.

He smiled. "Anyway, from what Charlie and Leif said about you, you have a reputation in certain circles for taking risks and coming back alive. I figure I'll be all right if I just stick close to you!"

She ate as she studied him. Not much deterred her from eating when she was hungry. Her lifestyle meant she took in a lot of calories and used them all.

You've been taken in before, she reminded herself. But the rabbi would have to be a diabolically skillful actor to fake this goofy artlessness, this seeming fundamental decency. He strikes me as kind, she thought. There's a virtue I encounter way too infrequently.

She sighed. "I hope I can live up to your expectations, Levi," she said. "I'll certainly try."

He lit up. "You mean you'll do it?"

"Against my better judgment," she said, "yes."

4

Annja was sitting at a table with a lot of men in a hotel conference room in Ankara, Turkey.

"You must understand," said the enormously tall, gaunt man with the eagle's-beak nose and dark circles under his eyes, "that there exist certain elements within my government who…resent American patronage of Kurdish separatists." He wore an olive-drab military uniform with a chestful of colorful ribbons.

The room air-conditioning worked with a nasty subliminal whine. It was a race whether it would slowly but inexorably give Annja a blinding headache or drive her mad. It worked though, keeping the temperature to arctic levels despite unseasonable heat in the streets of the Turkish capital outside, almost three thousand feet above sea level in the middle of the central massif of the Anatolian peninsula.

Unfortunately, it also reacted in some insidious way with the smoke generated by their host's harsh-smelling

Turkish cigarette to produce about the same reaction as tear gas in Annja's eyes. The Ankara Sheraton had a strict no-smoking policy. Apparently being a general of the Turkish army allowed you to opt out on that. Big surprise there, Annja thought.

"Well, General," Leif Baron said, leaning back in his chair and tapping a pen on the polished tabletop before him. "You should understand the Kurds have been our good friends in Iraq. They're the best indigenous allies we have there. What was that, Mr. Wilfork?"

"Nothing of consequence," said the man he'd addressed the last question to. He answered in what sounded to Annja like an Australian accent. It had also sounded as if he'd muttered, "The only ones who don't switch sides or bloody run away," under his breath at Baron's mention of the Kurds.

He wore a tan tropic-weight suit that fit his bulky frame as if he'd picked it off the rack, possibly at Goodwill: the suit was taut to near splitting at the shoulders, straining the buttons over his belly, the fabric bagging and rumpling at the chest. Despite the room's chill he mopped at his big crimson face with a scarlet handkerchief. His hair was thinning, combed over the top and white-tinged with yellow, although Annja had the impression he was only in his early fifties. She glanced at the equally tall and out-of-shape-looking Charlie Bostitch, who lounged across the table from the general at Baron's side, looking smug and at ease.

"Nonetheless, the United States has seen fit to provide assistance to certain Kurd groups internationally recognized as terrorists," the general said. "Indeed, the United States itself so recognized them, before they found a use for their services. Please, gentlemen—I do not raise these points in order to obstruct or cause complications. I, too, am eager for this expedition to take place. But it must be founded on a realistic appraisal of the situation, yes?"

"We've paid out plenty of money," Baron said, lounging back in his seat and crossing one leg over the other. He wore a pale yellow polo shirt, stretched tight over the bulging muscles of his chest and upper arms, and khaki trousers. "That ought to smooth our way."

"Now, now, gentlemen," Bostitch said, shaking his head. "Why don't we all just try to get along, here? We're men of goodwill. And the issues are bigger than all of us, after all."

General Orhan Orga gazed at him with his sad bloodhound eyes for a long moment before nodding.

"It is also true," he said, "that the army feels especially embattled now in its traditional role of maintaining the official secularity of our Turkish Republic against a rising tide of Islamism in political life. It is, I fear, a case of democracy in practice defeating democratic ends."

"Oh, I can understand that," Bostitch said, nodding his head. "And after all, you're fighting the good fight against the Muslim infidel."

"Dear Lord," Wilfork said out loud into a sudden silence. Annja noted that even the half-dozen young men, Rehoboam Christian Leadership Academy graduates all, who made up the bulk of the expedition were staring at their leader in something like dismay.

Orga's mouth compressed to a line beneath his magnificent brush of moustache. "Please understand that a majority of Turks, inside the army and out, are faithful followers of Islam. It is the job of the army, as outlined in our constitution, to maintain a clear distinction between religion and politics. That is all."

"Ah," Bostitch said, nodding and smiling. "Separation of church and state. That's—"

He stopped and did an almost comical take. He'd caught himself just in time praising a political concept he was quite famous for denouncing back home in the States. Annja scratched her upper lip to hide an incipient grin that she just couldn't quite hold in. She wondered if their fearless leader had been covertly hitting the bottle again.

Despite the whirlwind rapidity with which she'd been whipped from Manhattan's Chinatown to the Turkish capital of Ankara the process had still managed to entail lots of time sitting in airports waiting for flights. Using that time and Wi-Fi she'd done a bit more research on her current associates. She had discovered some interesting things about their employer. Including that he had a reputation as a real party animal, who every couple of years made a weepy public renunciation of his bad old ways, only to be caught in a few weeks or months half in the bag with his face between some stripper's boobs. Annja was experiencing more than a few second thoughts.

She shot a quick glance to Levi. He looked amiably befuddled. Still, he was being a good sport about it all.

He reminded her why she still felt committed to this project, increasingly weird and possibly, well, *doomed* as it seemed. There was his enthusiasm. And his innocence. And, oh, yes—the lure of uncovering ancient mysteries. And maybe a hint of adrenaline rush. Just a teensy, tiny bit.

"General Orga," Larry Taitt said with horrible playful-puppy brightness, "the key point here is that we're relying on you to smooth our way east to Mount Ararat. And I'm sure our fate, and the fate of our expedition, couldn't be in more capable hands."

Annja looked at the floppy kid—she couldn't help thinking of him that way—with a certain expanded under-standing. He may be a happy-go-lucky goof who'd had the bad judgment to lock himself into weird religion and weirder associates. But he clearly had something on the ball.

Orga was frowning still, but now it was with a sort of generalized concern. "I will certainly do what I can for this expedition," he intoned. "It is, after all, for science."

"Science," Wilfork said. He raised his glass of beer. "I'll drink to that."

Leif Baron, who had apparently decided to reclaim the "good cop" role, slapped his hands noisily on his thighs and stood. "We know you will, General Orga. Thanks for coming out."

Everybody else stood, so Annja did likewise. She wasn't sure what had actually been accomplished here. If anything. But now Baron and Bostitch were showing all hail-fellow camaraderie to the general, who himself was looking as jovial as he could with those bloodhound eyes. She was not a woman who yielded to gender stereotypes, for either sex, and if anything tended to consider herself, and be accepted as, one of the boys. But this scene baffled her. Maybe it was some male-bonding ritual she hadn't en-countered yet.

She found herself out in the curving hallway walking away. Aside from the smoking thing the Ankara Sheraton was a fabulous hotel. She felt a strong yearning to return to the extravagant comfort of a room she never could have afforded on her own. Then maybe a few laps in the huge indoor swimming pool would get her tuned up again.

"Ms. Creed," an Australian-accented voice called from behind her. "Wait one, if you'd be so kind."

She stopped and turned. Robyn Wilfork lumbered after her. His gait resembled that of a none-too-well-trained dancing bear. She couldn't attribute it to alcohol: he had a long torso and short, bowed legs for his height.

Well, maybe some of it was alcohol, considering how hard he'd been hitting the beer back in the room.

"Might I offer you a drink?" he asked. "The hotel sports an altogether splendid bar."

She was on the cusp of answering that she thought maybe he'd had enough in that department when she saw a knowing look come into his blue eyes.

"Nothing improper, I assure you," he said hastily. "It just strikes me that, since we appear to be the odd ones out—quite a striking fact itself, in this company—we might profitably get to know one another."

"Ah," she said, "sure. Why not?"

THE COPPER BAR OF ANKARA'S Sheraton Hotel and Convention Center was a splendid bar, Annja had to admit. The bar proper was a highly polished teak arc beneath outward-expanding concentric rings of copper hung from the ceiling. It was such a striking effect that she actually permitted, not altogether in accordance with her better judgment, the journalist to buy her a glass of wine. Having placed her order with the bartender, who appeared to be French, she followed Wilfork as he rolled like a sailor in a high sea to one of the blue-gray chairs. These proved to be quite comfortable.

The bar was almost empty. Soft chamber music played in the background. While the afternoon view outside the tall windows was pleasant, prominently featuring an out-door pool and the tall tower in which the rooms were located, she chose to sit with her back to them. She always liked to be able to see the entrance of the place she was in. The more so since there seemed to be some possible controversy concerning their expedition.

Which wasn't totally surprising, inasmuch as the whole enterprise was flamboyantly illegal.

"So, Mr. Wilfork," she said, "what brings you all the way from Australia?"

"Australia?" He laughed heartily. "Oh, no, no. My dear, you're grievously wrong. I am a Kiwi, born and bred."

Her eyebrows rose in surprise. "I'm sorry. I guess I don't know enough to tell a New Zealand accent from Australian one."

"You are quite forgiven. But I must say, the question you want to ask is, what is a confirmed atheist and semi-lapsed communist doing wrapped up in all of this religious mummery?"

That made her pull her head back and blink. "You're right. I guess that is a better question."

"Perhaps the answer is the same as what might bring a respected American archaeologist of decidedly skeptical bent into such an operation," he said. "Simply, money."

She frowned slightly. "It's not so simple," she said. "Not in my case. And anyway, what use does a communist have for money?"

"Why, all the use in the world. That turns out, perhaps, to sum up the history of world communism in a nutshell. Besides, I told you I've become apostate."

"And there you have it," she said, laughing. "I guess that's fair enough. And I have to admit that in my case the answer is partially money. But I'm legitimately interested in learning what really lies on top of that mountain."

The waitress, a trim diminutive woman with a tight bun of gray hair who appeared to be local, brought their drinks. "Gin and tonic with a wedge of lime?" Annja asked. "Isn't that rather…colonialist of you?"

"Well, I could remind you again I'm a lapsed communist." He shrugged. "Then again, I drank the same when I was fully communicant in the faith."

He held up the highball glass in salute. "Here's to Thomas Friedman's flat earth," he said. "Also to his flat head. What on earth ever possessed you Americans to give that self-inflated buffoon a Pulitzer Prize?"

"I'm not the one to ask. They didn't."

He sipped, smacked his lips and sighed. "Splendid. And splendidly retorted. You display a quickness of wit that they seem to be able to conceal quite well on that television program of yours."

"They don't exactly encourage spontaneity. At least, not from their resident skeptic."

"But they do in the case of the show's lead. At least if by *spontaneity* one means 'a remarkable gift for losing one's top in the most unlikely of circumstances.'"

She laughed. She was finding Wilfork and his self-satirizing bluster not just amusing but likable. Actually she so far found everybody on this trip, bizarre as it was, basically likable. Except maybe Baron, with his shark eyes.

And maybe the other Rehoboam Academy types, although they were polite and seemed a little less manically cheerful than Larry. Even if when she had been around them so far they had mostly been subdued out of due Christian deference to their elders. She still couldn't quite shake a distressing mental image of them as a pack of young wolves.

"So have you decided to throw over the whole voice-of-reason thing, then?" Wilfork asked.

She tasted the wine. It was sweet enough that she found it palatable. As far as wine-drinking went she was fated forever to provide a handy butt for jokes by wine snobs. She was resigned to that fate. Uncharacteristic, perhaps; but then, it didn't matter to her much one way or another. There were lots of other, more pressing fates to rebel against.

"Not at all, Mr. Wilfork. If you'll think back, you'll recall I said, *whatever's really up there.* Or words to that effect."

He nodded. "So you did. So you did. What do you think's up there?"

"If I knew, would I have to go?" She shrugged. "As you said, it's science."

"Did I? Ah, yes. My sardonic toast. Mostly I was trying to bait our employers."

"Isn't that kind of a dangerous game? Especially considering your background. What would they do if they found out about the whole ex-commie thing?"

"Oh, they're well aware of that, make no mistake. Our Lieutenant Commander Baron has access to things like secret dossiers, despite no longer being a member of your military."

"Is he CIA?"

Emphatically Wilfork shook his head. It made his yellow-white hair flop on his red scalp. "I'm fairly certain not. The agency rank and file seem to be quite disenchanted with ring-in-Armageddon fundamentalists of his ilk—and in any case, that lot appears on their way out. And bloody good riddance, too. But he still contrives to be plugged into a good old boys' network. It may just be among SEALs and other special-operations types. You know how warriors are—blood is thicker than water, unless it's that of bloody foreigners."

Belatedly Annja was having a cold flash at the prospect of those gray flat eyes scanning *her* dossier.

"How did they happen to hire you as their official chronicler?" Annja asked, eager to steer the conversation in a different direction.

"Back when I was a prominent international left-wing journalist I was often critical of Mr. Bostitch's attempts to influence foreign policy—especially since they all seemed peculiarly geared toward enhancing his own defense contracts. Also, if I may flatter myself, I proved something of a thorn in the side of special-operations murderers Mr. Baron so joyously served before deciding the grass was greener on the civilian-contracting side of the perpetual-war fence. I think it was because that established my objectivity—at least, gave credibility to the notion I wouldn't slant my reportage to suit my employers, even though of late I've become noted for my harsh criticism of my former comrades. All of it quite sincere, by the way—a bunch of humorless dolts, and most of them unacknowledged fascists.

"But I digress. A frequent weakness of mine. One among many." He sipped his drink.

"Also, in much of my recent writing I've been most critical of Islam, especially the more violent sectarians. That's made me more attractive to a good many people to whom I was once distinctly persona non grata. And finally, I suspect a certain element of revenge, as it were, my former foes making me subordinate to them."

"They must be paying you well."

He beamed. "Oh, they are. They are."

His expression turned troubled. He stared into his half-emptied glass as if seeking oracle there. "I only hope it's enough," he said. "I confess, I doubt things will proceed near as smoothly as our beloved pet Turkish army general is at such pains to assure us they will."

He tossed back the rest of his drink. It had no visible effect on him. He set the empty glass on the table with a decisive *thunk*.

"Ah, well," he said. "Our vicissitudes should make a ripping story, anyway. Perhaps I'll win a journalistic prize of my own. Or at least get a bestseller for my pains. A decent return on the sale of one's soul, wouldn't you say?"

5

The Museum of Anatolian Civilizations was a beautiful museum converted from an old covered marketplace situated close to the Ankara Citadel. It contained samples from Asia Minor's long cultural history, specializing in artifacts from the Paleolithic through Classical periods. Annja was admiring an ancient Hittite statue of a highly stylized deer of some sort, whose rack of antlers totally dwarfed its actual body, when her cell phone rang.

She flipped it open. "Yes?"

It was her team from *Chasing History's Monsters,* who had just arrived at Ankara's airport. Imagining what sparks might fly when a trio of doubtless liberal young New Yorkers came in contact with Charlie Bostitch's born-again culture warriors, she hastily offered to meet them at the hotel to help get them settled in.

Three hours later they were all sitting on the big mossy stone foundation blocks of the ruins of the stage area of Roman Theater. It also stood near the castle on its lava outcrop atop one of Ankara's many hills. Excavation of the theater's seating area was still ongoing; Annja hoped she'd have time before they took off for the wild, wild east to pay a visit and see if she could schmooze her way into the dig as a visiting archaeologist. She might even be able to make use of it for *Chasing History's Monsters*. The team told her they were looking for local-color shots to establish setting at stages of their journey to the forbidden mountain.

"I always thought Ankara was kind of a pit," Trish Baxter, the soundwoman, said. She was a pretty, medium-size blonde with a snub nose and ponytail. She dangled legs left bare by her cargo shorts over the edge of a block. A green slope stretched down toward the city center below them. "But it's really kind of pretty."

"There's a lot of green here," Annja said. "I was surprised the first time I visited Istanbul by how much greenery there was. I expected something more of a blend between desert desolation and cement-canyon modernism."

"Ankara doesn't seem to be much of a tourist Mecca," Tommy Wynock said. He was a stocky blond guy of medium height with a Mets cap turned around backward. He was the chief techie and secondary cameraman.

"So to speak," said lead cameraman Jason Pennigrew. A wiry black kid an inch or so taller than Annja, he had a brash but engaging manner and an olive-drab do-rag tied around his head. He sat with his back to a pillar and his long legs drawn up before him. "I wonder how much of that might be because of problems the government's having with Muslim fundamentalists."

"Actually, the government kind of *is* the Muslim fundamentalists," Annja said. "The democratically elected civilian government, anyway. They're in a state of more or less perpetual confrontation with the army, which turns out to be the guardian of Turkey's officially secular status. The religious-minded members of the government insist they don't want to turn Turkey into a full-on Islamic state. But it seems like a lot of people in the street do."

"I thought Turks were supposed to be, you know, kind of lax in their observance," Trish said. She'd impressed Annja as the most bookish and widely knowledgeable of the bunch. Television production types didn't always have the deepest understandings of foreign affairs or foreign cultures, even when they spent a lot of time traveling overseas, Annja had found.

"That's true, traditionally," Annja said. "And there's still a solid sentiment with the public for Turkey to maintain its secular status, even with a lot of very religiously fundamentalist Turks. Or that's the impression I have. Listen to me, sounding like Ms. Turkey Expert. The truth is I only know what the other members of the expedition tell me, and what I read on the Internet."

She nodded at Trish's bare legs. "You might want to change out of those shorts, just to be on the safe side. Ankara's a lot less cosmopolitan than Istanbul. And even if the real crazies are still a marked minority—well, it only takes a run-in with one to spoil your day, if you know what I mean."

"Oh," Trish said, "yeah. I wasn't thinking. It was so hot and stuffy on the plane, and then when it turned out to be hot here, too, I just wanted to kind of, well, air out."

"You're not going to have much opportunity to do that anyway," Jason said. "Ankara seems to be the only place in the Northern Hemisphere that's getting unseasonable warmth. Everywhere else it's even colder than last year."

"Great," Tommy said, shaking his head. "That's all we need. We already have too many people questioning global warming."

Jason unfolded himself from the stone pavement. "Okay, Annja. We've stretched our legs, which I gotta tell you was welcome after all those hours sitting around in airports and on airplanes. We should probably get back to the hotel. I could use a shower anyway."

"I think Annja wanted to prep us to meet the rest of the crew first," Trish said.

Annja made a humorless noise in the back of her throat. "And prep myself. This is liable to be a pretty hazardous undertaking. I hope that was all fully explained to you in advance?"

The new arrivals looked at each other and laughed. "Are you kidding?" Jason said. "Dougie? He assured us this was all going to be a piece of cake."

"My uncle back in Waco always used to say, 'Don't piss down my leg and tell me it's raining,'" Trish said, allowing a touch of Texas Panhandle she'd obviously been carefully suppressing before to slip into her voice. "It's like he knew Doug."

"Doug did admit this whole trip might be just a tiny bit *illegal,* once we got to Ararat," Tommy said. "But he tried to make it seem like it was really all just kind of a joke the locals like to play on tourists. You know how he is."

"I sure do," Annja said grimly. "There's a real-life war going on in eastern Turkey between the Turks and the Kurds. At the moment it's sort of…contained. But it could blow up at any minute into a serious conflagration involving Northern Iraq. And if that happens who knows where it'll go?"

"To hell in a hurry, sounds like," Jason said. He didn't appear overly concerned.

"So it's way important that everybody gets along. Let me stress that—*everybody*. I suspect that's not going to be easy on either side. So I wanted to get together with you guys off by ourselves, get to know each other, before we all walked into the lion's den."

"Are they that nuts?" Trish asked. "I mean, I thought the big guy, Bostitch, was pretty easygoing. I read up on him a little bit on the way out. Seems like he was the original good-time Charlie—never met a shot of booze or line of coke he didn't like."

"Or a babe," Jason said.

"He really isn't that bad. But he is deadly serious about his beliefs," Annja said.

She paused to inhale and marshal her thoughts. In general the crew made a good impression on her. But as she'd suspected, they were of a bent to see right-wing Christians the very same way the right-wing Christians saw them—the embodiment of dangerous evil.

"Listen. Everybody's polite as hell. Especially the rank-and-file expedition members, who it turns out all came out of this Rehoboam Christian Leadership Academy Charlie runs. And I'd like to keep things polite as much as possible," Annja said.

"How about this Baron guy?" Tommy said. "Even I've heard of him. He's supposed to be implicated in all kinds of war crimes."

Annja shrugged. "He's a bit tightly wrapped, I have to warn you. Seriously, seriously, do not tease the animals. But…please don't take this the wrong way. I don't condone war crimes—and I also don't know enough of the facts to have any idea of what he's guilty of, or whether he's guilty of anything at all except pretty vigorously waging an unpopular war. But the places we're going, he might turn out to be just the kind of guy we need to keep us alive, war crimes or no."

"The places we'll go," Jason paraphrased. "You make it sound like we're headed into an evil Dr. Seuss book."

"Hold that thought," Annja said.

"NOW FROM THE SMALL AMOUNT of research I was able to do before we set out," Jason Pennigrew said, "I understand that there are at least a couple of alternate sites for the Ark that've been proposed recently."

Annja was impressed by the crew chief's professionalism. The loosey-goosey black kid from Memphis and the University of Tennessee was gone. Jason hadn't quite gone so far as to put on a coat and tie, but he did wear a dark blue shirt and dark pants. His two companions went for a more informal, blue-jeans look. Annja wore her usual cargo khaki trousers, practical rather than fashionable, and a light blouse in abstract streaks of cream and yellow and rust and orange.

With the sun sinking behind the wooded western hills the view from the expedition's tower suite was spectacular. Orange light filled the room. Maps had been spread out on the large table. Charlie and most of his posse were there along with Annja and the recently arrived *Chasing History's Monsters* crew.

"That's right," Leif Baron said, sitting on the couch. He wore tan trousers, a white polo shirt and tan boots with pale crepe soles. Annja suspected the shirt was deliberately tight to emphasize his ripped physique. It *was* ripped, no denying—so much so that Annja suspected it wasn't entirely natural development. "A guy named Ron Wyatt was a big proponent for the so-called Durupinar site, eighteen miles south of Greater Ararat, where our Anomaly lies."

"Wyatt's great discovery is a big boat-shaped object, sure enough. Zeb, can you find us a photograph?"

Two of Charlie's Young Wolves—as Annja couldn't help thinking of them—stood side by side with their backs to one of the big picture windows. They looked as if reality had stuttered and produced the same image twice. Both were an inch shorter than Annja, athletic, their eyes blue in wide fresh faces with freckle-dotted snub noses. Like Baron they currently affected a casual style, salmon-colored shirts and khaki trousers. Everything about them lined up identically, from their blond crew cuts to the creases on their pants. Annja had a horrible sensation that if she examined them under an optical comparator they'd be identical to the microscopic level, as if made by machine instead of nature.

Since like their packmates the twins responded slavishly to Bostitch and Baron's every word, the one who came forward to the table was pretty much by definition not Jeb. She suspected uncomfortably that if Baron had said, "Jeb, do you think you can throw yourself into that molten lava?" he'd have complied with the same strutting alacrity.

Zeb bent over and searched through a number of large photographic prints from a folder. Straightening, he proffered one to Baron with a smile. Then in response to a slight inclination of Baron's shaved skull he handed it to Annja instead.

"Ms. Creed, I believe you have some training as a geologist," Baron said, smiling at her. "Maybe you could tell us what you think?"

Annja accepted it and scrutinized it under the light of the lamp on the table beside her. After a moment she looked up.

"That's a good shot," she said. "I'd say it's definitely a natural rock formation that looks a lot like a ship. I'm guessing it's basalt."

"You're good, Ms. Creed," Charlie said, nodding his head and smiling his big goofy smile. He sat sprawled comfortably in one of the black leather chairs, almost as if he'd been spilled there. "The samples Leif and I brought back from our little visit there last year have been scientifically confirmed to be basalt. No Ark. Unless it was a mighty heavy one."

"About what you'd expect from a nurse-anesthetist," Baron said. "Which is what Wyatt was."

Annja passed the print on to Jason, who pulled a long face and nodded, impressed. "Isn't there a supposed Ark site in Iran?" Trish asked.

"Oh, yes," Larry Taitt said, when Baron and Bostitch said nothing. He was dressed, as he always seemed to be, in a dark suit and tie. "There are several purported sites. We've investigated all of them thoroughly."

"We did produce some photographs of the site," Larry said. "Zeb, if you could please find those for Ms. Creed, thanks."

The blond twin handed her more prints with what seemed to Annja a lack of grace. The Young Wolves seemed willing enough to accept Bostitch and Baron's alpha and beta status. But having one of their own jumped over them in pack precedence didn't seem to be sitting too well.

"The one on top purports to be a view of the Ark itself," Larry said. "The other is of bits off stone they cut that some think are petrified wood planks from the Ark."

The first photo showed a ridge or saddleback, with snow drifts to one side and cloudy sky to the other, and slanting gently down to the snow a slope dotted with small rocks and dark green bunch grass. Jutting from the middle of the photo, right below the ridge-crest, was a dark outcrop with a pointy top that might have been a single big boulder. Annja made a face.

"This could be anything," she said. "Even some kind of hard volcanic extrusion with softer rock eroded away around it."

She handed it back, shaking her head. "I can't tell you much more about it. I doubt anybody could, on the basis of that picture alone. But I'd be extremely surprised if it was anything *but* natural rock."

"And these planks?" Bostitch asked.

"Look, I can't pretend to be a fully qualified geologist or anything. I took some courses—I have plenty of experience on digs. But I'm no expert. Still, what these look like to me are just slabs of some kind of fine-grained sedimentary rocks—shale or sandstone. Because of the way they've been cut out they look like planks. But see—" she pointed to some detail in the photo "—I think these patterns that look like grain in wood are probably a result of layers of deposition in some kind of marine environment. Like basically, years of silt filtering down out of the water."

"Nailed it again," Bostitch said from his throne. "That's just what the geologists we hired to look the pictures over said. One said he reckoned the so-called Ark was just a basalt dike—igneous, just like you said."

"Maybe we should have contracted with Ms. Creed earlier and saved ourselves some money on consultants," Baron said with a smile toward Annja.

"Not a good idea," Annja said hastily. "If you have real experts in a given field, you should listen to them."

"So what makes you think you've got a better candidate for Noah's boat?" Tommy asked, sitting perched on a table with his elbows propped on his knees.

The twins and the other two Young Wolves in the room, who'd been introduced as Josh and Eli, gave him slit-eyed looks as if not appreciating an outsider butting in. Annja was about to leap to his defense when Charlie spoke up.

"Well, that's a right good question there, Mr. Wynock. Luckily, we got us some good answers. And we'd better—otherwise we'd look like a bunch of damn fools coming over here and spending all this money."

At the pained looks that flitted across his acolytes' faces he blushed and added, "If you'll pardon my French."

Annja quickly outlined the evidence as they had presented to her. When called upon, Levi, who had gotten interested and sat leaning forward with his clasped hands between his wide-splayed knees, agreed that, at the very least, there might be a very valuable historical site on Ararat.

Jason looked to his companions. Annja caught a bit of an eye-roll from Tommy, but the others didn't notice. She hoped.

The television crew chief slapped his hands down on his thighs. "Well," he said, standing, "it does look as if we're in for some interesting times."

The intonation he gave the last two words suggested to Annja that any resemblance to a mythical Chinese curse was strictly intentional.

6

"It's bat-shit crazy," Tommy said. "But no worse than most of the wild-goose chases we get sent on."

"If the Kurds don't kill us," Trish said. "Or the right-wing fundamentalists."

They had gathered in Annja's room in the Sheraton Tower, just around the curving corridor from the suite where they held their meetings—or "briefings," as Bostitch preferred to call them. Annja wasn't sure whether he was following Baron's ex-military lead or his own inclinations. For all that Bostitch presented himself as an aw-shucks folksy businessman, the graduates of his leadership academy sure seemed to see themselves as holy warriors.

Though smaller than the suite, Annja's room was hardly less luxurious. She sat cross-legged on the wide bed. Tommy perched on the desk. Trish sat in one of the comfy chairs while Jason alternately paced like a caged leopard and stood gazing moodily out at the lights of the city.

"Might that mean it's a good idea to try our best to get along with the others, then?" Annja asked.

"Hey, we weren't that bad," Tommy said. "Don't bust our balls."

"I don't know whether to thank you or call you a pig," Trish said, laughing.

"Whatev. You know what I mean."

"Actually, you did fine," Annja said. "I just want to encourage us all to keep that up. You guys have been in the field. You know how once you start getting tired and thirsty and sick of being either too hot or too cold all the time, tensions tend to rise. So either we need to just bail on this or do our best to keep things from getting too tense."

"You'd do that, Annja?" Trish asked. "You seem to have, like, the most at stake here." She seemed honestly surprised.

In a heartbeat, Annja almost said. She decided it would be unwise. And anyway it wasn't really true. Although what Trish probably thought she had at stake in this expedition—the prospect of her own show on the network— barely registered in Annja's determination to see this through if possible.

"If I thought it was the right thing to do, yes," Annja said and that was true. Annja always did what she thought was right, whatever it cost her. And there had been times when it cost her greatly.

"What I don't see," Tommy said, "is how they can take all this Creation shit seriously."

"No kidding," Jason said. "Was it a pair of each kind of animal that went onto the Ark? Or seven of some and two of others? Doesn't Genesis do it both ways?"

"Yes," Annja said.

"Isn't the Bible, like, full of contradictions?" Trish said.

"It is. And I have to hand the literalists credit for their ingenuity in dreaming up explanations for a lot of them. Or maybe intellectual double-jointedness."

"I thought a lot of the fundamentalists just got by with announcing every word of the Old Testament is true, without actually reading much of it," Tommy grumbled.

"That's true, too. I don't know how well that applies to our employer and his associates, though. They seem to be a studious bunch."

"Huh," Tommy said. "Maybe they should study the evidence a little closer. I mean, look at the pictures they got."

He pulled his phone from its hip holster. "I was looking at some of the pictures online on my own. Take this oblique shot here from 1949. Tell me it doesn't totally look like somebody used Photoshop to add a toy tugboat in among some rocks. Badly."

"Dude," Jason said. "I could be wrong, here, but I'm pretty sure they didn't have Photoshop in '49."

"Whatever. You know what I mean. Cut-and-paste job with scissors and glue then. And what about this overhead from a satellite, with the so-called 'Anomaly' conveniently outlined in red pen? Give me a break. This just looks like someone took a picture of a random ridge and drew a boat shape around it. It looks like a fucking whale. Using that technique you could demonstrate that anything longer than it is wide is Noah's Ark."

"All right, you're right," Annja said. "All this is true. We do still have some fairly good artifacts that somebody close to Charlie brought back. And Levi—Rabbi Leibowitz— thinks there's *something* up there, if not a stranded ship."

"Yeah," Jason said. "But what about this rabbi guy, anyway? What's his story?"

"I think that's more a marriage of convenience. But Levi's based in Brooklyn. I think he's basically apolitical. He's into this because he thinks there *is* a mystery up here that could be really, really important to history. And I do, too."

"Whoa," Tommy breathed, mock-reverent. "Annja Creed, *Chasing History's Monsters'* resident buzz-kill specialist with all her skepticism, thinks there's really something there?"

Trish hooted. "Could you try to be more insulting, Tommy?"

He huffed and shook his head. Annja found herself just naturally envisioning him with a baseball cap turned backward on his head. "Sorry," he said.

"Speaking of climbing to the top," Jason said, "what do you make of the chances of old Charlie making it up alive? He looks like he'd be all out of breath walking across the room."

"Well, he did say he'd been climbing around Solomon's Throne in Persia—I mean Iran," Annja said. "Also illegally, by the way. He's tougher than he looks. I think he actually goes through his own academy physical-training courses in the summer."

"He must do a lot of training to keep that shape, then," Tommy said. "Like, at the buffet tables."

"And happy hour," Trish said.

"And what's with this Wilfork guy?" Jason said. "He looks worse if anything."

"Tommy says he smokes like a chimney," Trish said. "He always sees him when *he* sneaks out for a smoke."

"Dude," Tommy said aggrievedly.

"He's probably tougher than he looks, too," Annja said.

"When he was filling me in on the whole Turkish political situation, he said he'd spent his whole career chasing from one trouble spot to the next."

"Yeah," Trish said. "He's a pretty famous crisis journalist."

"As long as he doesn't have a crisis with his heart halfway up the damned mountain and we have to beg the Turkish army for a medevac chopper," Tommy said.

Jason grunted. "Be lucky if we didn't get a helicopter gunship," he said.

"Also, what's up with that whole mountain-peak thing, anyway?" Tommy said. "Fifteen thousand feet? God's supposed to have flooded the Earth three miles deep?"

"That's what our associates believe," Annja said.

Tommy shook his head in wonder. "Whoa," he said.

THE NEXT FEW DAYS PASSED slowly for Annja. It was a relief not to have the hassles of organizing and outfitting an expedition into hostile territory as her responsibility. Ankara's unseasonable warmth gave way to the equally unseasonable chill that had already descended on the rest of the country. Yet not running the show had one big drawback—it left her without much to do.

Although a vast and highly modern mall, the Karum, stood right across the street from the hotel, Annja had never bothered to venture inside. She didn't feel enough attraction to brave the crowds. She was not a shopping goddess, nor even particularly interested in shopping beyond what was necessary to keep her clothes from wearing out to the point of falling off her body. She'd rather be sitting on her couch in her apartment poring through her stacks of printouts of papers submitted to

obscure journals of archaeological arcana. Like Rabbi Leibowitz, basically, but with a few more social skills.

But she could always wander the archaeological sites
and museums. Fortunately, as she'd mentioned to the *CHM*
crew, the city abounded in those.

Even they palled eventually. Two days after the *CHM*
team's arrival from New York she decided to head south
on foot through the section called Kavaklidere, which
was a former vineyard. Its most prominent features now
were her own enormous hotel, the high-rise Karum and,
several hundred yards south, the equally ostentatious
tower of the Hilton.

She spent a pleasant, if cool and windy, day in the bo-
tanical gardens. The park occupied a hill south of the big
hill, *Kale,* on which the Ankara Citadel stood a few blocks
north of the Sheraton. Hill and park alike were dominated
by the Atakule Tower, named like so many things for
Kemal Atatürk, founder of the modern Turkish republic.
The tower was a spindly white four-hundred-plus-foot
spire with a sort of space-needle flying saucer at the top—
a similarity acknowledged by the presence of the UFO
Café and Bar within, along with two more upscale-looking
restaurants.

After the brief warm spell autumn had returned with
vindictive force that hinted at a truly brutal winter to
follow.

In her puffy down jacket Annja found the breezes
blowing down from the Köro lu Mountains to the north,
already well-socked-in with snow according to the
Internet, bracing rather than uncomfortable. Although no
blossoms survived in the park's beautifully designed and
tended gardens, and the merciless winds had stripped the

leaves from the deciduous trees, the park was planted thickly with evergreens, tall pines and fir trees. And even the bare limbs beneath which the numerous hill paths twined created interesting, intricate shapes against a lead-clouded sky.

Having spent so much time indoors of late Annja was content to walk briskly with no fixed goal in mind, stretching out her long legs. When she grew tired and chilled she bought a steaming cup of cocoa from a kiosk and then sat in the lee of the small building to read e-mail and check the latest news on her BlackBerry.

Nothing seemed likely to impact her situation directly—although as always the pot of occupied Iraq seethed on the verge of bubbling over, as did the U.S.'s perpetual grudge match with an Iran now backed openly by China and a resurgent Russia. If either of those situations did explode the best and possibly only shot at survival for the expedition would be to run like hell for the Bosporus. But Annja saw no reason to expect they would do so now.

Still, she felt a tickle of unsourced unease in the pit of her stomach. That's probably what I get for reading the headlines, she thought, and put her phone away.

The park closed at sunset, which came early this time of year. Ankara lay at about the latitude of Philadelphia, though considerably farther from the weather-tempering influence of a big ocean and considerably nearer to the monster-storm hatchery of the Himalayas. She had just reached the exit when a voice called, "Annja Creed? A word with you, please."

She stopped. Does every sketchy character in the world know my name? she wondered. Although she tried to keep her face and posture as relaxed as possible her body badly wanted to tense like a gazelle that thinks a wind shift at the watering hole has just brought a whiff of lion. The range of people who might conceivably wish her harm, or even just to talk to her in a none-too-friendly way, ranged from Turkish civic or military authorities less well-disposed to their endeavor than General Orga to any number of unsavory characters from her past. Among whom, of course, was the ever-prominent if publicity-averse billionaire financier Garin Braden, who might have felt a cold wind of mortality blow down his spine as he lay in his huge canopied bed that morning. When Braden wasn't trying to get the sword from her he was battling with his long-time nemesis Roux and dragging Annja into the battle.

Her interlocutor appeared to be no more than a solidly built man of intermediate height and apparently advanced age who stood by the white-enameled wrought-iron gates dressed in a camel-hair coat and a fedora that clung, despite the wind's best efforts, to a head of hair that, though as gleaming white as his trim beard, still managed to suggest it had once been blazing red. He smiled a bit grimly as she looked at him, and nodded.

"I have information that might prove vital to you. It concerns the expedition you are involved with."

Her eyes narrowed. "Please believe me," he said, holding up gloved hands. "I assure you I have no official capacity in this country. Nor in any other, for that matter. Nor have I any financial propositions to make to you. Nor any other kind, should you be worried about that."

His manner was disarming. Annja wasn't so easily disarmed. Then again, that was literally true; and her ever-active curiosity was excited. As for his disavowal of official standing she was far from willing to take that at face value. He spoke with an accent she couldn't identify—which itself was strange, given her expertise in languages, and wide travels.

Then again if he were some kind of Turkish secret cop all he'd have to do was snap his fingers and burly goons would magically appear on all sides of her, she thought. She knew it from past experience.

"Please allow me the honor of buying you dinner," he said. "In a suitably public place, of course. That should reassure you as to my intentions—although I doubt you have much to fear from the likes of me."

Her stomach growled. Her metabolism required frequent feeding. It hadn't gotten one in too long. Still, she was wary.

"All right, Mister—"

"You may call me Mr. Summer."

"Where did you have in mind?"

"Where but in the tower?" he said with a twinkle in his dark green eyes.

THE LIGHTS OF ANKARA by evening rotated almost imperceptibly by outside the window beside their table.

"It is good of you to indulge an old man's whimsy," her companion said around a mouthful of grape leaf stuffed with ground lamb and pine nuts. "The fare in the restaurant at the pinnacle, above us, is of higher quality. Or at least greater pretense. But this establishment, I daresay, offers quite acceptable local cuisine."

"I'm fine," she said. "I can get French-style bistro cooking anywhere. Good Turkish food, not so much." Although I halfway wish we'd stopped at the UFO Café, just on general principles, she thought.

The restaurant revolved once every hour and a half. It seemed to give Mr. Summer the pleasure a thrill ride gave an addict.

"I love the toys of our modern era," he said, green eyes gleaming, as if to confirm her impression.

"So what's this vital information you have for me?" Annja asked. Mr. Summer had made light conversation, mostly asking how she found the city and eliciting her views on the city's historical artifacts. His own knowledge of these seemed beyond encyclopedic; she wished she were able to take advantage of his knowledge. But she sensed that this meeting would be their one and only. She had carefully eaten until her hunger was almost assuaged before bringing up anything potentially controversial.

"Simply that your expedition poses great danger."

She frowned. "To me?"

"To you and to your companions, yes. To be sure. But also, quite possibly, to the world."

Her frown deepened. "Isn't that overstating things just a bit?"

He smiled thinly. "I wish I thought I was. For if your employers find what they seek it can be used to start the third—and likely final—world war. All the elements are in place, awaiting only a sign. Do you understand?"

She took another bite of rice and chewed slowly to give herself time to think. "Maybe," she said in a neutral tone. "I'm aware there are Christian millenarialists in my country who believe that Jesus Christ is waiting for a particular set of prophesied conditions to come about in order that he can return."

"And bring the Armageddon."

She shrugged. "That seems to be the general plan."

"You realize that certain such people are in what we might call a position to expedite the Last Battle?"

"Too well, as it happens. Are you telling me my employers are some of those people?"

"Not necessarily. But regardless of the particulars of their own belief, or their own degree of influence for that matter, if they conclude they have found that which they seek it could be more than sufficient for those who unquestionably do hold such beliefs and power."

She sighed and put her fork down. "If I let myself be intimidated out of an expedition," she said, "what kind of an archaeologist am I?"

"Spoken like the true heiress to Indiana Jones and Lara Croft," he said, shaking his head with a sad smile. "Unfortunately, this is not a movie."

"I can't bring myself to accept the argument that there are some things humankind was not meant to know, Mr. Summer. However it's couched."

"There is a certain nobility in your position, Ms. Creed. Even if it arises from a courage born of ignorance. Have you considered what the consequences might be if you learn a truth your employers *don't* like—for you and your friends?"

Anger stabbed through her. She let it pass without grabbing onto it. He seemed to mean well. He was clearly well educated and well-off—like some kind of Middle Eastern magnate, in fact, although he didn't strike her as Arab or Persian.

He had a most convincing manner. He also knew way too much. Yet words could never hurt her. Could they?

"Yes," she said, more tightly than she intended. "I have. But I'm just not prepared to throw over a commitment, professional and personal, simply because some mystical stranger utters Apocalyptic warnings. Please understand that."

He finished his food and laid knife and fork carefully across his plate. "I do," he said. "I also hope, most urgently, that you will reconsider. You are a most estimable young woman."

"Thank you. But I have to tell you it's highly unlikely. Thank you for the dinner, though. I enjoyed it thoroughly. The company as well as the scenery and the food."

He smiled and rose, taking up his hat and coat. "Please give my regards to young Roux and his apprentice Garin."

A light went on in Annja's skull. If that was the proper metaphor for something that felt like a hefty whack with a sledgehammer. Had that garrulous old fart Roux been running his mouth to his poker buddies again? she wondered furiously.

The man with the silver-brushed red beard was laughing and holding up his hands. "Peace, please. Don't be so hasty to blame Roux. Although indeed, it's easy enough to do. I come entirely on my own initiative. And he's not breathed a hint of your secret to me, although he's far too enamored of mystery and mumbo jumbo for their own sakes not to drop heavy hints. Unfortunately he's also so cagey that he never goes further, no matter how drunk one gets him. I will confess I've tried."

"Then how?"

"My dear child, when one's eyes have seen as much as these eyes have, one need see little indeed to discern the truth."

He touched his hat. "I bid you good evening, and leave you with my sincere wish that the gods go with you and keep you. I fear you shall need it."

He was gone then, disappearing around the curve of the corridor, before Annja had untangled his cryptic statement well enough to notice what else he'd said.

"Who calls Roux young?" she wondered aloud. She shook her head. "The old dude's got to be delusional. It's the only possible explanation."

LIKE A LOT OF OLD CITIES Ankara had narrow twisty streets right alongside broad well-traveled thorough-fares, giant skyscrapers rubbing glass-and-steel shoul-ders with brick tenements and blocks of modest shops. Some of that could be found in the Kavaklidere south of the Sheraton.

Annja preferred the dimmer backstreets to the bright modern lights. They allowed a more pleasant walk with a degree of solitude. Even if her thoughts were too roiled and dark for her to enjoy walking through the exotic Turkish capital as much as she usually would. She still found it both odd and pleasing that she had these streets, even this par-ticular relatively long and straight uphill stretch, pretty much to herself, when just a few blocks away on Talat Pafla Boulevard the traffic was flowing bumper to bumper and the nightspots were hopping.

A brisk wind edged with cold like broken glass sent dry leaves from the avenue's many trees skittering along past Annja's feet like small frightened animals. Not all the trees were bare; some were evergreen here, too, as in the botanic garden, and most impressive in size. The smell of spices and boiling water was stronger here than the inevitable city-center diesel stink. Floating from somewhere came the faint strains of Turkish music.

She didn't know what to make of the aged Mr. Summer.

It was tempting to dismiss what he said as nonsense. But there was the fact that he knew Roux. And Garin.

And also that she was off on a quest to prove the literal truth of the Old Testament, totally against the laws and wishes of their host country. Surreal? The whole damned thing was surreal.

She trudged up the hill toward the light-encrusted tower of the Sheraton. It was steep here. It didn't tax her particularly. In fact she was thinking of hitting the hotel's beautiful and well-equipped exercise room when she got back—maybe take a few laps in the indoor pool afterward. She was wary of jogging on the street under the circumstances; best not to attract undue attention to herself....

Striding down the hill toward her from the hotel she saw a familiar figure: the lean, beak-nosed general Orhan Orga. For all his near-depressive appearance at the negotiating table he walked with erect military bearing, looking taller than normal in his high-peaked cap, with his black leather greatcoat flapping around his stork legs. Behind him, and seemingly having to hustle to keep up, were a pair of huge and burly plainclothes goons. Apparently a Turkish army general worried more about being mugged on the Ankara streets than Annja. Then again, he probably had higher-level enemies than random street criminals on his mind.

A black SUV with dark tinted windows waited gleaming by the curb, nose toward Annja and two blocks uphill. Its lights flashed and its alarm system beeped reassuringly twice as Orga gestured grandly with a gloved hand. He thoughtfully slowed enough to allow one bodyguard to scuttle ahead of him to open the driver's door and lever his bulk inside. The other stepped fast to open the passenger door for his master, then clambered into the backseat.

She heard the car's big engine growl alive. The SUV rolled away from the curb toward her like a big black cat headed out for a nocturnal prowl.

Then it exploded with a brilliant yellow-white flash.

7

The heavy car flew skyward on a column of yellow flame.

At the same instant a sharp crack hit Annja's eardrums. She was already dropping onto her palms on the sidewalk, preparatory to flattening herself like a lizard on a hot rock. As a louder, heavier boom rolled over her on a breath of hot wind she realized she'd just seen a two-stage explosion going off. The first, sharper blast had been to rupture the car's fuel tank and turn the gasoline inside into an aerosol—which when ignited itself served as a high explosive.

The movies loved using two-stage blasts because they were showy, with lots of bright yellow fire. But out in the big bad world Annja knew they were relatively rare because they took extra effort and knowledge to plant. That meant they were reserved for those people who had really annoyed somebody who was really, really skilled.

I guess this means the Turkish government disapproves of our little scheme, she thought as chunks of debris began to rain down around her.

The blasts were still echoing around Kavaklidere when she thrust herself upright. She wasn't superstitious but she sure believed in bad luck. As in, it was bad luck to be the only person visible on the street when a car containing a reasonably major public figure blew skyward atop a pillar of fire.

With her usual gymnastic grace she snapped to her feet in a single spasm of effort. Time to get off the street and find a nice dark corner to fold myself into, she thought. She figured her next priority after that was a call to the Sheraton to let her friends know they needed a brand-new set of plans. In one heck of a hurry.

Before she could take a step a heavy hand clamped her right bicep. Another got her left one. They felt like iron bands.

Despite the length of her legs and her lean muscle weight, she felt herself picked up bodily off the ground. She smelled stale male sweat and harsh tobacco. Not a good sign. Not one little bit.

Looking hurriedly around, as she was dragged back down the street and around the corner, she saw she'd been seized by a pair of burly, swarthy goons in ill-fitting suits. One had a shaved head; the other took the opposite tack with a shaggy head of hair. Both had thick moustaches. Both also wore impenetrably dark mirror shades.

"I don't suppose the fact I've got an American passport will make much of an impression on you gentlemen, huh?" she said. "Huh. No. Thought not."

It had been purely quixotic to ask—mostly to reassure herself with the sound of her own voice, and assert her personal power with a smart-ass remark.

They bundled her into a four-door Mercedes sedan, black and shiny and imposing. Keeping a low profile didn't seem to be high on the agenda for this team.

One of Annja's captors slid in beside her, staying firmly latched to her arm while the other went around to the other side and got in, pinning her between their bulky bodies. The car slid away from the curb.

"Just to be fair," she said, "I'm giving you gentleman one last chance to let me go. Fair warning."

Dark sunglasses still on, they exchanged looks past her. Then as one they started laughing.

Annja formed her right hand into half a fist. The sword's hilt filled it with cool reassuring metal hardness. She leaned back against the luxuriant leather-upholstered seat, and jabbed before either man could comprehend what they had just witnessed.

The man to her right screamed shrilly as the blade's edge bit into his face. The man to her left was struggling to shift his bulk. She felt him bunching to deliver some kind of retaliatory attack. She couldn't get much hip into her own blows but she did the best she could, swinging her body hard to ram the sword's pommel into his face. She felt teeth splinter.

The other guy was thrashing and bellowing. Glancing back she saw his face fountaining blood from a long gash. Seizing the hilt with both hands Annja did quick nasty work in the tight confines. Periodically she gave his partner a quick slam with the hilt. The man on her right shrieked and convulsed. The inside of the driver's-side window and the rear window were sprayed with blood.

As he slumped into a bubbling mass of torn cloth and violated flesh his compatriot recovered from his facial battering enough to grab Annja's arm again. He was still strong; she couldn't break free, especially with too little room to really get her hips into it.

She opened her hand. The sword vanished. The astonishing sight made the assailant relax his grip slightly. Then she turned and jabbed him in the eye. He squealed.

His shades were broken and askew on his face. Half-blind he tried to grab her again. He still hadn't given up the notion that he was *big strong man* and she was mere *weak woman;* he was relying on muscles and now adrenaline rather than going for the gun whose butt she could see tucked beneath his left armpit.

As she fended off his blows Annja flicked a glance at the driver. He looked smaller than the two bruisers who'd picked her up—literally—but that was a relative thing. He was veering around some narrow street, dividing his attention between steering the big black SUV, looking in the rearview mirror to try to see what was going on in the backseat and bellowing what she thought were alternate curses and advice at the top of his voice.

The guy on her right cocked a fist to smash her in the side of her head. She couldn't afford to lose consciousness now or even focus.

Her problem was the car wasn't quite six feet side to side, internally. The sword was four feet long and there was no room to maneuver. She leaned way over the now quiescent, sodden body of her other assailant, held her right hand up and back at a wonky angle and formed it into a half fist again.

Again the sword came to her call. The way her wrist was bent her grip was very weak. She wrapped her left hand over the pommel again and, turning hard, drove the sword with all her strength into her enemy's thick throat.

She overdid it. She barely felt the blade's passage through the cartilage muscle and sinews of his neck, nor the seat padding. Only when the sword began to bite deeply into the metal of the car's body itself did she feel a shock of resistance.

And then the blade was well and truly stuck. The driver had finally turned his head to see firsthand what was happening behind him.

His eyes were wide with shock. The olive facial skin around his dark eyebrows and moustache was suffused with a dark hue that she figured was red; his blood pressure was headed toward detonation. Spittle flew from his mouth along with sounds Annja suspected weren't intelligible in Turkish or any other known human language. It was the primal speech of rage and terror.

But he hadn't lost enough touch to forget his own handgun. He was obviously grabbing for it, while trying to bring the car to a stop.

Annja released the sword. It vanished instantly back to the otherwhere. In the milliseconds she had to estimate, she didn't see any way to wield it effectively against the driver. Not before he got his own piece and started blasting her.

But she wasn't tied to the Renaissance and its tools. The butt of the handgun belonging to the man she'd just killed was prodding her in the right bicep. She needed no more hint than that.

Her left hand snaked over and dived inside his jacket. It was a wet mess, damp with a wider variety of fluids than she wanted to think about. Fortunately he didn't have one of those trick holsters that only work for a certain angle, or that you have to perform some kind of complicated ritual to get to disgorge its contents. For a while those had been all the vogue in law enforcement, to keep cops from having their guns taken away from them by suspects. Annja wasn't sure how that worked out; she personally thought that the point to carrying a firearm, which was at best heavy and inconvenient, was to have it instantly available at need.

The dead man's piece was a Glock. It was boxy, reassuring and reliable and best of all had no external safety to try to fumble to flick off. Annja was ready in an instant.

The driver came out with his own piece, a shiny chrome Beretta. Then he realized it was the wrong hand and the wrong angle to shoot into the backseat. His elbow was in the way, his shoulder not hinged to rotate far enough to bring the gun to bear.

In his moment of dithering Annja rammed the Glock's blunt muzzle up into the notch of the man's jaw, right behind the ear. He continued to try to get his weapon aimed at her. Knowing she had no other choice, she pulled the long, heavy trigger.

The gun's roar was astonishingly loud in the closed car. The brief, almost white muzzle flash illuminated a look of terrible terminal surprise on the man's face.

The driver slumped forward over the steering wheel. The car continued to roll down the street. Fortunately it wasn't going very fast.

It didn't matter. For any number of reasons, all of them good, all of them pressing, Annja was not going to stay in the charnel-house backseat a heartbeat longer than necessary. She threw herself over the slumped inert mass of the man on her right and yanked at the door handle.

The door opened. An icy blast of air hit her in the face. The diesel fumes of downtown Ankara smelled as sweet as the finest garden in the height of summer next to what she'd been breathing the last desperate minute or two. Which was all the time the fight had lasted.

She scrambled over the dead man and threw herself out the door. She tucked a shoulder and rolled. She still hit pretty hard, slamming her shoulder and then a hip. But she'd had gymnastic training and martial arts training in falling safely, plus way more experience at diving for safety on unsympathetic surfaces than she cared to think about. She wound up on her back staring up between dark, blank three- and four-story building faces at a dense, low cloud ceiling underlit to a sullen amber by the city lights. She was bruised, contused, but alive, conscious and with nothing she could detect broken or even dislocated.

The car rolled another twenty feet, hopped the curb and slammed into a darkened light standard. The car's horn began to blare.

Annja felt like just staying there a spell, enjoying the comforting cold hardness of asphalt on her back, the icy air on her face and in her lungs, the lovely, lovely clouds. Few beds had ever felt more welcome.

But she knew better than that. Anyway, her body did. Survival instincts kicked in. She got to her feet quickly and stumbled away into the nearest pool of welcoming dark she could find.

8

"Pick up. Pick up." Annja hated when people told her answering machine that. Now she was repeating it as fervently as a prayer, listening to the ring through her cell phone.

She'd found herself a nice, dark, narrow alley. The smell of garbage was appalling enough, she imagined hopefully, to discourage even street bums.

She was covered head to toe in blood drying to a sticky second skin. Although she was beginning to come down from the adrenaline rush, feeling shaky and clammy and not so happy in the stomach, her nerves still just stood out all over her like porcupine quills.

She had fumbled and almost dropped the phone as she punched in the number. She cursed herself for not having put it on speed-dial.

"Hello?"

Her knees buckled. Never in any moment of her existence had she ever expected to hear sweet music in the voice of a man like Leif Baron.

"It's me," she said.

She wasn't sure if hostile ears might be listening to her conversation—which was, after all, being broadcast over the airwaves like any other radio transmission. She had to presume that any hitters heavy enough to plant a bomb on a man as high-ranking as a general, and send three goons in a top-of-the-line Mercedes to sweep the street of any witnesses, could well swing the resources to listen in on cell phone calls.

There was a pause. Then, "Hello, me. What's gone wrong?"

A breath she didn't even realize she was holding gusted out of her in a sigh. Her hands were shaky with relief. Hang on, girl, she commanded herself sternly. You're not out of the woods yet. Baron was an unknown quantity. He gave good tough talk. She'd yet to see him in action when the hammer started coming down.

"Listen fast," she said, "our local chum just went up in flames."

"Shit," Baron said. "I copy. Wait one."

She did. She kept her head on a swivel, scanning up and down the blind alley, even up to rooftops black against the amber overcast. Whoever her assailants really were, they were powerful and there could be more of them.

She was good. She knew that. She'd seen plenty of danger, actual combat, in the last couple of years. She could handle herself.

She also knew when she was in over her head. At the very least she needed to warn her companions. Hopefully they could then all help one another get clear of the cross-hairs and safely out of the country.

In a moment Baron said, "Are you clear?"

"Affirmative. I had a…little trouble. I got loose."

"Roger that. Can you handle it?"

"Yes."

"I'll be in touch. We'll rendezvous later. Good luck."

The connection broke. She tucked the phone back in its carrier. She was surprised Baron actually seemed to think she might possibly be competent to look out for herself. It seemed not quite consistent with the fundamentalist view of womanhood. As she understood it, anyway. Then again, evidently they hadn't hired her just because they liked the way she looked on TV. Even if that had probably figured into the equation.

I sure hope Baron can come up with a way to get everybody out of the country safely, she thought. And fast.

Annja started off down the alley. Despite her circumstances she felt reassured. I may get a slightly creepy vibe from Baron, she thought, but maybe he is very good at what he does.

She headed toward the bright lights and the traffic sounds. Despite the fact it seemed a lifetime had passed—and for at least six men, it just had—it wasn't late.

Where she was going she had no good idea. Just away.

SIGHING, ANNJA STRETCHED OUT on her back on the bed in the little hotel in the middle-class bedroom suburb called Batikent, west of the city center. She'd wanted to go on to Sincan, farther out the recently added Metro line, mainly because it was farther, but a friendly middle-aged English-speaking woman in a conservative but Western skirt suit had advised urgently against it. Apparently both the district and the city were notorious hotbeds of Islamists. It wasn't a good place for a Westerner to be. Especially, all but needless to say, an unescorted woman.

After calling Baron she'd found a fountain in a deserted cul-de-sac and taken a quick field-expedient bath, clothes on. She'd been able to get her face, hands and hair reasonably clean, at least as far as appearance was concerned. And she had smeared the bloodstains enough that she hoped they'd look like some kind of fashion emergency, not the medical kind. Evidently it worked; nobody had screamed and pointed at her and fainted. In fact people looked pointedly away from the crazy Western woman. Which suited her fine.

The hotel she'd found near the Metro station wasn't bad. The staff spoke English. The rooms were clean, the water in the shower was hot and plentiful and her room had satellite television.

She'd spent an anxious half hour channel-surfing to make sure there hadn't been some kind of huge political upheaval in Turkey that had almost caught her in its overkill. But the absence of tanks or screaming mobs on the streets had not been a deception, at least as far as world or local news knew.

She was bone tired. She used the somewhat harsh soap offered by the hotel to cleanse herself all over, including her hair. It was good enough to get the crusted-salt feel and more important the smell of blood out. Yet her mind was spinning like a helicopter rotor. She knew how to compose it by meditation. But right now she let it freewheel.

She wanted to know what the hell was going on. She had clues—way too many, far too frightening. But how they fit together was a different question. It was still altogether possible that she'd been a happenstance observer of the results of some unfortunate lifestyle choice by General

Orga that had absolutely nothing to do with her or Charlie
Bostitch or Ararat coming home to roost. The fact that he
was involved in negotiations to allow a thoroughly illegal
undertaking meant he'd strayed from the narrow path by
definition. Annja doubted it was the first time.

But even if Orga's negotiations with the Americans
hadn't got him killed, his assassination was altogether too
likely to entangle them anyway.

She didn't know much about Turkish politics. Wilfork
had told her how the powerful Turkish army—NATO's
second largest—stoutly defended the country's official
secularism, even against a civilian government increasingly influenced by Islamism. He also told her that, despite
a long military alliance, resentment against the U.S. had
grown both in the army and among the populace at large
over the Iraq invasion and subsequent U.S. support of the
Kurds in that country.

Because the general had been assassinated, instead of
being arrested and bundled off to stand trial, she dared
hope that Turkey's ruling faction wasn't actively hostile to
the expedition, or maybe they were unaware of it. That
enhanced their odds of escape.

It wasn't as if she were uninterested in her own hide.
But she had gotten herself out of plenty of tight situations.
What really worried her was the rest of the party, cooped
up in that oh-so conspicuous Sheraton Tower. Especially
the innocent and otherworldly Levi—not to mention her
television crew, for whom she felt personally responsible.

I hate this, she thought. She could wait: that wasn't
the problem. What bothered her was the sense of utter
powerlessness.

Yet for the moment she was powerless. She could not

do anything more than make herself get the best night's sleep possible, to be fit and ready for whatever tomorrow would bring. Which she had a feeling was going to be…stressful.

Drawing a breath deep to the center of her being behind and below her navel, she tensed every muscle in her body. One by one she relaxed them, starting with her feet.

She was asleep by the time she got to her upper arms.

9

Annja's cell phone rang as she was getting dressed after another quick shower, mostly to refresh her and get her fully awake and alert.

"Hello?" she said, flipping open the phone. She continued to dress in the clothes she had washed in the bathroom sink and hung up to dry on the shower-curtain rod.

"It's Baron," the familiar voice said. "We're clear of the hotel."

Relief hit her so hard she had to sit down on the bed. She got that weak. "I take it we can talk in the clear."

"That's a big affirmative. No worries. I had to pull plenty of strings with both the Turkish government and our own. I won us a little operational space. Now the bad news—we have to get out of town quickly. We've got powerful interests on our trail."

Tell me something I don't know, she thought. After a breath she realized he was waiting for some kind of confirmation she had heard and understood.

"I copy," she said, feeling lame. "How are you getting us out of the country?"

It was his turn to let her hear dead air. "What are you talking about?" he said incredulously.

"I mean, how are you getting us clear? The expedition's over. We need to save our hides."

"Leave Turkey? Not going to happen. We drive on," Baron said.

"You've got to be…kidding me."

"Negative. This mission's a go."

"That's—"

She stopped herself. She was going to say *bat-shit crazy.* But she didn't talk that way. And she was sure nobody talked that way to Leif Baron.

Nor did she want to, truth to tell. Not after he'd gotten her friends and companions safely away from the Sheraton. She knew far too well how many ways their mysterious enemies could have turned that gleaming white tower into a death trap. She'd dreamed of at least half a dozen of them.

"You're not thinking of backing out on us, are you, Creed?" Baron's voice was harsh.

"No. Uh…no."

It was a lie, of course. She was *thinking* about it. But she wasn't about to admit it.

Because she wasn't about to *do* it.

I can't abandon Tommy, Trish and Jason. Or Levi. Nor did she like to think of herself as a quitter. And anyway, the Anomaly was still waiting, fifteen and a half thousand feet up a frozen mountain. It had gotten into her brain like a burr beneath a saddle. It would itch her until she learned the truth. Whatever that was.

She pulled in a deep breath. "Tell me how to rendez-vous with you," she said.

"That's more like it," Baron said. "I didn't think you'd wimp out on us."

ANNJA HADN'T BROUGHT MORE possessions to the hotel than she carried on her. She didn't exactly have any packing to do. Not vain, she still spent some time in front of the mirror trying to comb her hair out with her fingers. She figured it wouldn't be too discreet wandering the streets and subway looking like Medusa.

She had the TV on as background, a sort of synthetic company. The hotel had a CNN *Headline News* feed in English. The volume was turned low so as not to distract her.

Words nonetheless penetrated her subconscious. "—second car bomb, near the Haci Bayram Mosque in Ankara's Ulus district, awakened new fears of a resurgent of terrorist activity…"

Heart in throat, Annja spun. Ulus lay west of the castle, to the north across the city center from where the hit on Orga had taken place. And coincidentally, from the hotel where her group was staying. She saw somewhat washed-out news footage of a compact car burning fiercely with whitish-looking flames and surrounded by rescue vehicles with flashing lights and heavily armed men in camou-flaged battle dress.

"Two people are known dead in the attack at this hour," the television told her. The screen showed a gurney carrying a poison-green body bag being wheeled toward an ambulance. "Another dozen have been injured."

Head spinning, stomach suddenly surging with bile,

she sat heavily on the bed. It's just a coincidence, she told herself sternly. There can't possibly be any connection.

But the little voice at the back of her skull kept reminding her in an insidious whisper what a clever diversion a bombing like that would make for a mass escape. Just the sort of trick a seasoned special-operations vet might pull.

No proof, she thought. No proof. Her stomach wasn't waiting for more proof. She had to struggle to keep the bile down. A bitter taste and stinging sensation filled her mouth.

"I don't have time for this," she said aloud. She pushed herself off the bed and headed for the door.

She left the TV on, offering its unseen witness to an empty room behind her.

"LOOK! THERE'S ANNJA!"

Trish Baxter came running down a motley line of parked vehicles to hit Annja in a surprisingly strong hug next to an elderly schoolbus, sagging on its springs, with sun-burned white paint flaking away from its metal. Tommy and Jason followed, Tommy in his usual sturdy walk-through-a-wall way, Jason seeming to saunter as usual even though his long legs ate up ground at a good rate. Their breath steamed in the chilly air.

It was about ten in the morning. The sky overhead was blue, whisked by horsetail clouds. By Metro and city bus Annja had made it clear across Ankara, from the western suburbs to the development strung along the road to Kirikkale. On the way she had watched through grime-streaked windows as what seemed like mile after mile of ramshackle squats, some three stories tall, huddled close together as if leaning together for support. It gave her a fresh cause of discomfort along with the free-floating misgivings she had about the whole Ararat expedition.

Now, having coordinated with Leif Baron by phone—fortunately without need of talking in improvised codes, as Baron had assured her they could safely do now—she had made it to the truck stop on the road from Ankara to Kirikkale, in mountainous country a few miles short of the town of Elmada.

Annja hugged Jason and Tommy in turn.

An eighteen-wheeler with German flags flying from two aerials drove slowly past in a cloud of fumes and headed out on the highway. Some of the rest of the expedition came striding back, soles crunching on the white pumice gravel that covered most of the parking lot.

With his long legs the out-of-shape-looking Charlie Bostitch moved faster than he looked able to. He forged out front, pushing forward a hand and a big old smile. Leif Baron strode purposefully beside him. Larry Taitt, wearing a dark blue Rehoboam Academy windbreaker over white shirt and dark tie, came loping eagerly after them.

"The lost lamb returns to the fold!" Charlie said. "Welcome back, Ms. Creed. I understand we owe you quite a debt."

She shook his hand as perfunctorily as she could. "I thought I'd better let you know what happened."

"Good thing you did," Tommy said. "We'd've been stuck in that tower."

"You should've seen the way my man Leif got us out of there," Jason said.

"Yeah," Trish said, laughing. "We went out in these big rolling bins under piles of old sheets."

"It was so cool," Tommy said. "Slick."

"Little bit nasty, actually," Jason said. "Way better than the alternative, though."

"Yeah. The place was swarming with these goons in bad-fitting suits and shades," Tommy said.

Annja's mouth tightened. That description matched the three men she'd left dead in the Mercedes in Kavaklidere. Of course, it matched innumerable thugs she had known all throughout the world. She didn't disbelieve in coincidence, but she didn't believe in it *that* much.

Annja shook Baron's hand, and Larry's. Evidently the godless television crew and their godly cohorts on the expedition were all good buddies now, comrades of shared danger and a shared escapade. She hoped that would endure. She didn't like the suspicions rolling around in the dark depths of her mind concerning Baron's methods of pulling her friends and associates out of danger. Nor the way his eyes, barely visible behind his own Oakley sunglasses, seemed to linger on her after he released her hand.

"So where's our transport?" she asked.

Baron slapped the peeling white paint of the battered schoolbus. "Right here," he said.

"I FEEL LIKE SINGING BAND CAMP SONGS," Tommy said as they jounced along a questionable stretch of highway. It was a fairly major road here between Kirikkale and Sivas, four lanes wide and newish-looking blacktop despite the rough ride. It got a lot of traffic, including many burly eighteen-wheelers roaring both ways. Annja suspected the contractors of skimping on rebar.

The wide, flat-angled snowfields of the eastern Anatolian Plateau stretched out around them. Mountains like walls of white ice rose to the left and right. They seemed set to converge somewhere beyond sight ahead of the unlikely procession.

There lay their destination.

Ankara to Ararat wasn't much more than three hundred miles as an airplane might fly. Terrain and roads added plenty of distance to that, not just horizontally but vertically. Out front rode a glossy new Mercedes SUV, carrying Bostitch, Baron, Larry Taitt and their new local facilitator. Next came the weary white schoolbus that carried Annja, the *Chasing History's Monsters* trio, most of Bostitch's acolytes, Wilfork and the ever-amiable but bemused Rabbi Leibowitz, along with their personal luggage. Bringing up the rear rolled a pickup truck, once red, now faded pink, and piled with the rest of the expedition gear.

Tommy was playing an electronic game. Trish texted her friends. Jason sat reading a paperback novel.

Annja sat in the window seat next to the rabbi. Levi read some kind of book in Hebrew. Annja fretted, which she usually didn't do. It was cold in the bus, and noisy. She thought that if this vehicle had really served as a schoolbus, Turkish schoolkids smoked way too many cigarettes. The residual emanations from the upholstery made her eyes water.

"We can teach you some hymns," said Josh Fairlie, one of the bulk of the expedition graduates of various levels of the Rehoboam Christian Leadership Academy, along for whatever tasks needed to be done. "Would that do for you?"

He was built spare, older than the others, with a shock of thick, dark brown hair worn a little longer, and fair skin. He'd apparently served with the army in Iraq. He made no claim to have been Special Forces, and Annja, who knew a bit about the breed, guessed he wasn't.

Sometimes, as now, he seemed to kid around. Annja wasn't sure if she liked that better than the near-overt hostility of blond ex-marine Zach Thompson or even the suspicious cheerfulness of the twins Zeb and Jeb, whose last name was Higgins.

"Naw, really man," Tommy said. "It was only a joke, you know."

Josh got up and started walking forward, swaying and catching himself on the fraying seat backs as the bus lurched over frost heaves in the pavement.

"What," he said, a smile on his lips but his hazel eyes narrowed, "you don't like hymns? They're not good enough for you, maybe?"

"Easy, man. They're just not my thing."

Jason tucked his book away and sat up a bit straighter. The tension was getting thicker than the residual cigarette stink.

Robyn Wilfork, who'd been sitting by himself across from Rabbi Leibowitz staring moodily out at the snowscape with a half-open fist to his chin, brayed laughter. Josh almost jumped away from him, clearly offended. He was generally circumspect in dealing with the bulky New Zealander; Wilfork was in tight with the Man, Charlie Bostitch, and one of the foremost leadership values the academy taught was evidently unquestioning respect for the chain of command. It didn't mean these fit young men had to like Wilfork. Although most of them treated him as if they were more scared of him than anything else.

"Band camp songs, is it? Capital idea!" Wilfork's hair was a nest of disarray. The cream-colored tropic-weight suit he bizarrely still wore despite the intense and deepening winter outside the windows—with little delicate webs of frost beginning to form at their condensation-fogged edges—was rumpled, as if he'd slept in it. "I know a splendid one."

Tossing back his wild mane, he sang, "Bring me my bow of burning gold, bring me my arrows of desire. Bring me my spear—oh, clouds unfold! Bring me my chariot of fire—"

This time Josh recoiled from Wilfork as if he'd turned into a king cobra, reared up with hood extended. Thompson came up out of his seat as if it had suddenly gotten hot.

"What the hell do you think you're doing?" he roared. "What is that, some kind of devil stuff?"

Josh spun on him. "Language."

Thompson tried to lunge at Wilfork, who gazed at him with pie-eyed unconcern. Fred Mallory, an olive-skinned kid with black hair cut very short and even more muscular than Thompson, stood up and caught the ex-marine from behind in a quick bear hug.

"It's William Blake," Trish said loudly. Annja glanced toward the front of the bus. She briefly caught the Turkish driver's dark eyes in the big mirror over his seat. He had a bit of panicked-horse look to him. "It's from his poem, 'Jerusalem.' It really is used as a hymn in England."

"Bloody Americans," Wilfork said. "Don't even know their own religion. Aleister Crowley, now, he wrote some ripping hymns."

"Crowley?" Josh Fairlie blinked. "Wasn't he a Satan-worshipper?"

"That came later, or so they said," Wilfork declared grandly. "Although some might say he did the best work for the Prince of Darkness when he was still a faithful follower of the good old Church of England."

By this point Thompson's flash of anger had evaporated. Mallory released him. The three gave Wilfork a

deer-in-the-headlights look and retreated again to their
impromptu Bible study at the back of the bus.

Through it all Levi continued to read, unconcerned.
Annja was almost tempted to envy him his obliviousness.
But not quite: she couldn't afford to lead life in that state
of severely limited awareness. And truthfully, she didn't
really want to.

The driver began to expostulate and wave his arms
around. The bus swerved across blacktop dusted with
eddies and swirls of blowing powdered snow. Trish gasped
and grabbed the rail handhold over the seat in front of her.
Zach, who'd been standing obediently by his seat getting
a quiet dressing-down from Josh, was thrown on Jeb's lap.
Or possibly Zeb's. The blond twin unceremoniously
ejected him onto the floor.

Annja's cell phone rang. She flipped it open, held it to
her ear. "Yes?"

Leif Baron's clipped voice said, "We have a problem."

Her heart lurched. Because at that moment through the
pitted windshield she saw the flashing blue lights of the
police roadblock ahead.

10

The Turkish National Police wore bulky camouflaged smocks that looked blue-tinged in the weird afternoon light, with sun slanting in bright white slashes through rents in the clouds, only to be diffused by billows of blowing snow. Over them they wore even bulkier dark blue ballistic vests. One or two wore maroon berets. The rest wore small helmets. Annja thought they looked funny, more like batting helmets than combat headgear.

There was nothing remotely comical about the black HK33 assault rifles the troops carried. They milled around the three expedition vehicles, which had pulled to the shoulder short of the roadblock and stopped, but so far had shown no sign of trying to enter or search any of them. Leif Baron and Larry Taitt had gotten out of the lead car to talk to them. Charlie Bostitch was just climbing out.

"Is it time to panic yet?" Jason Pennigrew asked Annja. He smiled, but the smile was tight.

"I'll let you know," Annja said with a lightness she

didn't feel. Her main actual objection to panic at this point was that it wouldn't do any good, not that it wasn't called for.

"I'm just trying not to think about *Midnight Express*," Tommy Wynock said.

"Thanks for that image," Trish replied.

In the back of the bus the Young Wolves were pressing their noses to the windows and looking a lot less certain than they had a little while ago. Even Levi had set down his book and was gazing out with mild interest.

Annja didn't know yet whether anyone on the expedition packed any weapons. It wouldn't bother her if they had, not as much as she was pretty sure it would the television crew; given where they were going, into seriously hostile territory, it would make a good deal of sense. But the problem with weapons was if you needed them, and didn't have them, you were screwed. If they came out at the wrong time—such as in the face of overwhelming firepower, especially overwhelming *official* firepower in some third-world country whose outlook toward human rights was that there was no such thing—you were also screwed. She hoped the Young Wolves, if they did happen to be packing, had sense to leave the heat in their pants. Or wherever.

She found herself muttering all that to her seatmate. Levi smiled unconcernedly. "As we Jews say, it sucks to be the jug."

The front passenger seat of the lead car opened. "So who gets to sit up front when Himself rides in back, I wonder?" Wilfork murmured. The mystery passenger had entered the vehicle while most of the party were getting hustled onto the bus back at the truck stop.

What emerged into the uncanny light was a very stout man of medium height, wearing a dark blue business suit with the jacket opened. The wind instantly whipped a dark striped tie over one shoulder. He had on a red fez, which under other circumstances might have amused Annja even though it wasn't an uncommon fashion accessory in Turkey.

He bustled importantly up to where one of the maroon berets was standing with hands on hips scowling at Bostitch and his chief enforcer, Baron. At the sight of the tubby guy in the fez he straightened at once.

"Oh-ho," Jason said. "What have we here?"

"Must be some kind of major dude," Tommy said. "Otherwise the cops'd hand him a beat-down for stepping up to them like that."

Annja cast a quick look back at the Young Wolves. She reckoned them to be big law-and-order guys. But they might've reserved that for U.S. cops. Their own pallor and posture suggested they were as nervous about the National Police, whose manner definitely seemed to live up to their internationally fearsome reputation even if they hadn't actually done anything yet, as Annja herself was.

The man in the maroon beret actually saluted. Then he turned and started barking orders at the camo-clad troops.

"Whoa," Tommy said.

"Yeah," Josh Fairlie agreed.

The National Police started hustling back to their vehicles. The tubby guy bustled back toward the bus. He was grinning hugely beneath a colossal black moustache.

The driver opened the door for him before he reached it. Either he knew the man or figured, wisely, that anyone who could make the National Police hop like that was not somebody a mere bus driver wanted to keep waiting. An icy gust whipped fine snow into Annja's face.

The man mounted the steps and stuck his head in the door. "Never to fear, dear friends!" he called out in thickly accented English. "Atabeg is on the case! The police, they pull back and let us go."

"Thank God," Josh said. He seemed to have the most acute understanding of all his crew of just how deep a pot they were in.

"Yes, yes!" the newcomer chortled. "Thank God! And also Mr. Atabeg."

"Thank you, Mr. Atabeg," the whole bus chorused as one.

He smiled, bobbed his head, waved cheerily and withdrew. As he waddled back to the car Tommy said, "What do you suppose *that* was all about?"

"No clue," Jason said. "Just be glad he's on our side."

"Amen, brother," Josh said.

THE CITY OF SIVAS LAY in eastern Anatolia, halfway between Ankara and Erzurum. Erzurum being the point, Annja gathered, at which things would get really interesting.

"Once upon a time," she murmured, half to herself, "this would've been a caravanserai."

"And nowadays," Jason Pennigrew said, "it's a crappy building made out of cinderblocks, with attached truck-stop café."

"The Brits call a place like this a transport caff," Trish said brightly.

"Ah, the Pommies," Wilfork sighed, plummily seating himself in a booth with a cracked vinyl back. "Masters of euphemism."

The restaurant on the strip development outside Sivas

had been closed when they pulled in. Apparently Mr. Atabeg, probably with help from money, had talked the motel management into unlocking the restaurant and letting the group in to fire up the grills and cook themselves a late meal. Like a lot of fairly similar facilities Annja had visited in the interior USA, the look and general feel of the place suggested it had been all chrome-and-Formica shiny and clean when new. It was chilly and shabby now. About a quarter of the fluorescent lights were lit, casting a jittering, dispiriting illumination that made the place feel closed. The diner smelled of stale cooking oil and illicit, harsh cigarette smoke.

As if to add to the ambiance, Wilfork lit his own smoke.

"Do you mind not smoking in here?" Jason and Josh said in unison. They looked at each other and grinned sheepishly.

"Yes," the journalist drawled. "In fact I do mind not smoking in here."

He took a deep drag. "Welcome to Sebasteia," he said.

"What was it called in the Bible?" Eli Holden asked. He sat with most of the other acolytes around a table in the middle of the room. He was a wiry guy, an inch or two shorter than Annja, with red hair curly on top and shorn short on the sides of a head that seemed to sprout on a stalk of neck from shoulders well-roped with muscle. He had lots of freckles and his eyes were a murky green. He said little. When he did the others listened, with what seemed more like wariness than actual attention. He seemed to specialize in doing what he was told and asking no questions—which made this one doubly surprising.

"It belonged to the Hittite Kingdom in those days," Levi said. "Not much is known of the place before Caesar's fellow triumvir Pompey built a city here called Megalopolis, or Big Town. Around the end of the first century, though, the name was changed to Sebasteia, deriving from *sebastos,* a Greek translation of the title assumed by the first Roman emperor, Augustus. The current name evolved from that. The name Sebastian originally meant, 'a man from Sivas.'"

"Wow," Tommy said. "You mean everybody named Sebastian's named after this dump?"

Levi smiled and bobbed his head. "Yes. Exactly."

The Young Wolves looked at him as if they didn't know what to make of him, as if a winged squirrel had landed in their midst or something. Annja didn't think they'd normally be the types to take too kindly to being lectured by a know-it-all. Especially one who happened to be a Jew. Yet if anything they had been well trained to obedience, and Rabbi Leibowitz had been hired by their master Charlie precisely *to* know it all.

Anyway, unlike way too many intellectuals and academics of Annja's experience, there was no smug air of superiority about Levi when he engaged in one of his info-dumps. It all came out matter-of-factly. If you asked what he knew, he politely told you. And her associates from New York were staring at the rabbi about the same way the acolytes were.

"No fooling?" Josh asked, a little weakly.

"No fooling," Levi said solemnly.

Annja was with Tommy. She hadn't known about the origin of the name Sebastian, either. She disagreed about his opinion of Sivas, though. She could see how he'd be a bit prejudiced right now. The adrenaline rush of their early-hour escape from the potential death-trap of the Sheraton

Tower had subsided into the usual ash-and-cold-water gruel of depression and vague dissatisfaction; the sudden vengeful fall of winter further chilling their spirits; and the encounter with the surly, heavily armed National Police more a cattle-prod shock to the fear gland than anything to produce even another temporary adrenaline-dump high.

All that, plus the not-very-inspiring nature of the closed truck-stop café, may have colored his judgment on Sivas. Or not. The city lay in a wide valley along the Kizilirmak or Red River, amid wide winter-fallow grain fields and sprawling factories, whose lighting, actinic blue through blowing snow, suggested they never lay fallow. It might have been a pleasant setting in spring.

A gust of wind threw some larger clumps of snow against the big front window, making everybody jump and turn. The door opened, admitting a swirl of wintry air. Charlie Bostitch stomped in, hugging himself and blowing, followed by Leif Baron and Mr. Atabeg. Larry Taitt brought up the rear like a puppy following its humans. Charlie wore a tan London Fog trench coat, Larry a black version of same, Baron a bulky jacket and a pair of earmuffs clamped over his bald dome. Atabeg wore just his suit and fez and seemed comfortable as well as indefatigably cheery.

"Well, we're good for the night," Baron announced, moving into the center of the room. "We won't have to show our passports, either."

"Under the circumstances," the local guide said, "the management saw the wisdom of such a course of action. Atabeg helped them see the way, of course."

"Whatever," Jason said. He stood up out of a booth. "So who's cooking?"

"We can play rock-paper-scissors for it," Tommy said, holding up a fist.

Baron showed teeth in a brief smile. "Not necessary. Zeb and Jeb—kitchen. See what they've got and report back."

The twins disappeared into the kitchen. One of them came back a moment later. He was still wearing his heavy jacket open over a blue shirt. So was his brother, so it was no use for identification purposes.

"They have ground beef in the freezer and even burger buns," he reported.

"It's a truck stop," Trish said to no one in particular. "What'd you expect?"

"Something Eastern European, given most of the long-range lorry drivers on this route," Wilfork said. He stubbed the cigarette out in a red ceramic dish. "Still, burgers do seem peculiarly appropriate. Cook on!"

Everybody else agreed. So did Annja, somewhat to her surprise. She enjoyed eating the food of the area she was working in, and particularly liked Turkish food, as it happened. But sometimes a hamburger just sounded right.

Trish seemed to read her expression. "Me, too," she said. "We're such Americans."

Josh frowned. "You say that as if it's a bad thing."

"What about you, Rabbi?" Annja asked hastily. "Are you all right with burgers?"

"Hold the cheese," he said with a smile.

What Annja thought was the other twin came out wearing a white apron. "Good news," he said. "We have the makings for milk shakes, too. Chocolate, vanilla. Strawberry if you don't mind it made out of preserves."

"Any soy?" Trish asked.

"No. 'Fraid not."

Trish made a face. "I'll take yogurt. It's Turkey. Surely they have yogurt."

The twin nodded. "There's yogurt."

"Well, I don't know about anybody else," Charlie Bostitch said, "but I could go for a milk shake. What about you, Ms. Creed?"

"Absolutely," she said with a smile.

Trish turned her a look as if to say, you traitor. Annja started to smile it off, but then got a weird unsettling feeling Trish was actually mad at her.

She shook her head. You're getting weird and silly, she told herself. Fatigue poisons are messing with your mind and emotions, that's all.

Everybody else wanted milk shakes, even Jason and Tommy. The twin returned into the kitchen, from which the sound of sizzling beef now came. Everyone seemed to sink into a sort of mellow fugue state. Pleased to be alive and free and safe for the moment.

Whatever happened next.

11

"So," Trish said, peering out the window at the landscape rolling by the battered, drafty, rattling bus, "do you think these sheep are where they get angora from? I mean, it's named after Ankara, right?"

The provincial capital of Erzurum lay in high country at the eastern end of Anatolia and Turkey. Annja, who had been charmed by Sivas, ancient Sebasteia or not, was less enamored of Erzurum.

They passed through mountains and tall mesas, and between them snow-covered plains dotted by occasional herds of depressed-looking sheep, huddled closely together against wind that was often snow-laden and never seemed to let up buffeting the bus.

"We're a long way from Ankara, man," Tommy said. He sat with his Mets cap turned around backward and a disgruntled look on his face.

"It's still the Anatolian Plateau, isn't it, Annja?" Jason asked.

"Yes."

He shrugged. "So maybe."

"Angora is made from the hair of goats," Robyn Wilfork said authoritatively. He laid aside the copy of *Der Spiegel* he'd bought along with a sheaf of other multilingual magazines at a truck stop west of Sivas. He sat behind the *CHM* contingent, between them and the Rehoboam Christian Leadership Academy group at the back of the bus, in front of massed luggage. "Also rabbits, peculiarly enough."

"Seriously?" Trish asked.

"Seriously," Wilfork said, sounding sober as a bishop. Which he was, unless he'd managed to smuggle a hip flask aboard and hit it while nobody was looking. Annja didn't think he had.

"Is that right, Annja?" Trish asked.

"I think so. Textiles and fabric arts are a little out of my line, though. I'm more up on old manuscripts and stuff you dig up out of the ground. Artifacts, I mean. Not metals and minerals or anything."

"So you don't know anything about sheep."

"No."

Trish sighed and turned her snub-nosed face back to the window.

"If it makes you feel better," Wilfork said solicitously, "Erzurum did garner a modicum of fame for massacres during the Armenian genocide."

Trish had nothing to say to that.

The roadside motel where they overnighted outside of Sivas boasted beds with the consistency of butcher blocks. Exhausted from sheer stress, Annja had slept as she usually did—totally, deeply, bonelessly and ever alert to snap to instant wakefulness. She had slept in worse places. Many and *much* worse.

Most of her companions on the bus, it seemed, had on the other hand slept badly, fitfully, and were prone to complain loudly about it.

"Are we there yet?" Trish asked from the seat where she sprawled across from Annja. She had her arm laid across the foam stuffing spilling from the split seat top. "God, I sound like a little kid. But I'm so bored."

"You can join our Bible study group if you want," Larry Taitt said brightly. For the current leg of the journey Charlie Bostitch had Josh Fairlie driving for him, Baron and the irrepressible Mr. Atabeg. Larry was in full-on tour director mode, doing his bright-eyed, toothpaste-ad-smile best to keep everybody's spirits up. If anything it was having the opposite effect.

Annja turned to peer out the window. Although it was only the middle of the afternoon the iron-colored overcast sky and the sporadically falling light snow turned everything to twilight. Half of the scene was fuzzed out by condensation on the window caused by the cold. Hoping no one would notice, she began to draw stick figures in the condensation. Growing up in hot New Orleans she'd had little chance to do that as a little girl. It still secretly fascinated her.

Snow, on the other hand, had already long since lost its capacity to thrill her. If it hadn't the last couple days would've killed it off for sure. And she hadn't even had to be out in it much yet.

"So, Rabbi," Jason said. He sat two seats up from Annja on the far side of the bus, with his long legs stretched out into the aisle. "What do you think? Is Noah's Ark really up on this mountain we're going to?"

That awoke a growl from someone in the back of the bus. Annja tensed. But Levi laid aside his own reading matter and sat up adjusting his glasses on his nose with a happy smile. The only thing he loved as much as his studies was talking about them.

"Well, Mr. Pennigrew," he said, "you should first understand there are numerous Flood myths."

"That's why we're so sure of the truth of the Biblical account," Larry said. "Well, along with our faith, of course. But the worldwide accounts of a deluge corroborate the Genesis story."

"Ah, but do they, Mr. Taitt? The ancient Akkadians and the Sumerians had very similar Flood myths that predate Genesis by a millennium or more," Levi said.

"Sure," Jeb said. "They're talking about the same thing."

"They certainly could be recounting the same myth," Levi said. "The staying power of myth is simply wonderful."

"Of truth," said Zach Thompson, the muscular and to Annja's mind overly tightly wound ex-marine. "The power of truth."

"Perhaps," Levi said, head bobbing happily, eyes alight. "Ah, but which truth?"

"The truth of God," Zeb said, sounding more puzzled than anything else. "What other kind is there?"

"To be sure, my young friend. But how well do we discern the truth? For example, in the Biblical account, Ararat clearly refers to a mountain range. In all probability it has nothing to do with the giant cinder cone which currently bears that name."

"Aren't there, like, two different accounts of the whole Ark thing in the Old Testament, anyway?" Tommy asked.

"I seem to remember from my Sunday school classes that one says there was one pair of each kind of animal, and then there's like another than says there were seven types of some animals and only pairs of others."

That was what Annja remembered as well. She felt it better to stay out of this. Sure, her sympathies lay with her fellow *Chasing History's Monsters* staff from New York. But she was acutely aware of being stuck in the middle here. Taking sides wouldn't help things go smoothly, and the worst risks and hardship still lay ahead. She knew how tensions could build up to the point of erupting in unreasonable outbursts of anger on the most conventional expedition. This one was anything but.

Larry laughed. "But that's easy," he said, sounding genuinely delighted to be able to clear everything up. "If there's seven of some kinds of animals, there's at least a pair of them, right? So there isn't any contradiction."

Both Jason and Trish sat up straighter, ready to hit that like a bass spotting a juicy worm. Levi spoke before they could, obliviously. Or maybe not; Annja wondered.

"If only things were so simple," Levi said. "There are other explanations, too, after all. The Babylonian account claims the gods determined to flood the whole world basically because humans made too much noise, and it bothered them. In that version the ark-builder is named Utnapishtim. He was a friend of Gilgamesh, of Epic fame."

"Wasn't he the dude that won immortality?" Jason asked.

"Well…the standard accounts claim that Gilgamesh tried, and failed. But certain tablets claim he made it. Then again, there's a Flood account in the apocryphal *First Book of Enoch,* apparently dating to the second century BCE, as you secular archaeologists like to term it, which claims it was intended to wipe out the Nephilim, a race of evil giants gotten by angels on the daughters of men."

"That's different," Trish said.

"Musta worked," Tommy said. "Seen any giants lately?"

"Well, of course the giants were among those who failed to survive the Flood," Larry said. "Like dinosaurs."

The three television crew members stared at him. "Dinosaurs?" Jason managed to say at last.

"Of course," Larry said. "Dinosaurs and humans lived together before the Flood. That's why there are dinosaurs in the fossil record."

The *Chasing History's Monsters* trio all started to talk at once, tending to drown each other out. Words like *insane* and *messed-up* bubbled to the conversational surface.

Seeing the hackles rise on the Young Wolves, Annja said sharply, "Hey! Enough."

That silenced the three. But only for a moment.

"Look," Jason said, "I still have trouble with this whole thing. Are you people seriously saying a flood plopped this ship down fifteen and a half thousand feet above sea level? That's like three miles. Where'd all the water come from? Where'd it all *go?*"

"Why, the same place it came from," Larry said. "By the will of God the waters fell from the sky. By the will of God they returned to the sky. It was a miracle."

"But if God could do that, why bother with a flood in the first place? Why not flick all the sinful off the Earth at once like boogers?" Tommy said.

Some of the others snarled at that. But Larry shook his head with a smile. "The ways of God are not the ways of man."

"Wait." Annja held up her hands. "Wait, now. I don't think we're all going to agree on things here. So can we just agree to disagree?"

"Are you going to let them get away with mocking the word of God, Larry?" Zach asked.

"Turn the other cheek, Zach," Larry said, still indefatigably cheerful. "That's what Charlie would say to do."

The invocation of the holy name—Charlie Bostitch's—quieted the others right down. Annja wondered if Rehoboam Academy students—and graduates—weren't encouraged to snitch on each other over signs of dissent or heresy.

"We have to work together," she said. "We have a tough road ahead. Maybe even before we get to the mountain. And once we do we've got a tough climb ahead of us. So let's all just step back and take deep breaths and save our energy. Because we're going to need every bit of it later."

Slowly Wilfork clapped his hands. "Oh, bravo, Ms. Creed. Bravo. When controversy rears its ugly head, dodge the issue. Intellectual cowardice to the rescue."

Cheeks burning, Annja wheeled on him. But Rabbi Leibowitz laughed.

"Oh, Mr. Wilfork," Levi said. "These arguments have been going on now for thousands of years. Do you think they're going to be settled this afternoon here on this bus?"

12

They passed their night in what Leif Baron called a "safe house" in Erzurum. It didn't look much like a house to Annja, nor strike her as especially safe, as flashlights held by her companions swept across and around it in the early evening gloom. It was a rambling ramshackle block of structures rising as high as three scary-leaning stories, thrown together of cinder blocks, bricks, wood, sheet metal, plywood, what seemed to be field stone and God knew what else. Random segments were painted a grim mustard-yellow. The whole thing was cheerless enough to be a prison, an effect heightened by its being surrounded by high chain-link fences topped with coils of razor wire.

"A *gecekondu*," Robyn Wilfork said with his usual assurance as they dismounted from the schoolbus, blinking in the unexpected brightness of afternoon sun shining through big breaks in the clouds and staring in consternation at their quarters for the night. "It means 'built overnight.' There is a loophole in Turkish law that forbids civic authorities from tearing down unauthorized structures if they are entirely built between sundown and sunup."

"Just the kind of place where I want to spend the night," Trish said, with her pack on her shoulder and a green ball cap on her head.

"Might be worse," Jason said. "Might be raining."

Annja looked reflexively upward. A few brave stars greeted her eyes. Only a few brushstrokes of cloud were visible. Rain did not seem to be in the offing. Nor, thankfully, did more snow. The air was cool, redolent of petroleum fractions and what she suspected was a nearby stockyard, but not cold. She thought again about conditions on Ararat with the early onset of winter weather and shivered anyway.

The *gecekondu* lay not far from the Euphrates, which the ragtag caravan had crossed at dusk. Levi said the headwaters weren't far from here. This was an industrial part of town, near another rail yard, and seemed mostly derelict at that. Certainly there were no other residential-looking structures in the area.

The Young Wolves set up portable generators to power lights inside; there was no electrical supply. Inside the walls were bare and whatever plumbing and wiring had existed had long since been ripped out by metal thieves or scavengers. There were pallets on the floors but they smelled, Trish remarked, as if generations of people had died on them. The newcomers inflated air mattresses, with which they were thankfully well supplied, and unrolled sleeping bags on them.

While this was going on, along with a certain amount of sweeping and waving things in the air in hopes of stirring it and cutting into the mustiness, and much grumbling, Larry and the Higgins twins were sent off in the lead car with Mr. Atabeg to forage for provisions.

"How come we have to skulk into this hole in the middle of post-Apocalypse urban nightmare number three, and then the Bible Scouts get sent off on their own without adult supervision?" asked Jason, fortunately out of earshot of the remaining Young Wolves. Baron and Bostitch had repaired with Wilfork and the rabbi to quarters on an upper story, presumably more sumptuous than what the ground floor offered. If you set aside the risk the floor might collapse under you. But, it occurred to Annja, if that happened the floor would collapse on them, so it was probably kind of a wash.

"I think they want to get them experience on their own in potentially hostile territory," Annja said. "Then again, they didn't tell me."

"What if they, like, screw up and bring whoever it is we're supposed to be hiding out from here down on top of our heads?" Tommy asked. He was disgruntled because Bostitch had forbidden them to take video of their current surroundings.

"My guess? That's good for at least three demerits each," Annja said.

After a short while Wilfork came down to step outside for a smoke. Annja happened to be outdoors in her shirt-sleeves doing stretches to work out the day's kinks.

Wilfork noticed her as his large face, florid as always and looking puffier than usual, was underlit rather diabolically by his lighter. Puffing furiously he turned away, as if hoping somehow that if he couldn't see her, she wouldn't see him.

She marched up to him. "Hey, Wilfork," she said.

He turned around. "Ah, Annja. I didn't—"

"Save it. I wanted to know what was up with your sharp-shooting me on the bus today about trying to cut short potential conflict. Did I step on your shadow or something?"

For some reason he seemed to go a shade paler at that. "Be careful what you say," he said in a semicroak.

"Look. I'm not okay with what you said. I'm trying to prevent bloodshed on this expedition. At least among its own members."

"Surely you're overdramatizing."

"You think so? Really? We've got a bunch of militant, and in fact trained paramilitary and even military types, who are fervent right-wing Christian fundamentalists. Then we've got a contingent of equally militant lefty atheists, or at least scoffers, from Babylon itself—New York City. Throw in the sort of stresses you get even on a regular expedition—one where you're not actually on the run from the authorities, you know? And where your official contact doesn't explode in flames right in front of your eyes? And you've got a high-explosive mix with the stability of a speed freak at the wrong end of a three-week binge. What the hell were you thinking?"

He shook his head. "Really, I am sorry. I just have an impish impulse to stir things up."

"So you can report on it when it all blows? Are you *that* hard up for a story?"

"Well…hard up may not be too far off the mark."

"What do you mean?"

"This crisis journalism may not be a young man's game. But I somehow don't find it as easy as once I did. And I find it is my misfortune to grow old in a world that values youth over experience—and the bottom line above all. It's easy to look at a 'seasoned' journalist and see someone doing a job you could hire a fresh-faced journalism graduate to do for half the money."

"That's your excuse?"

"Very well. I confess it bothered me that you seemed to be successful in calming the waters. Lack of controversy makes for lack of interest in my chronicle. And then where's my bestseller?"

"So you're looking to hit one big score and then retire? That sounds like something from a caper movie."

"Well, thank you for so perceptively comparing me to a professional criminal."

"Sorry. I'm still a little hot over this. You of all people should know how nasty this could all get in a big hurry, given all that crisis experience you talk about. Don't imagine that journalistic detachment is going to keep it from getting all over you if it does blow up. And, by the way, my crew from New York are here as journalists, too, aren't they?"

"By a definition shockingly liberal even by my standards," Wilfork said.

"Which may say more, or maybe less, for your own prejudices than anything else. But think about this—if things really start to fly, do you think your status as direct employee of Charlie Bostitch will shield you? A reformed commie and alcoholic is not the sort of person the religiously enthusiastic are going to give too much slack to. Unless you out and out convert to their brand of muscular Christianity, which I doubt you have."

"Really, Annja. I'm sorry. I meant it as a joke. I see now that it was inappropriate, as the current cant phrase goes. I'll try not to do it again," Wilfork said.

He screwed his big pink face up in what was at least a good imitation of contrition. "I have to confess there's more at stake here than my final payday and its contribution to my retirement fund—which, yes, I must admit, does enter into my calculations. I—I still find myself drawn to the excitement. The sheer adventure. My age and avoirdupois notwithstanding."

"So kicks keep getting harder to find," Annja said. She regretted it the moment it left her mouth: she didn't mean to sound so witchy. She never intended to; and she didn't want to participate anymore in any kind of potentially destructive melodramas.

But instead of taking offense he nodded enthusiastically. "Precisely. I fear that along with my numerous other addictions, under better or worse control as they may be, I am also what's currently called an 'adrenaline junkie.' But I promise to try to restrict my…fixes to what our enterprise provides in the natural course of things, rather than trying to generate my own."

"Good," she said. "Because if I catch you causing actual danger to my people, or me, I'll totally kick your ass. That simple."

"You know," he said, "I believe you could, at that." But he said it with enough of a hint of a smirk to make her think he was simply humoring her.

Let him find out for himself, she thought furiously, if he really wants to so badly. Then, taking a deep abdominal breath, she forced herself to cool down.

Don't start pouring gasoline on the fire you're trying to put out, she told herself sternly.

"Ms. Creed, I bid you good evening."

"You, too," she said with a genuine smile.

AN HOUR LATER THE FORAGING PARTY came back bearing cardboard cartons filled with Turkish takeaway. They ate by the garish light of generator-powered trouble lamps, on folding tables set up in a one-story segment on one end of the *gecekondu* that seemed to have served as a garage. The smells of old accumulated grease and oil were far more appetizing than what pervaded the rest of the structure. The food was good, washed down with some kind of unearthly Turkish fruit drink and the inevitable bottled water.

Annja fended off several invitations from Bostitch to share the upper-floor accommodations. He seemed still elated at their action-movie escape from the hotel in Ankara, with spots of color glowing high upon his cheeks. Annja wondered if he might have fallen off the wagon again. His manner was jovially avuncular. It wasn't far from that to creepy uncle, though, and Annja was pleased when he didn't press the issue too hard.

"And keep in mind," Josh called to them as they and the Young Wolves headed for separate but adjoining compartments, "no lewd cohabitation."

It sounded to Annja as if the kid were trying a joke. "Hey, now," Jason said, sounding sharp. "I just had my heart set on lewd cohabiting. Just couldn't wait to get right on down to it."

Josh blinked. He seemed more puzzled and a little hurt than offended. Predictably Zach and a couple of the others growled, though, and seemed set to start woofing back.

"Jason, stop being a dick," Trish said.

Jason jerked around and shut his mouth. It surprised Annja to hear the blond woman speak up like that to one of her comrades. Annja had been thinking much the same thing. She had felt constrained mostly because it wasn't her style to call somebody a dick.

She didn't have any moral qualms about bad language, nothing like that. Nor even residual fear of the nuns with their ever-ready bars of startlingly corrosive soap. It was just that having devoted much of her life to the study of language, making herself fluent or at least conversant in the major Romance tongues, past as well as present, she should by God be able to come up with something better than to just call somebody a dick.

After all, mincing words wasn't her style, either.

With no further static the groups went their ways. Annja likewise refused an offer from the three *CHM* staffers to join them huddled in a corner of the room they had staked out as their own to share a pint of whiskey thoughtfully donated by Wilfork. They muttered about the way Leif Baron had told the Young Wolves to patrol the perimeter by two-hour watches, a pair at a time. They speculated in tones half scandalized and half fearful whether the sentinels were actually armed.

For her part Annja hoped they were. And she was glad there were guards. That was something she could say for Baron—she doubted anyone would slack off on his watch. She actually felt secure enough to sleep the whole night through. And no compunction about doing so—watchstanding wasn't her job.

THE NEXT DAY FOUND EVERYBODY semirested and grumpy. Not even Annja had been able to muster much enthusiasm for a breakfast of cold rice, ground lamb and pine nuts, wrapped in grape leaves and washed down with grape soda with an especially acrid bite to it, as if made with too much battery acid.

In a few hours the inevitable battered bus was jouncing and clattering down what was nominally a paved two-lane road through the broken terrain of the Ağri plateau, beneath an overcast sky that suggested their respite from snow was nearing a decisive end.

"Ağri Province once was part of the ancient Kingdom of Urartu," Levi was telling an audience of Young Wolves. The Rehoboam Academy alums never seemed to know quite how to treat the rabbi. They listened attentively, with eyes wide, as if on the one hand not wanting to miss a drop of the wisdom he was imparting, and on the other fearing he'd at any moment start trying to seduce them into worshiping pagan idols. "Urartu is the source of the name Ararat."

"It might as well be mud, lads," Wilfork said with patently false heartiness from the seat ahead of Levi's. "Someone blew up a Turkish-Iranian natural gas pipeline hereabouts in August of 2006. Since then fighting between Kurd separatists and the Turkish army has escalated into open but unpublicized warfare."

"Good news is everywhere," Trish said.

Annja's cell phone rang.

Everyone turned and stared at her. Feeling conspicuous she took it out and flipped it open. "Hello?"

"Creed, this is Baron. Look alive. We might have a situation, here."

At the same time Tommy Wynock pointed out the front window and shouted, "Whoa! Roadblock!"

13

"Again?" Tommy said.

"No worries," Trish said. "Mr. Atabeg will wave his hand and make it all okay."

With much shuddering and squealing of brakes the bus slowed to a stop. Their forward passage was barred by a stake-bed truck parked across the road.

"Maybe not," Jason said. Tall men in dark caps and long black coats stepped out into the road in front of the block, pointing Kalashnikovs at the lead car. "These guys don't look all that amenable to sweet reason."

"Tell everybody to just stay calm back there," Baron said over the phone. "Atabeg says he's on top of it."

He hung up. Annja passed along the injunction and re-assurance without being able to fake much conviction.

She had to admit Atabeg had proven effective so far. Twice since leaving their miserable hideout in Erzurum they'd been stopped by army checkpoints, and once pulled over by a national army motorized patrol. Each time Mr.

Atabeg had dealt with it with his trademark blend of cheeriness, gesticulation and, she suspected strongly, a good strong dose of bribery.

But this roadblock was a different thing entirely. Annja hoped this bunch proved as acquisitive as the National Police were.

Tommy hauled his black camera bag down from the overhead wire-mesh rack and started to zip it open. "Hey, what're you doing?" Josh asked.

"Gotta get some shots of this, man."

"Not a good idea." Fairlie's handsome young face was pale.

The lead car had stopped. Baron and Atabeg climbed out into the road and walked toward the men at the road-block. A moment later Bostitch emerged, and Larry Taitt from behind the wheel.

"He's right," Annja said to Tommy.

"But this is some great shit!" Tommy protested. "It'll make for wicked-awesome TV."

"Think how much more gripping the viewers back home will find it when you videotape your own massacre at the hands of peevish tribals with medieval attitudes and thoroughly modern weapons," Wilfork said.

"They have guns," Trish said, as if that were a surprise. "I hate guns."

"Me, too," Jason said.

Annja looked at them in surprise. She thought they were a fairly seasoned crew. Apparently they either had only visited the tamer parts of the world on their shoots for *Chasing History's Monsters,* or Doug sprang for a better quality of local fixers to insulate them from the harsher local realities than Annja would've given him credit for. Whether you *liked* guns or not was beside the point. In most of America, especially the sanitized if not quite so safe as advertised New York City, somebody sporting fully automatic weapons was cause to alert the media. In much of the third world, it was part of the scenery.

Annja had no trouble with guns per se. What she had trouble with was people *pointing* them at her. Which unfortunately seemed a form of trouble that was just about to recur.

"Those aren't the Turkish National Police," Josh said, getting out of his seat to lean over and look out a window.

"Not army, either," said Fred Mallory. Like the carrot-topped Eli who sat across the aisle from him the dark-haired bodybuilder seldom said much. Both seemed content to let others do the talking. And probably the thinking.

The men at the block weren't uniformed, as such. They wore long sheepskin coats over long smocklike wool shirts and baggy trousers, which was the basic dress of South Asia from Iraq to Pakistan. Some had on black wool hats, others knit caps.

The tall man who seemed to be in charge, whose splendid beard and piercing eyes made him resemble a younger Osama bin Laden, had a flat cap and a 1911-series Colt .45 or reasonable facsimile thereof stuffed down the front of his trousers, which were a gray-white-black camouflage pattern. The hammer was back, Annja could see. It didn't mean the safety was on. In fact the odds were good it wasn't.

He stood with thumbs tucked on either side of the big angular handgun, listening as Atabeg expostulated at him. Or so Annja guessed from the way the short, dumpy Turk, dapper as ever in his utterly inappropriate suit, waved his arms and hopped around.

"Ladies and gentlemen," Robin Wilfork announced grandly, "I have the pleasure of presenting to you the Kurds."

"Great," Jason muttered. Annja couldn't tell if that was irony or not. "And we can't even shoot stills?"

"That verb, *to shoot*," Annja said. "That's kind of key here. It's the sort of idea we don't want people getting."

"Are they *peshmerga?*" Trish asked hesitantly.

"I'd rather say so, dear, given the Kalashnikovs and beards," Wilfork said.

Trish was so anxious she neglected to bridle at being called *dear.*

"In Kurdish the name *peshmerga* means 'those who face death,'" the journalist added helpfully.

"That's encouraging," Jason said.

Annja's cell rang again. It was Baron.

"I thought you were tight with these guys," she said.

"There are *peshmerga* and there are *peshmerga,*" Baron said. "These aren't my guys."

Annja looked uneasily out the window at the lean bearded men in their long sheepskin coats and black sheepskin caps. Wolves in sheeps' clothing for a literal fact, she thought.

"What do you want us to do?" Annja asked.

"Sit tight and stay frosty," the former SEAL said. "I told you, Atabeg's got us covered."

Right about then the *peshmerga* leader pulled the .45 out of his pants and shot Atabeg point-blank. The muzzle was about a handspan from the stickpin of the smaller man's necktie.

"Shit!" she heard Baron shout. He grabbed Charlie and threw him bodily into the ditch by the roadside. He flung himself on top of his boss.

Trish screamed.

Atabeg staggered back. A dark stain spread across the front of his shirt and his necktie was burning with a smoky blue flame. The *peshmerga* leader shot him again and he fell on his back with arms flung out. The fez came off his head and rolled a few feet away, revealing the bald spot on top of his head.

As the other *peshmerga* raised their Kalashnikovs and began to lash the ditch where Baron had thrown Bostitch with bullets the bus door was kicked open inward. From outside came a billow of new falling snow, a knife-edged chill, and a spate of angry Turkish. The bus driver leapt from his seat, dashed out the door, ran off up the side of a hill, and was swallowed from sight as the blizzard outside intensified.

"Cowardly heathen," one of the Young Wolves spat. Annja sympathized with the driver. He hadn't signed on for this. He sure wasn't getting paid enough.

An immense-looking broken-nosed AKM assault rifle came in the door, seeming to tow a tall man in a cap behind. He swept the bus with dark eyes and the muzzle brake of his rifle. He favored Annja with a gap-toothed leer and then started toward the back of the bus, evidently intent on securing the men—the only opponents he considered worthy of notice.

Eyes blazing, Annja watched him. As he came abreast of her she lunged at him in a tigerish leap.

She caught the gunman totally unaware. Her sudden onslaught sent him staggering several steps backward, slamming his head into the steel pole behind the driver's seat. At the same time she grabbed the forestock of his weapon, controlling it, driving the barrel up.

He triggered a burst, shatteringly loud in the confines

of the bus. Though she felt the sting of flame from the flashes from the cuts in the muzzle brake, Annja scarcely heard the terrific noise. She was totally intent on her target as a burst ripped through the ceiling over Wilfork's head, causing the journalist to vanish to the floor with a yip of dismay.

It was an old-school Soviet-era rifle and it packed quite a kick. The full-auto recoil jarred the weapon loose in the stunned man's grip. Annja wrenched it away. She buttstroked him in his bearded face.

He fell to the floor, holding up an arm to defend himself. It didn't help. Gritting her teeth in rage she smashed the metal butt-plate into his face and the side of his head, battering him into the slushy, gritty rubber runner that covered the steel floorboards.

She stopped. Slowly, she straightened. The gunman lay unmoving at her feet. Blood totally obscured his face.

The bus was silent as the tomb. The firefight crashing merrily away outside sounded like fireworks from a distant stadium.

"That ought to hold him," she said. She was aware that all of them—the *CHM* crew, Young Wolves, even hardened trouble journalist Wilfork—were staring at her as if she'd just turned into a pterodactyl. "Watch him anyway, in case it doesn't," she said.

Jason raised an ashen, trembling face to her. "Annja, what are you doing?"

"What needs to be done. Keep your heads down."

She was out the open door into the snow. The Kalashnikov was a familiar, comforting weight in her arms. I'm glad I could take care of that one without the sword coming out, she thought. We might actually survive this fiasco, and I don't want questions asked that I definitely don't want to answer.

She barely felt the bite of the air, the snowflakes hitting her face like tiny wet slaps. She ran straight up the same ridge the driver had disappeared over, headed toward a clump of rocks already thoroughly mounded over in white. If she was going to do any good—if she was going to do anything other than catch a round and go down—she had to get to cover fast.

Fortunately the gunman on the bus had been flying solo. Apparently the *peshmerga* felt one bus full of foreign infidels only required one fighter. The others, maybe a half dozen or so including the leader, still stood blasting happily away at the defenders in the ditch.

The Americans were shooting back gamely. But it was handguns against assault rifles. It was not as hopeless as it might seem at that close a range. A burst from a Kalashnikov wasn't going to kill you any deader than a good handgun hit to chest or head, Annja thought. And presumably the Americans were bothering to aim. That was more than the Kurds were doing. They were ducking down behind rocks or the vehicles to reload, then standing bolt upright to blaze off their whole magazines in the general direction of the foe.

But there were only Leif Baron and Larry Taitt, who had joined his boss and bodyguard in the ditch, to return fire. Presumably one or the other was sitting on Charlie Bostitch's head to keep it down. Their worst problem was they could seldom get a shot of their own off for the torrent of bullets streaming their way. It was one of the relatively few circumstances where handheld full-auto fire really did provide an advantage: the superior if unaimed Kurd firepower kept the American pair all but suppressed.

We're about to change that, Annja thought grimly. Using the big metal lever on the side of the stamped-steel receiver she switched her weapon from full-auto to single-shot with the famous loud "Kalashnikov clack." She winced at the sound.

No one noticed. The noise levels were too high, and anyway, as she knew too well, when somebody was shooting at you directly, your whole world tended to narrow to pinpoint focus on that person. And his gun. Even a highly trained and seasoned special warrior like Baron would be able to spare little perception for anything but the enemies firing him up.

She snugged the rifle's steel butt-plate against her shoulder. Having been trained in classic rifle marksmanship by one of the many military mentors, serving and ex, whom she had sought out, the first time she'd tried to shoot an AK, she'd gamely thrust her face down to try to get a proper cheek weld on the wooden stock. It was uncomfortable and felt unnatural with the rifle's upright design. She'd persevered.

Her reward was a savage whack like a home-run swing from a baseball bat that left her cheekbone first numb and then aching for two days. She missed a target she could have dead-centered with a handgun at that range by a good five feet. Not just the silhouette, either: the whole piece of paper, *and* the three-by-four-foot piece of plywood it was stapled to.

With that sharp lesson she'd meekly accepted instruction in proper AK technique. With an assault rifle like that you didn't press your cheek to the stock, but rather held your head up, as one of her older Special Forces teachers had taught her. It was easier to sight that way, anyway, since the Kalashnikov's profile was much higher than a bolt-action rifle's. It did make for a less stable shooting platform. Then again, assault rifles weren't designed to engage targets three hundred yards away with minute-of-arc accuracy, either.

But the farthest enemy gunman in sight wasn't fifty yards from her, and at that kind of range even a bunged-up third-world AK was more accurate than a pistol. Fortunately the Kurds fought the way most third-world fighters did: standing right up in the open and blazing away, either from the hip or holding their rifles up and out in front of them with the butts actually clear of their shoulders. Which worked fine if your enemy fought the same way. Or was shooting full-auto from more than a hundred yards away or so, where they'd hit man-sized targets only by accident.

To the side of her field of vision Annja saw one Kurd fall backward, downed by bullets from one of her companions. Almost directly in front of her, though, was a cagier fighter, better trained or better seasoned. He knelt behind a rock with the buttstock held to his shoulder and pulled off short bursts instead of hosing the landscape a magazine at a time. Clearly he was the most dangerous opponent. Aside from the fact he was more likely to hit one of her friends he was also hard for one of them to hit, since he actually used cover.

She lined up the black-capped head between the ears of the rear sights and the hooded post of the front sight. Using the best form she could she let out half a deep inhalation, caught it and squeezed the trigger. It was like working a rusty gate latch but she managed to hold true until the trigger broke sear and the gun went off with a ringing bark and kicked her shoulder hard.

She let the weapon ride up in recoil then brought it down with proper follow-through. Then she moved toward another target. Even before the rising barrel had obscured her vision she'd seen the shooter's head jerk and a cloud puff out beyond it, dark in the dull afternoon light.

He didn't concern her anymore.

None of the other half-dozen standing enemies had noticed the fall of the marksman behind the rock. She put down two more with solid hits to the torso before the survivors broke and ran, realizing with a sudden adrenal fear-jolt that someone was firing at them from the flank. Abandoning their own vehicle they rabbited off over the nearby hills. Baron and Larry Taitt swarmed out of the ditch, grabbed up fallen Kalashnikovs, and fired after them with quick shoulder-aimed bursts. One threw up his arms, his rifle soaring up over his head theatrically, before collapsing over the top of a ridge out of sight.

And silence descended like a steel curtain.

14

Annja sighed and slumped to the cold ground. She let herself just lay there and quiver with reaction for three whole breaths. Then she stood and walked back toward the bus, brushing snow off the front of her jacket and pants with one hand.

She held the Kalashnikov ready in the other. She doubted the Kurds would stop running for some time as they'd taken terrible casualties in terms of their small numbers. But she wasn't going to bet her life on that.

"Nice job, Creed," Baron said as she came back to the road.

With obvious effort Charlie Bostitch hauled himself out of the ditch where he had taken cover. "Annja!" he cried. Brushing snow-damp bits of dead vegetation from his trench coat he lumbered quickly toward her.

"Thank the Lord you're all right!" Before she could elude or try to dissuade him he'd caught her in an enfolding embrace. Fortunately it was no more than a sort of clumsy dancing-bear hug. If he harbored any impure ideas beyond that they didn't come through. Of course that might have been tricky, given that he'd trapped the heavy Russian rifle crosswise between their bodies.

Releasing her, he held her out to arm's length for a moment. Out of politeness she didn't try to squirm away. Still wired from the fight she was determined that if he got out of line she'd give him a fast knee where it'd do the most good, boss or no boss.

Instead he said, "You've done a remarkable thing. But why didn't you let the men handle it?"

In light of whom she had agreed to work with she'd already performed the necessary attitudinal self-adjustments not to give in to reflex resentment at a question like that. Besides, she had to admit it wouldn't take a dyed-in-the-wool male chauvinist to ask it; in her place most women would've said the same thing. And most women would probably have been right to.

"He had the drop on the men, sir," she said, quite truthfully. "The man on the bus did, I mean. He was also pretty focused on them. I saw my opening and acted. And then because I knew what to do next, I went ahead and did it."

"That's a pretty concise after-action report," Baron said.

They took stock of the situation. Mr. Atabeg was dead. So were six of the roadblock party. If any of the Kurds had gotten injured their companions had carried them off with them.

Although Bostitch, Baron and Taitt were soggy and dirty and chilled through from diving into a ditch partially filled with snow none of them was hurt. Neither was anybody on the bus.

There was no sign of the bus driver. The *CHM* crew and

several of Bostitch's pack wandered around the ridges calling his name, which was Ali. They got no response.

The worse news was that neither the lead car nor the school bus was going anywhere anytime soon. The shine had definitely come off the Mercedes SUV, with bullet holes speckling what looked like every square inch of its bodywork and the starred and sagging windows. Meanwhile the engine compartment of the battered white school bus had gotten shot up; the radiator was gone, the engine block probably cracked. Or so Baron, Tommy and a couple of the Young Wolves who knew a lot more about cars than Annja did said after prying up the damaged hood.

However, all the full-auto/high-power rounds had gone one way. Aside from a hole in the windshield the truck blocking the road was intact. It started immediately when Baron tried it.

Unfortunately the stake-bed was too small to accommodate both the luggage and the passengers from the deceased bus. The pickup that brought up the rear was untouched, although its driver had likewise departed for parts unknown at some time during the proceedings. But it was already overloaded with the expedition's equipment.

"The good news is," Baron said, "we're getting into the area where I have contacts."

"Yes, our contacts with the Kurds have been highly gratifying so far," Robyn Wilfork said cheerily. Everyone ignored him. Although Annja admitted to herself he may have had a point.

Taking Josh Fairlie with him Baron motored off down the road in the truck in search of more transport. Charlie

Bostitch and Robyn Wilfork clambered back on the dead bus and sat sharing a seat with their heads together while Larry Taitt enthusiastically oversaw the unloading of the gear from the back.

Annja went off to the side and sat with Rabbi Leibowitz and watched. "Should we help?" Levi asked.

"Under most circumstances I would," she admitted. "But I think we probably need to preserve our standing as expert consultants, not grunt laborers. Besides, it'll do the Young Wolves good to work off some of that adrenaline."

He blinked at her through the thick round lenses of his glasses. "'Young Wolves.'"

"Sorry. Private nickname I gave them. It, ah, wasn't supposed to come out."

"They do seem lupine, somehow," Levi said, watching the Rehoboam Academy contingent joke and hoot as they hauled out the baggage. "They show distinct pack behavior, I believe. Very appropriate name, Annja."

"Thanks. So, how are you holding up?"

"Me? I'm fine. Why?"

"Well, I mean…being caught in the middle of a firefight and all."

He shrugged. "I leave handling that sort of thing to others," he said, as casually as if he were talking about the heavy lifting going on. "As for the danger, I'm a student of the Qabbala. Not in the sense that's received all the publicity the last few years."

"I understand the distinction. I've run into several flavors of Qabbalist the last few years. All of whom spell it differently," Annja said, laughing.

He laughed, too. "The Semitic tongues don't fit into Latin transliteration very well, I'm afraid. In any event, I suppose I have a philosophical attitude toward such matters. Perhaps it's merely being an otherworldly scholar."

She felt a rush of warmth for this strange, genial man. "Don't worry, Levi. Wait, I guess you don't. Keep on not worrying. I'll get you up the mountain and down safely."

Whether I make it or not, she mentally added. Not that she had any reason to expect things to go bad.

Aside from the occasional ambush, bombing and assassination, all before coming in sight of the stupid mountain, of course. No reason to expect trouble on the climb at all.

She thought Levi might be caught out by her declaration, imagine it was bravado, coming from a mere woman. Instead he smiled.

"Well, of course, Annja," he said. "I knew you would. It's what you do, protect the innocent."

The *Chasing History's Monsters* team came down the ridge—the same one over which Ali the bus driver had fled into the snowy wastes of Ağri province, and from whose flank Annja had fired up the roadblock gunmen—carrying their gear. Once the shooting had stopped they had bailed out to record as much as they could of what had happened. Thank goodness they couldn't catch any video of me shooting, she thought.

They looked oddly deflated. They seemed to be studiously ignoring Zeb, who'd accompanied them to the crest line with a Kalashnikov recovered from one of the dead gunmen hung around his neck on a waist-length Israeli-style sling. Annja thought it a good idea. There was no telling whether the Kurds might decide to come back with reinforcements to avenge their fallen comrades. She wasn't sure whether the trio from New York were in deep denial over the danger or just uncomfortable around an armed man.

She got a quick hint as they came up to her. All three stared at her as if she'd turned into a scorpion.

"I feel like I don't know you," Trish said. "I feel like I don't know if I *want* to know you."

"Yeah," Tommy said. He still had his big camera perched on his shoulder. "That whole thing totally creeped me out. That dude is dead, Annja. You smashed in the whole side of his head."

A voice at the back of her skull said, Good. It scarcely penetrated her lead emotion, which was surprised hurt at the reception she was getting from her compatriots. She had steeled herself to take whatever her fundamentalist employers from the other side of the culture wars chose to dish out. But the raw fear and loathing and sheer rejection from what she thought of as her own people felt like an ice-cold bucket of betrayal thrown in her face.

"But why are you angry with her?" Levi asked. "She saved your lives. She saved all our lives."

"She should've let the authorities handle it!" Tommy said.

"Authorities?" Annja echoed.

Jason shook his head. "Violence never solves any-thing, man."

Levi looked at them quizzically. "Violence would seem to have settled that gunman on the bus, yes?"

"Now that is one sorry-ass motorcade," Jason said, peering up the road at the approaching procession of vehicles.

Fortunately the Young Wolves had had plenty of jockish energy to burn up; after Bostitch made a quiet suggestion to Taitt the dead had quickly been gathered up and carried away out of sight over the nearest ridge. What they did with poor Mr. Atabeg, his sunny positivism forever dimmed, and his Kurdish assassins Annja didn't know and didn't ask. The local burial customs and whether they got respected or not didn't much matter to her right now; she wasn't an anthropologist. The *CHM* crew, whose résumés presumably didn't include TV news, were freaked out considerably by the sight of the bullet-riddled corpses. And even more by the sight of the man Annja had been forced to kill.

Two hours had passed before Baron called Bostitch to let him know he and Fairlie were inbound with new transport, and requesting nobody fire at them as they approached. Actually seeing the vehicles Annja quickly understood that "new" only applied as a manner of speaking.

There were four of them, two sedans and two pickups. Proudly leading the way was a slab-sided old Citroën 2CV with square headlights. Its gray color seemed to be what it normally was, not a product of the cloud-filtered afternoon light.

Annja stood up from the pile of baggage where she'd been sitting. Levi sat beside her. He hadn't spoken a word since their earlier conversation—had never taken his nose out of the Hebrew paperback he'd pulled out of a pocket. She figured he was trying to give moral support in the face of her apparent ostracization from the New York contingent by continuing to sit with her.

Annja had rebuffed efforts by Wilfork to strike up conversation. She wasn't prepared to deal with his foibles, especially since he seemed to keep intruding deeper and deeper into her personal space. If he chose to interpret her unresponsiveness as shock reaction to taking human lives, or post-adrenaline slump, let him. The latter was at least partially true, anyway.

The unlikely vehicular procession pulled up alongside the baggage mounds, which had been covered over with blue tarps against a restless wind that sent powdered snow scurrying and eddying everywhere. Baron himself was driving the front car; another man sat beside him. It wasn't Josh, whom Annja recognized driving the Isuzu pickup next in line.

Baron got out. Charlie lumbered over, relief and concern washing over his big slack features like ripple echoes from two sides of a narrow pool. "Great! You found us more vehicles."

"Yeah. But we got some news, too," Baron said. "The Turkish army's really locking Ağrı province down hard. We'll need to stick strictly to the back roads and camel trails from here on."

"What about the *peshmerga*, dear boy?" Wilfork asked. As always he had his small digital voice recorder out and waving like a stubby magician's wand. "They'd seem to be of more immediate concern."

"Maybe not," Baron said. "Allow me to introduce my man, Hamid."

A man unfolded himself from the other side of the gray Citroën. When he straightened he was taller than Annja, at least as tall as Charlie, but lean and wolflike, with coal-smudge eyebrows over dark, dangerous eyes. He had a thick moustache, but beard shadow covered the whole lower half of his face; the top edges of it, angling from ear to mouth, were so precisely straight it looked to have been stenciled on. He wore a colorful wool knit cap and a sheepskin jacket over weathered blue jeans.

Behind her Annja heard Trish Baxter gasp. Hamid looked that way and scowled. He said something guttural under his breath to Baron. It might even have been English. Then he stepped forward and waved his hand.

"No camera, no camera!" he exclaimed.

Jason and Tommy were both filming. With practiced ease Jason stepped toward the tall newcomer, lowering his camera while Tommy kept his up and recording. "Not a problem, my man," the *CHM* crew chief said, tone soothing but eyes cutting to Baron. "Not a problem. We're not a news crew. We edit this before we send it back, and we can block out his face if that's what he wants."

Baron said something sharp to Hamid that definitely wasn't English. Hamid stopped and lowered his hands. But he didn't stop glowering at the television crew.

Baron introduced Bostitch, Levi, Wilfork, Larry Taitt, then Annja. Under other circumstances Annja might have been mildly amused at the pecking order. Josh and the drivers of the other two vehicles came up, and introductions became more general. The local drivers might have been Kurds, too, but they were smaller and altogether less intimidating than Hamid.

Annja waited until she noticed Baron standing momentarily apart from the others. She walked up to him. "Are you sure this is a good idea?" she asked quietly.

"We lost our local guide and fixer, you may have noticed," he said. "Under circumstances that maybe suggest we need one now more than ever. I know Hamid—I've worked with him before. He knows how to get things done."

Annja was prepared to swallow her ambivalence about Baron and his own ability to "get things done," at least in the absence of firm evidence of actual wrongdoing. And as long as he seemed to be using his competence to keep everyone alive and moving forward. She wasn't happy about extending that kind of grace to a stranger in an even stranger land.

"How well do you know him? It's not as if our relations with the local Kurds have been cordial so far," Annja pointed out.

Baron shrugged. He seemed impatient, shifting his weight from foot to foot and speaking with more than a hint of tension. "Look, I've worked with him, okay?"

If anything that set more alarm bells ringing. Annja knew they were not very far from the borders with Georgia and Armenia, two former Soviet republics affected by violent unrest, one of which had recently fought and lost a short if vicious war with its former masters. Not to mention how near they were to Iraq and Iran as well. It was not a tranquil part of the world. Nor did the possible kinds of "work" Hamid and Baron might have found to do together in the region allay Annja's many misgivings.

"As I told you before," Baron went on, "there are Kurds and there are Kurds. Some of them shoot at us. Some are listed by the U.S. State Department as terrorist groups.

"Hamid, here, will help us deal with the bad ones. Look, why don't you just leave this part of things to the professional and not worry your pretty little head about it?"

Annja just stared at the arrogant man. Did he really say that? she wondered as he moved off with quick lizard motions to consult with some of the acolytes who were coming back from loading gear from the dead bus into one of the pickup trucks. It left her shaking her head.

"Well, it troubles *my* scabby old outsized head, too, if it's any consolation to you, Ms. Creed."

Annja spun to find Robyn Wilfork looming behind her.

"So sorry. Didn't mean to startle you. I thought post-

adrenaline reaction had set in and you'd be more...
relaxed," he said with a smile.

Reaction had indeed set in, with its attendant mental
dullness, sense of wondering what anything was worth
and incipient nausea. The aftereffects of adrenaline overload were all way too familiar to Annja.

"Under the circumstances relaxation doesn't seem to be
much of an option, Mr. Wilfork," she said.

He shook his imposing head. The wind ruffled his
yellow-white hair as he gazed around the uneven horizon,
with white-peaked mountain walls rising to the sides and
in front. The breeze came from the west, though, and was
warm. It wasn't snowing anymore.

"I suppose not," he said. "I have to admit, dinosaur that
I am, that under most circumstances, or I suppose if any
other woman were involved, I'd quite agree with the bel-
licose Mr. Baron. But given the somewhat...startling and
indeed impressive faculties you've displayed, I'm just glad
you're on watch as well. You may well see things our masculine egos blind the rest of us to."

He didn't say anything about Trish, the only other
woman in the party. Annja tended to agree with the tacit
assumption that Trish wouldn't be much use in danger. She
wasn't at all abashed about that judgment, either. It wasn't
about being male or female but about experience and
courage. Abundantly blessed with physical courage, Annja
tended not to be awed by it. She was more interested in
the moral kind, herself. That to her mind was what separated true heroes from the psychos and blunt instruments.
From what she knew of Trish, she wasn't likely to rise up
in the face of real danger.

But she wasn't willing to let the journalist off the hook.

"I would've thought old-school socialists had a more en-lightened outlook on women, Mr. Wilfork."

He laughed gustily. "Oh, my no, my dear. Not us gray-beards who were around when Marcuse and Che walked the earth. There were giants in those days, at least in their own minds. No, our prevailing wisdom was the dictum of Brother Stokeley Carmichael, that the only place for women in the revolutionary movement is prone."

And he ambled amiably off, suit coat hiked up and hands in his trouser pockets, leaving Annja with her eyebrows climbing up her forehead.

15

Leif Baron hadn't been kidding about camel trails. They came equipped with real camels.

"Okay, are we officially having an adventure now?" Trish Baxter called from the back of her beast. Wedged between the furry humps, she swayed alarmingly in her saddle with each lurching step the camel took.

"Well, if you're cold, miserable, uncertain where you're going to spend the night, hoping it doesn't snow again, and your butt and the insides of your legs are chafing," Annja said, "that's definitely an adventure."

It was cold, although not currently snowing, and the winds weren't strong as the group threaded their way among hills where the steep rocky sides were dotted with bare scrub. Annja and her mount were cresting a low gravelly pass between ridges. Half of the long column had already passed over it.

Annja wasn't at all miserable. Oddly enough the transfer to the camel and mule train had perked up the spirits of the whole *Chasing History's Monsters* crew. In fact, everybody's moods had improved. It was as if the transition from the familiar modern world to the *Arabian Nights* version had signaled an entry into a fantasy realm. Annja held no illusions that they were any safer than when they were clanking along in their collection of ramshackle vehicles. And she didn't know if any of the others actually harbored any. But she still shared the general high spirits.

THEY HAD DRIVEN PERHAPS twenty miles from the point of the ambush, along roads that started out as goat tracks and got worse from there. Charlie had brought Annja and Levi into the Citroën to ride with him in the lead vehicle while Larry drove. Baron and Hamid followed in the truck right behind.

"So what's the CV in 2CV stand for, anyway?" Larry asked, trying to play tour director, as usual.

"Cheval-vapeur," Annja said. "The full name means 'two steam horses.'"

"Steam horses? You're kidding!"

"Not at all," Annja said, smiling despite herself. It was a relief to get away from the *Chasing History's Monsters* crew and their silent reproach. Their stares had gotten a little hard to take while waiting for Baron's return. She'd struggled to keep from telling them to grow up and face the reality of their situation. "It's a measure of engine power," she continued.

"Surely you don't mean this car has only two horsepower?" Charlie said, turning around in the front passenger seat to stare at Annja in alarm.

She shook her head. "Different measurement system. And no, I don't have any idea what it really means. I just always loved the name steam horses."

"You're quite a remarkable woman, Ms. Creed," Charlie said.

"It's simple French, Mr. Bostitch," she said.

Half an hour later the car had come to a stop next to what appeared to be a large herd of camels and donkeys standing in a draw. Everyone had gotten out of the cars, believing they were only stretching their legs and lower backs—welcome, after jouncing over miles of washboard track. The *Chasing History's Monsters* crew unloaded their gear and set to shooting the herd, grateful to have something to do.

Baron put his head together with Hamid and a little wizened man with a skullcap and a spectacular gray beard falling halfway down a long blue robe that hung almost to the high tops of his green Converse knockoffs. The small man seemed to have charge of the beasts.

When the conversation wrapped up Baron came striding purposefully back shouting orders to the acolytes. Looking bemused they started unpacking gear from the trucks. Suddenly, Annja saw a large group of men rise from behind the rocks up a slope to their left.

Then she realized with some surprise that the men weren't armed. Instead they were throwing away cigarettes they'd been squatting out of the wind to smoke, which she hadn't smelled because the wind was blowing away from her. The men hadn't even been hiding,which unnerved her since she hadn't spotted them. They started gathering up the ropes trailing from the halters on the enormous shaggy two-humped beasts.

"What's going on?" Jason demanded of Baron.

Baron showed him a mirthless smile. "There's only one way around the Turkish army patrols, and the cars can't go, junior. So we're saddling up to ride. Old-school."

"SO DO THESE THINGS, LIKE, BITE?" Tommy Wynock sang out. The travelers rode in front of the long line of baggage animals. He had a video camera propped on one shoulder. With his other hand he hung on for dear life to the high pommel of his camel saddle.

"Yes," Baron called. "Keep any fingers you want to keep away from their mouths."

"But they're, like, so much fuzzier than real camels," Tommy said.

"They are real camels, you dork," Trish said.

"No, I mean, like, those ones on the old cigarette packs, like you always see in old movies with Arabs in them. The ones with one hump."

"Those are dromedaries, these are camels," Jason Pennigrew said.

"How much longer do we have to ride these ambulatory skeletons?" Robyn Wilfork called out. "Have pity on an old man's bones."

"Not up to it, Wilfork?" Baron said.

"Oh, cut him some slack, Leif," Charlie said. "I feel the same way." Annja had the strong impression he was aching to add the words *I need a drink*.

"We've got some distance to make yet," Baron said. "Just a little longer tonight, though."

"Aren't we past the army patrols yet?" Jason asked.

"Nope."

"Hey!" Larry Taitt called out. He fumbled his glasses, which had slipped down his nose, back into place and pointed.

Looming up suddenly before them against the mauve evening sky was…a block, almost a cube, huge and featureless, with a white or sand-colored wall tinged pink and orange with light thrown horizontally beneath the canopy of clouds by the near-setting sun.

"What's that?" Trish asked.

Hamid had turned his camel and, swatting it lightly and deftly on the flanks with his whip, brought it trotting back along the line.

"It is what they call here a *khaan*," he said.

"It's a caravanserai," Annja said in amazement.

"What's that?" Josh Fairlie asked.

"It's, like, a Holiday Inn for camel caravans," Tommy said.

Everyone looked at him in surprise.

"You don't mean to tell me you've ever actually cracked a history book," Jason said.

"I think I read it in an old *X-Men* comic," Tommy said.

One of the other men, stocky and middle-aged, rode out in the lead on a mule. He was already halfway down the slope toward a high and broad arched opening in the wall. As they got closer Annja realized there were narrow windows around the upper stories. They looked like arrow slots. Or rifle loops.

Both Jason and Tommy had their bulky video cameras balanced on their shoulders, with the rubber eyepiece guards pressed to their faces. "Loving this," Jason said.

The arched door was actually a passage at least twenty feet long. As they rode through Annja craned her neck to look upward. In the gloom she couldn't see anything but shadowed stone.

"Looking for murder holes?" Wilfork asked cheerfully.

"What are those, Mr. Wilfork?" asked Levi, who rode right behind Annja clinging to his saddle with both hands.

"They put them in the ceilings of the entrances to

medieval European castles," Annja said. "They used them to pour stuff like boiling oil on unwelcome visitors. And yes, Mr. Wilfork, I was looking for them."

Trish, who rode right in front of Annja, had passed into the open courtyard inside the caravanserai. She twisted around in her saddle. "You guys are sick," she said while scowling at them.

"Not Levi," Annja said. "He was just asking a simple question."

Trish glared at Annja for a moment then turned and rode away.

They emerged into a wide courtyard. The tan ground was swept bare of snow and tamped hard. Around the courtyard the lower floor was lined with stalls with broad but pointed arches similar to the ones they entered through. A well of yellow-stuccoed mud-brick occupied the center of the large open square. Snow huddled in clumps against the south and west walls, dirty and with the glazed look that suggested it had partially melted and frozen over.

Some of the stalls held animals. Some held men sitting cross-legged on carpets, smoking and arguing. Others stood empty. A gallery ran around the second floor. Beyond it were what looked like small rooms—or cells. Between the armed men walking along the gallery and at least a couple more on the flat roof, Annja got an impression of a prison more than of a hostelry.

As the procession wound inside and around the central well the animals came to a halt. They brayed greetings to the beasts in the stalls. The human guests eyed the newcomers with an interest Annja hoped was only curiosity.

"Holy crap, we're not actually going to stay here?" Jason said.

"No," Hamid said. "You'll be at the Hilton over the next ridge where you cannot see. Paris Hilton herself, she will carry your bags."

"But it's medieval," Trish said with disbelief.

"It is Asia," Hamid said. "Not the Asia of the Chinese infidels or Singapura with its shiny skyscrapers. The *real* Asia. We are poor here. Things go as they always have, with little change."

Annja couldn't help noticing that wasn't strictly true. She doubted, for example, that carvanserais in the heyday of the Silk Road had boasted any appreciable number of bicycles. Nor had many of the guests in Tamerlane's time sported Kalashnikov rifles, or auto-pistols thrust through their sashes. Much as they no doubt would have liked to.

The caravan master had dismounted and gone to talk to several large men who stood not far from the entrance. Hamid joined them. Instructing the others to hang loose, Charlie followed Hamid. Larry Taitt trotted obediently behind.

Stiffly everyone else climbed off their mounts. Annja stretched. Her back made interesting noises, creaking and popping, but it felt wonderful.

The other inmates of the caravanserai either ignored them or eyed them with frank interest. "These totally look like the dudes who held Tony Stark hostage in the first *Iron Man* movie," Tommy said with fanboy fervor.

"Hold that thought," Baron said.

"What kind of people do you think they really are?" Tommy asked.

Jason shrugged. "Smugglers. Drug runners. Terrorists."

"I don't know about you," Baron said, "but I intend not

to go sticking my nose in their business, and hope they'll extend us the same courtesy."

Trish glared at him. "What, you're not going to do anything about it?"

"What, like call in an air strike on my cell phone? Then where would we spend the night?"

"I thought you were the big law-and-order type," she said.

He shook his head. "What you think of as the law doesn't reach here and never has. Most likely never will. Regardless of what you and I might prefer. But there's law here, just the same. The Old Testament patriarchs would feel right at home. And I think we'll find all the order we need."

"You really think that?" Jason asked.

Baron shrugged. "What I know is that we're a long way from home, and it's probably not a good idea to go making enemies. This isn't New York City and *we're* the foreigners. Satisfied, junior?"

Jason, Tommy and Trish all moved closer to each other and looked unhappy but they kept their opinions to themselves.

The caravanserai turned out to be run by an indeterminate number of brothers, each one larger and more formidable than the last, and ruled over by an even bigger patriarch, who looked like Omar Sharif if Omar Sharif had turned into the Incredible Hulk, and whose white moustache was the largest Annja had ever seen on a human being. Then again she wasn't sure she'd ever seen a larger human being to go with it; but even at that he barely lived up to its magnificence.

"Bismarck himself would go palsied with envy of that brush," Wilfork murmured. "I've only ever seen one greater, and that was on a Sealyham terrier."

"The rules are simple," Hamid said, coming from the darkness and gesturing for the party to gather together near the well in the compound's center. He explained that the caravanserai was run by Gypsies—which he seemed to disapprove of—and that they were good Muslims, which he heartily approved of.

"You want anything, you pay," he said. "You cause disturbance, they beat you with sticks and throw you out in the snow. You steal, they chop off your hand. You use a weapon, or threaten one of them, they kill you. Then it's your body they throw out in the hills."

"They don't even give you a proper Muslim burial?" Wilfork asked.

"They leave you for the wolves," Hamid said, nodding with approval.

"Wolves?" Larry Taitt asked, his eyes saucer-like behind his glasses. For once his compulsive amiability seemed to have deserted him. It was such a startling transformation Annja suspected their guide had touched a raw phobia.

"Like that's a big deal," Trish scoffed, her hands in the pockets of her thick down-filled jacket. "Wolves are never known to attack people."

Hamid fixed her with a baleful dark eye. "This may be true in the land of clean sheets and the MTV. Our strong Kurdish wolves have steel in their spines," he said menacingly.

Despite the talk of wolves, after piling the gear and saddles in several stalls, the caravan master and a couple of his drovers led the unloaded camels and mules back out into the cold evening. Hamid explained there was an enclosure on the far side of the caravanserai from the one they'd come in through.

"Aren't they worried about bandits?" Josh asked.

"Why?" Zeb asked.

"They're all inside with us," Jeb said, finishing his twin's thought.

16

Jason Pennigrew sighed with satisfaction.

"It's all right out of the *Arabian Nights*," he said. "Except, of course, for the ridiculous French techno-pop blasting from somebody's iPod speakers. This may be Asia, the *real* Asia, but the modern age had made some inroads, looks like."

"Hey," Tommy said. "We've got a whole wall to ourselves. Both floors."

"There's benefits to traveling with a bazillionaire," Trish observed, lying back and stretching on a genuine Bokhara carpet—rented from the Gypsy proprietors—that covered the floor of one of the stalls. The trio shared it with Annja and the cheerful, myopic Rabbi Levi, although the coolness they still showed Annja indicated it might be a temporary arrangement at best.

"But, how does he pay?" Tommy wondered aloud. "I mean, I doubt the Angry Moustache Gypsy Brothers take travelers checks, or will just, like, swipe his Visa plutonium card for him."

"I wouldn't be too sure about that," Trish said. "I don't know if Charlie would use plastic, though. I don't think he wants to leave that kind of paper trail."

"At any rate," Annja said, "we're probably better off not asking."

Jason gave her a puzzled frown. He'd seemed more pained than censorious, as if trying to understand her rather than condemn. But now things seemed to have changed.

"I don't get you, Annja," he said. "I thought you were one of us. Then you go all Rambo on those guys at the roadblock. And you sure seem to want to play the good German where our right-wing fundamentalist pals are concerned."

Annja took a very deep breath to calm herself before responding. "The right-wing fundamentalist pals are paying for this expedition," she said. "*Chasing History's Monsters* is paying for you to tag along. And they've hired me as an expert."

"Me, too," Levi said. He didn't seem to be interested in the political subtexts here, far less the cultural ones—neither impinged much on his personal solar system. But he seemed determined to show solidarity with Annja. Apparently he considered her a friend.

And what better reason is there? Annja thought appreciatively. One way or another, his support comforted her.

"Do you really think you should have taken the law into your own hands like that?" Trish asked.

Annja sighed. "It looked to me as if it was me or nobody."

"But you killed that man," Trish said.

"His friends had just shot down poor Mr. Atabeg in cold blood. His friends were trying their level best to kill Charlie, Leif and Larry. And he didn't look as if he'd boarded the bus to give us a language lesson in Kurdish. He had a gun and he looked ready to use it. I saw my chance to stop him. So I did."

The *CHM* trio passed tight-lipped, furrowed-brow looks all around.

"But, you don't seem…upset," Trish said tentatively.

"Why should I be? It's been hours since it happened. My heart rate's had plenty of time to settle," Annja said impatiently.

"I didn't mean that. I thought…shouldn't you be overcome by guilt for taking a human life?" Trish asked.

"Why should I feel guilty? I figured it was him or one of you. Or all of us. Why should I feel bad about the choice I made? I doubt he would have."

"Cops always have bad dreams when they shoot somebody," Tommy said solemnly. "They have to go through mad therapy."

"Some of them do," Annja said. "And they're all taught to say they are. But I've talked to plenty who haven't really been traumatized or anything like it."

"But…why not?" Trish asked.

Annja shook her head. "Listen. I may have nightmares tonight about what happened today."

They looked relieved. She was starting to fit the profile again.

"But I'll have nightmares about what could have happened if I didn't kill those men. If I'd missed. If they'd hurt or killed me. Or my friends. What they might have done to any survivors they captured."

She paused for a moment to let that sink in. She hoped they'd be able to understand the position she was in.

"But as for feeling bad about stopping somebody intent

on doing something bad, intent on commiting murder—
no. I don't feel remorse for that," she said plainly.

Trish's eyes glittered with tears. She shook her head.
"Oh, Annja, you seemed like such a nice person. And now
I'm afraid you might be some kind of sociopath or some-
thing."

"If you'd feel more comfortable I can go somewhere
else. I'll find someplace else to room, too." She and Trish
had accepted Charlie's offer to share a chamber upstairs
for the night.

"No. No. I don't want to…abandon you," Trish said.

Don't want me to abandon you, Annja thought with a
sudden stab of annoyance. She realized that Trish feared
the other occupants of the caravanserai—including, most
likely, some of the Young Wolves.

It must be so weird and unhappy to live like that, she
thought. To require so much violence to protect your lifestyle, and to impose your views on others yet be so terrified of those who exerted violence on your behalf. For all
that she disagreed with them on just about every point,
philosophically, Annja had great respect for pacifists. But
that was *real* pacifists. Not those who smugly felt themselves morally superior while relying on men with uni-
forms and guns to do their dirty work for them.

Still, she admitted to herself, we're not here to agree
with each other. Nor to serve my bruised ego. She forced
herself to smile.

"That's very good of you," she said to Trish. "Look, I
appreciate your concern. And I just have to ask you,
please, to accept that we're different people with some
different outlooks."

Trish pressed her lips together. Annja guessed that for

her part she was biting back on saying how glad she was that they *were* different.

"Okay," Trish said. "I—"

A figure loomed out of the courtyard darkness. Everybody tensed for a moment. Seeing it was Baron caused incomplete relaxation.

"Chow's on," he said. "Better hustle your butts if you want to eat."

"What is it?" Jason asked, standing and stretching like a big lean cat. "Meals Refused by Ethiopians?"

"Got it in one."

"Why use up our own supplies?" Annja asked. They might need their MREs to fuel them once they started their mountain-climing expedition. "I thought they sold food here," she said.

Baron shrugged. "We put heads together and decided we didn't have a high trust level in what the Gypsy Bros have on offer."

"So they're typical capitalists," Jason said, "selling tainted food to their customers."

Baron snorted laughter through his nose. "More like, the kind of food their usual patrons can afford, and are happy to eat, wouldn't settle too easily in tender Western tummies. Too many rat and insect parts per million. To these people, it's all just protein."

"There was an Indian mathematician who moved to Britain in the early twentieth century," said Robyn Wilfork, who had wandered over munching from his own MRE tray. "He starved to death because the British rice was lacking in just those proteins—the bug and rat ones. Too clean, you see. Not like Mama served back in Bombay."

"I think you're talking about Ramanujan," Levi said

shyly. "Actually, he didn't starve to death, exactly. But he did suffer a severe protein deficiency that probably contributed to his death at the age of thirty-two."

Wilfork raised an eyebrow at him. "I'd think he and his area of expertise was somewhat different from yours."

The rabbi shrugged. "It's a nerd thing," he said.

"Hey," Tommy said, getting to his feet. "I'm a committed carnivore, I'm not gonna lie to you. So why make a big deal about it?"

"Yeah," Trish said. "I guess I trust the mystery meat in MREs over the rat bits."

"Always assuming the Meals Ready to Eat aren't made of rat parts themselves, you poor naive creature," Jason, said, laughing.

"Hey," Trish said, a little defensive. "At least they're sterile rat parts."

They walked off, following Baron to dinner like school children, bantering as they went. Wilfork gestured with the travel fork he'd taken from a pocket and unfolded. "A moment of your time, if you please, Annja."

"What is it?" she asked, staying behind.

"That Baron is an interesting man," Wilfork said, pointing after the furloughed security-company executive with his hobo tool. "With emphasis on *man*. Charlie's still an overgrown schoolboy. As am I, for that matter. Levi's a scholar, which is another thing altogether. And our muscular Christians—they may be of the age of majority, but they remain at core boys, with the happy feral fury of adolescence."

After a moment's silence, broken only by the tinkle of bells as a camel was led out through the eastern door and the tinny strains of Algerian hip-hop, Annja said, "So you were going to warn me about Baron."

Wilfork snorted a laugh. "Perceptive and tenacious! You're a formidable woman, Ms. Creed. Yes, indeed I was. Perhaps I'm wasting my breath."

"I appreciate the thought. I respect Baron. He seems to be good at his job. He's certainly the only thing that's got us this far. He may have kept us all alive."

With a little help from me, she thought. But she was just as happy that part wasn't widely known. "Otherwise I wouldn't associate with him if he were the last man on Earth."

"That's certainly decisive. Let us hope you never have cause to regret it."

"It's always a risk, isn't it, Mr. Wilfork? But isn't life risky?"

"An excellent point, my dear," Wilfork said. "'No one here gets out alive,' as the poet said."

THE *CHASING HISTORY'S MONSTERS* crew, Levi and Annja brought their food back to their stall. The topic of conversation was the other twenty or so guests of the caravanserai.

"Seriously," Annja said, "that's something about the developing world you really find out when you spend enough time there—often the most villainous-looking people turn out to be the sweetest, most honest, generous people you could ever hope to meet in your life."

"And you think those guys are like that?" Trish asked, looking skeptical.

"Well…no," Annja said, assessing the other guests and going on her gut feeling rather than judging by appearance alone.

"I'm going to keep my hands clamped firmly on anything I don't want to lose," Jason said grimly.

"If I did that I might look as if I was *inviting* attention, if you know what I mean," Trish said.

"Are you still worried?" Hamid asked. He was showing a distressing tendency to loom up suddenly next to private conversations. Of course, Annja realized it was possible the man was just lonely. "Do not be afraid. If anyone molests you, just cry out and the Gypsies will come and hit them over the head and throw them out in the snow," he said.

"Good to know," Jason said.

They finished eating their food. Annja had definitely had worse. Then again, she spent a lot of her time in some fairly severe parts of the world.

Shortly after eating they all decided they were ready to turn in. Jason, Tommy and Levi had decided to share the cell at the back of the stall where they'd been hanging out. Trish headed up the stairs. Annja stayed down to do some stretching in a shadowed area of the big courtyard where she hoped she wouldn't attract unwanted attention. The other occupants stayed within the scope of their own lamps—kerosene lanterns or battery-powered—and nobody seemed to notice her.

When she finished her workout she headed for the stairs at the corner of the yard. A voice suddenly called out. "Yo, Annja. Hold up."

She stopped and turned. A familiar bald-headed silhouette strode toward her at what had become an equally familiar thrusting gait.

"It seems like you've been avoiding me," Baron said. "What's up with that?"

"Avoiding you? I've been a bit busy to pay much attention to social interplay. I figured it was the same with you."

He laughed softly, with his jaws wide like a wolf. "Fair

enough. Well played. But I think it's time we remedied that situation. Come up to my room with me. Relax a little. Let's get to know each other."

"I'm actually going to turn in now, Mr. Baron. In my own room. I'm in desperate need of a good night's sleep."

He stood for a moment with his hands in the pockets of his khaki trousers.

"If I won't take no for an answer, hypothetically, would you call the Gypsy Brothers to come hit me over the head?"

"What makes you think I'd need the Gypsy Brothers for that?" Annja said. "Good night, Mr. Baron," she said firmly. She turned her back on him and walked away.

BY NOON THE NEXT DAY, with the caravanserai already many rump-tendering and lower-back-knotting hours behind the swaying two-humped camels, the expedition had transferred themselves and their gear back to a collection of vehicles even more motley than the last. Evidently the Turkish army's zone of control had been successfully crossed. How Baron—or Hamid—knew that, Annja wasn't sure. She decided to sit on her curiosity. She didn't feel at all eager to talk to either man more than was strictly necessary, right now.

But once again she had to acknowledge their competence at what they did. Twice that day they'd encountered roadblocks by unmistakable *peshmerga.* In both cases Hamid got the party through with minimal dramatics, even if that didn't keep Annja's pulse from spiking both times.

And then in the late afternoon they rolled over a saddle between two jagged hills, ancient drifts of black lava now fanged and pitted, to see the mighty mountain thrust up into the sky before them, its snow-clad flanks shining silver and rose in the light of the declining sun.

17

"Tell me again," Jason Pennigrew called out over the howl of the wind, "why anybody thought it was a good idea to climb this damned mountain in the winter?"

"Language, Mr. Pennigrew," Josh Fairlie called back down over his shoulder.

They staggered through snow, both shin-deep on their bulky boots and blowing hard into their goggled faces, angling up the southwestern face of the great cinder cone. From the days before Ararat's being designated a restricted military zone by the Turkish army, the mountain had been a fairly popular climb for serious mountaineers. Some fairly well-established routes had been mapped.

But this expedition used none of them. The explanation was the terse word *security,* offered by Leif Baron.

"Christ's name, put a sock in it," Wilfork hissed at Jason and Josh from behind Annja. "You want to bring the whole bloody mountain down around our ears?"

Fairlie turned away. Annja thought his cheeks burned

pink beneath his goggles. It might have been from the frigid wind. For some reason he had no response to the New Zealander's blasphemy.

While there turned out to be no such thing as an extinct volcano, as geologists had long believed, Ararat had been dormant a long time in human terms, suggesting it might be likely to stay that way and behave itself while being climbed. Or alternatively, it was long overdue to blow up like the Death Star. Annja reckoned it was a half full, half empty scenario.

Fortunately she had more immediate considerations pressing on her. Being a cinder cone, Ararat had a fairly gentle, consistent slope, at least in its lower reaches. After five thousand feet or so the way became increasingly difficult. Or so Baron had assured them during their planning session in a little isolated building near the mountain's base, the size and shape of a boxcar and made of adobe, with a satellite dish on the roof, from which they'd launched their assault on the peak.

And then there were the glaciers. Especially the one on the west and northwest sides, at the edge of which, a little less than a mile and a half from the summit, the Anomaly lay like a half-submerged log.

But even on a clear path winding up the slope to the south the footing was tricky. Snow fresh-fallen on earlier layers of snow and ice provided uncertain footing at the best of times. Sometimes it also hid serious stumbling blocks or gaps. And the wind kept trying to push the climbers off the path, to send them rolling back down the long white slope.

Plus Levi and Annja, it seemed, were Team Awkward on this climb. Annja had done some climbing but wasn't truly trained or skilled at it. Levi had no experience what-soever. It turned out the Young Wolves had all studied mountaineering techniques at the Rehoboam Christian Leadership Academy, possibly with an eye toward this very climb—although Annja had no doubt it was used also to foster more mundane survival and leadership skills as well. Charlie Bostitch, for all his unwieldiness, had appar-ently successfully completed the same course and knew what he was doing. So had Baron, of course, who'd also had mountain warfare training as a SEAL—which seemed bizarre to Annja, but she knew these days even marines got it, too. The *Chasing History's Monsters* team, unused as they may have been to combat zones, clearly were all ex-perienced climbers. Annja had to give credit to Doug Morrell for choosing a trained crew for the job. Even Wilfork, as he said, "Did a spot of mountaineering in my misspent youth."

At midmorning they paused for a break at a relatively level spot. Jason took a panoramic shot of the surround-ing landscape. Conveniently the snow had stopped falling.

The sun broke through the seemingly perpetual cloud cover to drop a beam of golden radiance on the neat black cone of the four-thousand-foot Little Ararat not far from the main peak to the southeast. To the north rose the Pontic Mountains. The Eastern Taurus range trailed away to the south.

Like many volcanoes Ararat was its own lord and master. It rose from the midst of a rising plain, largely lava shield. Around it lay terrain rumpled like a sheet on an unmade bed. Most of the landscape was covered in snow.

"It's really beautiful up here," Trish said, looking around in awe.

"Do not be fooled," Hamid said darkly. "For once the Turks do not lie. They call it the Mountain of Pain."

"That's reassuring," Jason said. "What do the Kurds call it?"

"Fiery Mountain," Hamid replied.

Wilfork sat, breathing heavily on his pack. "We're up a bloody volcano, are we?"

"Yes," Annja said. "It's a stratovolcano. Built up of many layers of activity."

"*Activity*. What a charming euphemism. I presume that means bloody great belching and fuming and emitting of molten lava?"

"Pretty much. But don't worry. It's been dormant for millennia. Well, unless you count an earthquake in 1840."

"Smashing," the journalist said. "So it might be due for another bloody great blast."

"Don't sweat that, Mr. Wilfork," Larry Taitt said. "The Lord won't let that happen to us."

"He knows we're doing His work," ex-marine Zach Thompson said ominously. "He's keeping a tight watch on us."

"No doubt," Wilfork said, rolling his eyes.

Hamid thrust an arm toward the north dramatically. "That way lies Armenia. On a clear day you can see its capital of Yerevan."

Tommy turned his camera that way. "I don't know," he said, blinking his free eye. "Looks pretty hazy up that way. Like smog or something."

"It is smog," said Baron, who was tramping tirelessly up the line checking gear and making sure everybody was holding up. He seemed totally relaxed and in his element. "Not many clear days up that way. That's the big city for you."

Hamid swept his arm around to the west. "There lies a part of Azerbaijan, cut off from the rest of the country by Armenia. And there, farther south, is Iran. And south of us—Iraq. And all of it belongs by right to the Kurds."

"I guess you'd get some argument from the Iranians and the Azerbaijanis," Jason said. He was filming the climbing party as Tommy shot the scenery. "Like you do from the Turks. But I guess the U.S. has you guys set up pretty good in northern Iraq, huh?"

Hamid's fierce brows knotted. "The Americans allow us to administer the north for them, so long as we help them fight in the south. But they prevent us from cleansing our land of the Arabs and Turcoman interlopers."

"Hey, if it were up to me, you'd have free rein to wipe the towel-heads off the map," Baron said. "The Arabs are just scum. You can have the Turcomans, too, for all I care."

"But your government stands aside and lets its allies the Turks shell and bomb our people in the north!" Hamid said angrily.

Baron shook his head. It glinted in the afternoon sunlight that managed to make it through the cloud layer. "Hey, big guy. Ease off. You're preaching to the choir here. But I don't make policy."

"I thought in your country, all Americans could make policy, through this democracy you try so hard to make everyone obey."

"A surprising number of Yanks suffer under that delusion, too," Wilfork said. Annja noted that his comment won him black looks both from the Young Wolves and the *Chasing History's Monsters* crew.

Frowning, Baron said, "Enough slacking off. Time to climb."

HAVING APPROACHED FROM the west—the Turkish side—
they worked their way around the mountain's flank to the
eastern side. And up. The slope on this side, with the
smaller satellite cone on their right, was more gradual.
They could gain a fair amount of altitude without any scaly
vertical climbs with ropes and crampons.

Of course that meant the sun set early behind the
mountain's bulk. As a blue twilight descended on them,
while yellow-gray light still fell across the broken land to
the east, they pitched their tents on a broad, level patch of
ground. The quiet, red-haired Eli Holden passed out food.
With his stalk neck and not much by way of a chin he
tended to remind Annja of a carrot, although a carrot with
jug-handle ears. His murky green eyes were neutral as
stones passing over her as he handed her her meal pack.

"He's a real ball of fire," Jason said as Eli passed on.

"Bummer," Tommy said. "I got the chicken fajitas.
Anybody want to trade?"

"No," a chorus of voices said. The chicken fajitas were
legendarily bad.

They gathered into a circle. The tents gave some shelter
from the wind, which had thankfully begun to die away as
the sun set in the greater world beyond Ararat's bulk.
Bostitch had insisted on taking full tents along, even
though he'd warned them they might find themselves
needing to pass at least one night hanging from a sheer precipice by bivouac bags. But he said, and Baron backed him,
that they'd need as warm and comfortable a sleep as they
could get every night on the great mountain.

There was no need for Annja or the *Chasing History's
Monsters* crew to worry about the excess weight in their
packs. The Young Wolves all toted massive packs and the

bulk of the gear, without complaint and apparently with little deleterious effect. Annja could hardly complain about a burden she wasn't, after all, being asked to bear.

And for all their weird notions, and for that matter the bone-crazy notion that underlaid this whole expedition, her employers seemed to have a firm grip on the essential things of this world. At least as far as the expedition went.

"It was always tough, growing up in the old man's shadow," Charlie was saying. Earlier he'd been strutting around like a bantam rooster, which he certainly didn't resemble in any other particular, cheeks glowing with pink patches of health. Now that bloom was gone, leaving gray cheeks that sagged. "I could never measure up. No matter what I did."

"I hear you," Baron said. "It was the same way with me. Nothing was good enough for my father. If I didn't do just what he said, just when he said it—" he made an open-handed sweeping gesture across the front of his body "—boom!"

Slowly Charlie nodded over his self-heated tray of food. "Yeah. Yeah, I know just what you mean. My dad was the same way. High expectations, iron discipline."

Given your notorious lifestyle, how well did that turn out? Annja wondered. She didn't feel it was her place to say so. She took no pleasure in picking at other people's psychological scabs. She noticed that the three New Yorkers were staring at the two expedition chiefs in wide-eyed horror.

"You dudes were like, seriously abused as kids, man," Tommy said.

"No, no, nothing like that," Baron said quickly. "We're not whining about it."

"Spare the rod and spoil the child," Charlie said.

"Kids need discipline," Baron agreed.

Trish set down her half-eaten MRE on the rocky soil, slapped her hands on her thighs and stood. "I can't believe you're justifying your own abuse like that. There ought to be some kind of law!"

"I hear you," Jason said.

"The state should just take over care of all abused children," Trish said. "Maybe they should take an extra-close look at Protestant fundamentalist families."

Josh gave her a narrow look. "How about unbelieving households, where their mortal souls are in peril?"

Trish turned to Annja. "How can you just sit there and not say anything?"

"It's not my business. I don't have any kids, or intend to for a while yet. So it's not really something I feel competent to have an opinion on, at this stage." She took another bite, chewed, winced a little at the flavor. The lasagna tasted a little…used.

"Anyway, if you think taking kids away from their families and putting them in orphanages is such a great idea, you should trying growing up in one," she said quietly.

"Why do you always take their side?" Trish said.

"I'm not taking sides. I'd really prefer there not be any sides. Can't it just be all of us against the mountain and the elements?"

"Coward!" Trish said and turned and marched off to her tent.

"My old man always said the Bible gave the father dominion over household as it gave Man dominion over the beasts," someone said.

Despite Annja's having spent the last few days cheek-to-cheek with pretty much the whole group she almost didn't recognize the voice. It was low, just above a whisper.

Fred Mallory was the olive-skinned bodybuilder with his black hair cut high and tight like a marine's. As far as Annja knew he'd never served in the military, although passing through Baron's rigorous course of instruction, that might not make much functional difference. She didn't remember hearing him say anything at all.

"He used to use this big heavy old belt. He'd use the buckle end. If we cried out he'd just hit us harder. He said…a Bible-believing man had the right to do anything he wanted with what God give him. He made us serve him…all kinds of ways."

The wind had died down. The silence seemed to echo. The faces of his Rehoboam Academy cohorts were no less horrified as they stared at him.

"Dude," Tommy said. "Dude."

"That's a whole lot of information," Josh Fairlie said. "Maybe too much sharing, you know."

"It was God's will!" The young man's muscles all seemed to be swelling to the point of bursting. Veins stood out on his forehead and the sides of his neck. Annja worried he was about to give himself a stroke.

"We had to obey it, or we'd be damned," he said.

"Face it, Fred," Josh said, rearing back a bit. "Your father was wrong and that's all there is to it."

"You can't talk that way about my daddy!"

"I'm just saying you should face facts. It's part of being a leader. And a Christian. Facing up to unpleasant realities with the Lord's help and asking the Lord for strength to deal with them."

"He's right," Zach Thompson said.

Fred shot to his feet like a piston and stamped away into the night. Josh shook his head. "Poor guy needs to pray for the strength to hear truth."

"I don't know," Jeb said. "I think he's right."

"The Bible says honor your father," Zeb said.

"St. Paul says the father's the boss in the household," Jeb said.

Jason scowled at the twins. "Okay, now you're starting to get into scary territory, too."

"Just shut up about that," Baron said, standing up more deliberately than the last two to do so. "Now see what you jokers have done. I'm gonna have to go talk Fred off the ledge."

"Fred always was a bit tightly wrapped," Zach said.

"So, I GUESS IT GETS PRETTY cold out here on the mountain," Jason said. Annja sat among the tents, rummaging through her pack for things she needed to get ready for sleep. She was annoyed at not having everything on hand; she was the world's most seasoned traveler, young as she was.

"I usually have everything right there when I need it," she said. "It's just, these last few days have been so crazy."

"I hear you," Jason said, hunkering down near her. "Maybe you should share a tent with me. Might help take the edge off."

She flicked a wary glance at him. "I'm supposed to be sharing one with Trish."

He shrugged and showed teeth gleaming in the fugitive starlight sneaking through the clouds. "I bet I could warm you up better."

Scowling, she put her toilet kit down and turned her face

to him. "Listen. I like you, Jason. But I'm not interested in hooking up on this trip."

He flushed, and his eyes got a little wild. "I know. I know. I'm a brother, right? It's the same old racist story. You white people. You act all accepting. Then when it comes down to it—back-of-the-bus time."

"That isn't fair and it isn't okay," Annja said. "I'm not going to bother defending myself to you. And I think throwing cheap accusations about racism around are like throwing around false accusations of rape—it devalues the whole concept, and makes life a whole lot harder on the real victims."

Shaking his head, Jason straightened back up. "I guess you're one of those who's only interested in sleeping her way to the top," he said. "I thought better of you, Annja. I really did."

"Sleeping my way to the top? With Doug? You have *got* to be kidding. Anyway, isn't Kristie on top? She's the face of the program."

She was just realizing what an unwelcome visual image she'd created for herself when Jason said, "Everybody knows this gig is your big opportunity to get some face time as something other than a boring dry-stick librarian type nay-saying everything. Maybe even get your own show if it goes well. But don't worry about it, I wouldn't want to do anything to interfere with your ambitions, lady."

He turned and walked off. It seemed to be kind of the theme for the evening.

"Now what?" she said to the cold air surrounding her.

She knew the answer, though, all too well. The same thing happened on archaeological digs all the time. You had people spending too much time isolated with only each other for company and you started having soap operas. If there was less booze and dope on this trip than on a lot of digs she'd known—which was to say none, unless Wilfork had a hidden stash, and maybe Charlie— the tensions caused by danger and culture clash were impairing people's judgment. She knew that sharing deadly danger was supposed to bring people together like nothing else. She'd experienced her own share of that.

Now, it seemed, she was experiencing the opposite.

Out of the night Trish suddenly appeared. Annja felt a stab of irrational relief at the arrival of the expedition's lone other woman.

"I can't believe it," Trish said.

"Can't believe what?" There were so many possibilities.

"That you're actually a racist. What do you think they'd say back at the studios if they knew about that?"

"How would they react to Jason's trying to coerce me into going to bed with him by throwing out some wild accusations?" Annja said.

Trish opened her mouth, closed it, frowned.

"Listen," Annja said, "who I have sex with is my choice. Do you really think you can take that away from me? And I'm not discussing any 'racism' talk any further. It's absurd and insulting and I'm not going to play."

Trish shook her head. "I just wonder if you've been…infected by these people. You sure seem to stick up for them."

"Mainly I try to stick up for keeping the peace and not causing conflicts over trivial stuff like who doesn't like whose opinions. We've been in a lot of real, live danger already. It's only going to get worse."

Trish crossed her arms forcefully. She seemed dissatisfied, but unsure how to phrase her dissatisfaction.

"You know, you guys don't really strike me as a whole lot more tolerant than Charlie's angels," Annja said.

"Of course we're more tolerant. It's just that some things can't be tolerated."

"That makes a whole lot of sense."

"Listen," Trish said, "we just feel like you're not standing with us on this. If you're not with us you're against us."

Annja raised her hands in the air and let them fall helplessly by her sides. "That's it. You're starting to quote George Bush now. You guys sleep where you want and don't worry about me."

She got up and went off to share a tent with Levi.

18

Inside the tiny tent Rabbi Leibowitz seemed nervous, almost terrified, at Annja's presence. But he was too much of a gentleman to say so. They got into their sleeping bags back to back and fell asleep after the briefest interaction in which Annja announced her intention to spend the night in his tent, then asked his permission and reassured him her only interest was sleep. Which it was.

The next day dawned bright. Annja's spirits rose with the sun, although she knew too well both could be a deception.

They wound their way up the great mountain. By noon they reached a place on the north face where the easy climbing ended and they faced what the seasoned mountaineers termed a technical climb up a sheer rock face. "Technical" meant that to ascend would require the use of protection such as pitons, and ropes fastened to the harnesses they all wore.

Fortunately the cliff was mostly bare rock, granite with occasional extrusions of basalt. From her training in geology Annja knew granite was extremely hard. It would resist attempts to drive in pitons, but when hammered into cracks they tended to hold quite well. Of course, over millions of years even granite could be weakened by endless cycles of freezing and thawing, cracking into chunks from pebble to boulder size ready to peel treacherously away at the rap of a hammer or even the pressure of a climber's body.

Because this was a journey, not a sport climb, Bostitch and Baron wisely chose not to take chances. Confronted by a sheer hundred feet of rock they sent the two strongest climbers to scout a way and secure ropes with anchors at the top. The others could then climb up with the aid of ropes, belayed by Baron, who would wait at the base and come up last. Worst-case they could simply haul exhausted or hopelessly incompetent climbers up they same way they would their own heavy packs, which they shed before starting off for maximum agility.

Annja found herself somewhat surprised that the lead— meaning most proficient—rock-climber was Larry Taitt. Apparently he was more than a Future Bureaucrat of America with an uncharacteristic floppy-puppy attitude. Going first he swarmed up the rock with the skilled assurance of a spider monkey, driving spring-loaded camming devices into cracks in the rocks at intervals, both to protect himself and provide surety to following climbers. After sneering thoroughly at what the others were doing as mere "trad climbing," Tommy Wynock free-climbed, paralleling Larry and staying a little behind, so as to shoot his entire climb with a smaller helmet-mounted camera. Baron tightened his lips slightly at what he had to consider a lack of discipline. But although as expedition leader, or at least executive officer, he considered himself responsible for the welfare of everyone on it—rightly, in Annja's estimation—he had to face the fact that the *Chasing History's Monsters* video and sound crew did not consider themselves to be in his chain of command.

In any event Tommy proved to be an expert rock climber. Knowing that, Jason, the crew chief, was content to stay at the bottom getting longer shots of the ascent. Earlier he had taken some panoramic shots of the wide, tortured land of eastern Turkey. Trish kept track of the dancing colored bars on the monitors of her recorders and fiddled with her gear.

"Have you ever done anything like this before, Ms. Creed?" Charlie Bostitch asked, craning his head to watch the climbers scale the forbidding dark gray rock.

"Some," she admitted. "I didn't really know what I was doing, though. I've never had much formal instruction. It was mainly a matter of not having any choice but to go ahead and do it." Which was how she wound up doing a lot of things, now that she thought about it.

Charlie had a wide orange double-knit headband on that clashed horribly with his apple-red cheeks. His breath came in great dragon puffs of condensation. He seemed elated, elevated, as if he were getting more oxygen at this altitude than he was used to, rather than significantly less. It made Annja look with concern from him to Baron and back again, remembering that euphoria was a possible symptom of hypoxia. But Baron's expression remained unreadable as his eyes were invisible behind his dark goggles.

Off to one side Hamid stood, slightly stooped, like a vulture perched on the stiffened leg of a dead wildebeest. His expression was fierce. Then again, with a nose and eyebrows like that Annja wasn't sure he could look any other way.

Once ensconced at the top Larry and Tommy set anchors and fed ropes through. They tossed the lines down to their waiting companions. The Higgins twins inspected everyone to make sure their crampons were set to the front of their boots for a climb up a vertical surface—they were adjustable, and could also be worn on the bottoms of the climbers' boots for walking across ice. The climbers also used ascenders, metal grippers designed to slide up the climbing ropes but not down, helping the user do the same.

From that point the climb came off with few dramatics. Levi did manage to break loose twice. The second time those above simply hauled him the rest of the way up like a backpack.

The actual backpacks came up next. Baron waited at the bottom until the last climber was securely perched on the cliff top. Then making an ostentatious point of using the safety ropes and all the proper safety procedures he clambered up himself, retrieving all the climbing equipment out of cracks in the granite as he came. When he reached the top he wasn't even breathing hard, despite the fact they were well above eight thousand feet now.

So the afternoon progressed, in a serious of vertical stages punctuated by hikes, often along narrow icy trails. As always Annja found these the scariest, even though the party roped itself together for all questionable crossings. She knew that for a party like this the greater dangers, statistically speaking, were likely to be the deceptively gentle snow and ice fields, where hidden crevasses and the ever-present danger of avalanche were greatest. But she'd seen too many people come to grief on narrow cliff-face ledges to feel complacent about them. Even if she'd actively helped some of those people come to grief on them.

The party, it seemed, had been well screened for fear of heights. Annja herself lacked phobias of any kind, so far as she knew, although she did have what she considered a healthy regard for gravity.

The least experienced member of the party, Levi, was cheerfully unathletic and not much more coordinated than a newborn foal. However, he was happily amenable to going where he was steered. In the face of dizzying panoramas—and even more dizzying sheer drops to certain doom—he kept a smiling, calm demeanor. Annja was unsure whether that came from fatalistic philosophical detachment or a self-induced nerd trance. When he explained to her at one rest break that he occupied his mind contemplating a slew of ancient and abstruse Qabbalist commentaries on construing the nature of the Creator, it didn't exactly clear things up for her.

"Near-sightedness helps, too," he added with a smile.

Hamid bore the climb the same way he seemed to bear everything including sunshine and happy tidings—with the smoldering demeanor of a pissed-off martyr.

Still, even Levi's inevitable peelings, as the seasoned climbers referred to them, failed to produce much excitement. "That's why we use protection, people," Baron said in a voice of suitably heavy irony as Levi swung like a stoic rabbinical piñata over the latest terrifying void. As always his dark tinted goggles hid his eyes, but the set of his jaw when Zeb and Jeb tittered at his words promptly shut them down.

As the sun dropped, swelling and reddening like a boil, toward the Anatolian Plateau behind them they began the day's last and most difficult ascent. Annja followed Levi to help bolster his confidence as he made his halting way aloft. His best efforts weren't enough to keep him from bumping into the rocks again and again. Annja was climbing on her own but was bent onto the safety lines by a quickdraw, which consisted of a pair of carabiners—basically snap rings—held together by a synthetic strap. She helped the rabbi as best she could. This mostly took the form of stopping him when he broke free of the cold unforgiving rock and began to spin, helping to stabilize him and get him oriented the right way, and generally encouraging him. He kept grinning down at her in an almost manic way, and she guessed that only shortness of breath caused by thin air and the tightness of his harness on his chest kept him from babbling his gratitude in a constant stream.

At last, both pushed and pulled, the gangly rabbi reached the top. Feeling thoroughly wrung out by the last spasm of effort Annja hauled herself over the black rock lip.

She quickly found a scene turned to nightmare.

Levi had gotten to his feet and stood blinking in confusion through his glasses and the goggles strapped over them. He held his gloved hands up before the shoulders of his puffy jacket.

"Come on, vessel of unrighteousness," a harsh and thickly accented voice commanded. "Clear the way. You will be dealt with later."

Hamid the Kurd guide gestured with the muzzle brake of the short rifle he held in his hands. His own heavy jacket lay open to the wind that was kicking up powdered snow all around the ledge, which was about the size of a theatrical stage. The wind was also sweeping some fresh snow down from the dark, thick clouds that had gathered like vultures around the peak. Did he have that thing under there the whole time? Annja wondered, gingerly obeying his command. It must have gouged and battered his ribs unmercifully.

She recognized the gun as a Russian-made AKSU. It was the submachine gun–sized version of the AKS-74, although it shot the same powerful 5.45 mm cartridge as the full-sized assault rifle. As a result it produced a fearsome noise and muzzle blast. This wasn't the first one Annja had encountered.

Although by the wild look in Hamid's dark eyes, it could well be the last.

Bostitch and Baron stood together with the sheer dark wall of the next cliff at their backs, their own gloved hands upraised. Bostitch blinked incessantly and his features were slack with befuddlement, as if he couldn't wrap his mind around this turn of events at all. Baron, though, seemed to be nearing dangerous pressures; Annja half expected at any instant to see white steam vent suddenly not just from his tightly compressed mouth, but from nose and ears as well.

"I don't understand," Bostitch was saying, shaking his head. "Why are you doing this, Hamid?"

"How can you not know? It is because your people have betrayed ours. They have denied us the promised prize for helping them seize Iraq—the north. And they have allowed their lapdogs the Turks to assail us there, to destroy our dreams of a free and united Kurdistan once and for all!"

Her mind racing, one question crowded its way out of Annja's chapped lips. "Why did you wait until now?" she asked.

"Silence, unclean thing!" Hamid jabbed the AKSU at her like a dagger. "Stay out of the way."

"That's twice," she muttered under her breath.

She saw about half the party stood on the ledge with gloved hands upraised or clasped behind hooded or color-fully capped heads. Bostitch, Baron, Taitt and Levi were with her. Also the darkly muscular Fred Mallory, whose black eyes smoldered beneath charcoal-smudge brows and his army-like haircut. Next on the rope came Wilfork, and then Zack Thompson. Josh Fairlie belayed from the bottom of the hundred-foot face.

To one side Jason stood, his café-au-lait features wooden and gray as driftwood, shooting the whole evil scene with the video camera that squatted on his shoulder.

The gunman stood just to the left of where Annja had emerged onto the narrow ledge. Obedient to his command, or at least his gun, she had moved both away from the edge and counterclockwise. She kept moving, gently, gently. The movement took her to what she judged was the edge of Hamid's peripheral vision.

The Kurd promptly turned his back on her to jab his AKSU down at Wilfork's startled porkpie face, for once drained of its florid color. He screamed at him to stay where he was. *As I thought*, she told herself. *He doesn't think I'm worth paying attention to.*

Male-chauvinist contempt had never been so welcome. She was a little far away from him to make a move. The last thing she wanted was to startle him into triggering a burst into poor Wilfork's face—and rain bullets down onto those climbing below him.

"What do you think you're going to accomplish, Hamid?" Leif Baron said in a voice reminiscent of a metal rasp over wood.

"This faithless one here records the vengeance of the

Kurdish people upon you double-dealing capitalist infidels."

"Capitalist?" Larry said, sounding far more perplexed than scared.

"The Kurds are devout socialists," Baron said tersely. "Put a sock in, boy."

"For daring to speak," Hamid said, "you shall have the honor of cutting the rope that holds your friends. Then I shall shoot you all, except the *kafir* with the camera, and roll your bodies down on the rest. Then I shall drop rocks on any who still cling to the cliff. Then this worthless dog and I shall descend the mountain together to show his footage to the world."

"Can you make it down this route alone?" Bostitch asked.

Hamid laughed wildly. "If I cannot, I die a martyr. And this one dies a dog. And in the fullness of time, Allah willing, his camera will be found, and the world will see our vengeance. We Kurds are patient, as is Allah."

He pointed the stubby little Kalashnikov from the waist at Larry Taitt and gestured imperatively. "Now! Cut the rope. Quickly, quickly, or I shall shoot your master, the decadent plutocrat Charles Bostitch, in the belly. Move!"

The color dropped from Larry's face like a curtain falling. Snow began to blow in thick swirls around them. The clouds pressed close to the merciless mountain, enclosing them in a microcosm of fear. Larry flicked his eyes toward his boss. His right boot trembled on the verge of taking a step.

Without a sound Fred Mallory charged at Hamid.

All this time Annja had been edging into position. Hamid couldn't have paid less attention to her if she were ten thousand miles away hearing about all this over her cell phone. She had gotten well away from the others and behind the man with the gun.

Fred charged along the cliff from Hamid's other side. The Kurd, who had taken a step back from the edge once he froze Wilfork floundering five feet down from the top, wheeled, thrust out his AKSU and sprayed his attacker with thunderous yammering gunfire.

Annja watched in horror as the muzzle blast hit Fred in the chest. Fred gasped aloud as the bullets lanced through him. He went over the edge and fell away without another sound.

Annja watched in horror. But not *helpless* horror. Even as Hamid fired she launched into furious motion, sinuous with long practice. It was a classic fencing advance lunge—a quick step flowing into a long driving step off the left leg. As she began the accompanying thrust she formed her right hand into an open fist.

The sword's hilt filled it. The mystic tip crunched into Hamid's back just below his left shoulder blade, just outward of his spine.

For many hours she had drilled the move, in relentless and unsparing practice of modern and Renaissance sword-play techniques alike. She had calculated her thrust to give him about six inches of steel—enough to do maximum damage to his internal organs without poking betrayingly out the other side.

He stiffened. He screamed. Praying the tip hadn't protruded from his chest far enough for her companions to see, Annja opened her hand. At once the sword vanished back to the otherwhere, where it was no more than a reach away.

Keeping her forward momentum she spun a back-kick

into the small of Hamid's back. He was pitched over the ledge, narrowly missing Wilfork, who let go the rope and cried out in alarm as he spun.

The Kurd screamed and fired wildly as he fell. Annja leaned out perilously far to watch him. Now coming in hard, the snow swallowed him inside of thirty feet; the muzzle flashes continued to illuminate the whiteness from below and the slamming reports continued until his weapon jammed or ran dry.

The screams continued considerably longer. It went on and on, until even Annja felt a mad desire to press her gloved hands to her ears to blot them out.

"Jesus," Jason whispered. No one took him to task for his blasphemy.

19

For a moment, no one moved or said anything. Annja wasn't sure anybody even dared to breathe. She had to remind herself to do so, and that only happened when the already razor-thin membrane keeping hypoxia at bay began to fray, and the blackness crowded forward threatening to crush her vision to a pinpoint, and then extinguish it completely. She swayed then went to one knee. She focused on taking in deep breaths. Otherwise she risked following Hamid and his victim Fred into white oblivion.

It was Larry Taitt who came to her side and helped her to her feet. His thickly gloved hand trembled on her arm. The face behind his goggles was the same color as the snow.

"Ms. Creed," he stammered. "A-Annja. Are you all right?"

"Yeah," she said. "I guess so."

She was shaken. She had just stabbed a man in the back and watched another brave man fall to his death. She'd seen many people die since the sword had come into her possession but she was sure she'd never get used to it. At least she hoped it would never become un-remarkable.

"You took your bloody time booting the traitorous bastard over the edge," Wilfork bellowed as he scrambled up over the ledge as lithely as a skinny adolescent. Baron grabbed his arm and hauled him away from the drop. "Were you taking time to admire his rhetoric, or what?"

"Waiting for my chance," Annja said.

But the question did bother her. Did I wait too long? she asked herself mentally again and again. Did I buy my secret's continued security with the life of that poor boy? Even if the "boy" was likely the same age she was.

While Hamid had obviously dismissed her from his consciousness, it didn't mean he didn't keep cranking his head left and right like a feral Brooklyn tomcat navigating an unknown alley. Once he caught the flash of purposeful movement in his peripheral vision it wouldn't matter whether it was caused by man or mere woman— he'd instantly wheel and shoot.

But was I too concerned about trying to hide the sword from the others? she wondered. She feared she would see the grimace of pain on Fred's face as he fell for a long time in her dreams.

The rest of the climbers reached the top quickly and safely despite the full-on blizzard that had descended around them. Tommy and Josh came up last. The survivors basically clumped into two shocked groups huddled against the now-howling storm. The Young Wolves moved to one side, the *Chasing History's Monsters* trio to another.

Jason was babbling excitedly to his companions. His voice was lost to Annja in the greater voice of the wind. They cast the occasional wide-eyed look at Annja but sent no recriminating words her way. She dared to hope they'd finally grasped that her act of violence, shocking though it was to their tender sensibilities, had been to save them. Had been the only thing that saved them.

More likely, she thought, they're too scared of me to speak to me now.

Levi stood close to her, making soothing noises he seemed to hope were helpful. She appreciated his solicitude but tried to tune him out. She was sitting with her back to the granite wall, trying to sort out her own chaotic seethe of thoughts and emotions. The thin air didn't help.

Wilfork also loomed nearby, his ski cap off, his white-yellow hair ruffled by the wind and rimed with snow. He kept looking at her strangely.

"You actually kicked him off the cliff," he said, several times. To Annja it sounded as if he was trying to talk himself out of something. Did he think he saw something?

She was questioning, now—oh, blessed hindsight—whether she'd even needed to use the sword. But as tightly wound and wary as Hamid had been, could she realistically have been sure of getting close enough to land a solid kick before he turned and shot her? The three-foot steel length of the sword's blade had been her margin of success.

She knew she'd got a clean heart shot, even if she'd slightly misjudged the range. Trying to reach a man's heart through a man's stomach was taking the long way around, she knew from anatomy classes. And also experience. But the additional kick that sent him over the edge hadn't just been to hide the fact he'd been run through. She'd also seen firsthand how even a clean heart shot wasn't always instantly lethal. Especially on someone totally stoked on adrenaline. She couldn't afford him the chance to pull the trigger and wave goodbye to her companions with his automatic weapon.

Blood spills, burned deeply into fresh snow and already cooled to the point they no longer steamed, spattered the edge of the sheer drop. Nobody, Annja figured, was going to be in position to analyze them and find out they belonged to Hamid as well as his victim. It was relief, but a small one.

Bostitch and his acolytes had formed an inward-facing circle linked with arms on shoulders and heads together. They seemed to be going through some kind of ritual for their lost friend.

"Have they done this often before?" Levi asked. He'd shoved his goggles up onto his forehead so he could scratch the bridge of his nose beneath his thick glasses.

"Good question," Annja said, feeling suddenly colder than even weather and circumstances called for.

"We have to push on," Bostitch announced as the circle broke up with some kind of joint exhalation of prayer.

"What?" Annja and Wilfork asked at the same time. The television crew echoed them a moment later. Jason had recovered his presence of mind enough to take up his big video camera and start filming again.

"Didn't you hear the man?" Baron snapped. "He said we have to move. Get bodies in motion, people. Daylight's wasting."

"It's still daylight?" Trish asked.

"You can't be serious," Jason said. His voice shook but he held the camera steady as stone. Annja had to admire his professionalism. "Somebody just died here," he said.

"We have to go back," Trish said. "The expedition's over. I mean…isn't it? Surely it is." She looked pleadingly at Annja.

"And let Fred's sacrifice go in vain?" Josh snarled. His own face was so white that for a heartbeat Annja feared he was on the verge of massive frostbite.

"This is crazy, man," Tommy said. He also looked to Annja for support. "You tell 'em."

But she shook her head slowly. "I'm not going back," she said. "We're within a day of our goal. We didn't quit when Mr. Atabeg got killed. I don't see why we should quit now."

Trish and Tommy stared at her, white-faced beneath the goggles they'd pushed up on their heads. Jason shook his head.

"We're just used to covering imaginary horrors," he said. "Not real ones."

"We're moving on," Bostitch announced. His own voice wobbled like a relapsing alcoholic after a couple of stiff ones. "Move on. Up. We have to get away from here."

"What, man, are you afraid it's haunted?" Wilfork demanded.

"Does this look like a debating society?" Baron shouted. "The man says move, people. Now, do it!"

Even the Rehoboam Academy grads seemed to move slowly in response, although that could well have been residual shock from the sudden horrible death of a friend. But move everyone did.

Annja realized with a little shock that she hadn't even raised a peep of protest herself. Did I just realize it was futile to argue with the boss, she asked herself, or am I as eager to get away from this place as Bostitch is?

The day, such as it was, grew dark around them. Annja thought it reckless to the point of craziness to continue to climb. But Josh took point and they struggled upward over a hundred feet higher through the snow and twilight. Annja moved in an internal fog almost as chill and blinding as the hell of half-lit and darkening snow whirling around her, compounded by physical fatigue and emotional overload. A good dose of adrenaline-buzz letdown had been thrown in, too.

Perhaps in desperation, both to escape the scene of horror below and to find some kind of relatively safe harbor before darkness and the storm trapped them dangling on the sheer gray face like flies on a single spider-strand, they took more risks than they should have. Perhaps mental numbness and physical fatigue took its toll on the others as well as Annja.

Jason, though not the most skilled climber in the television crew, insisted on accompanying the lead climber, now Josh Fairlie, as he blazed a trail while the others rested as best they could suspended in midair, roped closely to pitons and spring-loaded camming devices jammed in cracks in the rock. He also insisted on making his own way, paralleling the Rehoboam graduate from the right and slightly below.

Annja thought that was a foolhardy risk to take for the sake of some grainy snow-filled video in a gloom even the camera's built-in light did little to dispel. But the crew from *Chasing History's Monsters* didn't seem to be listening to her right now. Possibly they thought she'd gone over to the "other" side, as they apparently saw it. Or maybe they were so creeped out by what she'd done they couldn't bring themselves to deal with her.

During the desperate storm-whipped scramble tempers had frayed. Below her Annja could hear Trish and Tommy snarling at each other with voices held low to prevent dropping some shelf of snow and ice hanging over them unseen down in their faces. The odd acoustics of storm and stone both muffled their voices and oddly amplified them.

For his part even Levi seemed too exhausted for the usual cheerful banter he tried to fill time with when circumstances kept him from his beloved reading. He gave her a smile, weakly, slowly blinking long lashes behind his goggles and thick glasses. Just below the soles of Annja's boots, Robyn Wilfork groused to the Higgins twins beneath him, past an untalkative Zack Thompson, who climbed right after the New Zealander to help secure him. What, if anything, Jeb and Zeb said in reply she couldn't hear.

It happened, as disasters did, with a suddenness that stole the breath like a plunge into icy water. Somewhere above the vertical procession a rock gave way with a crack and a rumble. Josh cried out a frantic warning and caught himself by sinking his ice ax with a ringing clang into the rock as his legs swung free.

The falling rock was about half the size of a human torso. It struck Jason's shoulder and knocked him free. He cried out sharply and fell off the mountain's face.

Continuing down the rock missed Annja by the breadth of her outspread fingers. Whether it had struck Charlie Bostitch or not she couldn't tell. But the bulky shape twenty feet above her dropped toward her goggled face with shocking speed. At the same moment she heard Wilfork bellow in terror below her and knew he'd lost his grip, too.

"Hang on, Levi!" she shouted to the man above her.

Jason plummeted past. Annja caught a nightmare glimpse of his face, eyes and mouth strained wide. His arms and legs moved as if he were trying to swim on air. His camera's brilliant beam wheeled around him like a spoke of yellow-white light.

Annja pressed herself against the rock, clung with outflung hands as well as boot-tips to the rock. She thought the plentiful safety anchors and lines should keep anyone from falling too far.

That was the idea, anyway. But the more climbers who peeled, the greater the risk that pitons would rip free of rock, or the ropes themselves might break. Annja's body took a brutal shock as Wilfork's considerable weight hit the length of the rope that separated them. She gasped for breath and clung for all she was worth.

A second shock almost tore her from the cliff. Bostitch's hurtling mass had plucked Levi right off the wall. The rabbi flailed as he dropped the short distance toward Annja.

"Grab onto me!" she screamed. She probably didn't get it out in time to do any good.

But somehow Levi managed to get a grip on her right leg. He clung with both hands, his own legs swinging wildly above white emptiness that swirled into oblivion.

For a moment Annja seemed to be single-handedly supporting the combined weight of several helplessly flailing men, more by strength of will than body. Below her she heard more cries as other climbers fell. She braced herself.

But she knew she couldn't take any more. As it was she could only hope to hold out seconds more against the killing weight that hung from her climbing harness. She felt her fingers weaken, seeming to squeeze the handholds out like watermelon seeds.

No further shocks hit her. The mountaineering training the Rehoboam grads had received evidently kicked in. The party was still anchored. They'd survive, she told herself. If only I can hold out…

She heard Baron's voice, low yet penetrant, speaking

reassuringly to his boss. The former SEAL and current security-contractor mogul hunched like a big dark spider. He had lost his cap. His bare head jutted from his jacket like a bullet from its casing.

Annja felt the relief as Charlie Bostitch's weight came off her harness. Baron had taken up the slack. A moment later the tycoon himself had gotten his own purchase on the rock and even found the presence of mind to screw in a fresh camming device to help hold him.

At the same time the load from below diminished further as somebody secured Wilfork once again. And then Zack was alongside Levi, snapping a safety line onto the scholar's harness, lashing them together. Levi released his death-grip on Annja's legs as Thompson made both fast to the wall.

"Are you okay, Ms. Creed?" the young ex-marine called softly, his words echoing between cliff and cloud.

All she could do was nod weakly.

As if they had passed some kind of test the sky cleared. The snow stopped. The wind died. Shafts of golden late-afternoon light stabbed past the mountain to either side, illuminating the rolling few miles of land between Ararat and Iran. Annja found the side-scatter light almost blinding after the terrible white night of moments before.

By the golden fading sunset light they hauled themselves up to a substantial ledge, perhaps twenty feet deep and fifty long. Josh had been on the verge of laying a gloved hand over the actual lip of safety when the big rock had broken loose.

They all made it up to lay gasping, exhausted and safe, on ice-sheathed stone. All except Jason.

Examining the lines they quickly learned that tempers weren't the only thing that had frayed on the climb. The television crew chief's belaying rope had parted. Jason had fallen away down the steep northern face of the Mountain of Pain, to vanish forever in the storm.

20

Before Annja even caught her breath Baron had his men busy checking all the other ropes.

"Are you all right?" Levi asked, hunkering down beside her. His skin looked paler than normal behind his goggles and he was breathing raggedly through his mouth.

From somewhere he pulled his red asthma rescue inhaler and took a puff. His breath came in such short frenzied chops he could barely hold the medicine in for an entire second. The thin air was torture to Annja, who was in splendid shape. It must have been unimaginably brutal for him. Even though she'd performed more strenuous activity than the rabbi, fear and panic and the strain of clinging to her had to have left him starved for air.

"I'll be fine, Levi, thanks," she managed to gasp. "But no. I'm not all right." He collapsed beside her, wheezing like a landed trout.

Desperate guilt about Jason's death all but overwhelmed her. Part of her knew that was irrational. She'd never had the slightest chance of doing anything to arrest his fall. A far greater argument could be made that she was culpable in Fred's death. But not Jason's.

And yet…they wouldn't be here if it weren't for me, she thought. Steeling herself she glanced toward Trish and Tommy. Their duties to record the expedition forgotten in disaster's bare face, they huddled together up against the cliff face like lost puppies. They didn't even glance her way. Somehow that hit her harder than reproachful stares or even words would have.

She became aware of a big shape looming over her. It was an effort to raise her head and look up.

"Thanks for saving me," Robyn Wilfork said. Then he lumbered off to sit down somewhere.

If he planned to take a hit from his hypothetical hidden hip flask, she reckoned, he was entitled to it. She wished she could find such easy sanctuary.

Baron was a whirlwind of activity, a raging demon. Or as he'd probably put it, an avenging angel. Though his Young Wolves were themselves completely wrung-out and shaken he raged at them until Larry Taitt volunteered to climb down and search for the fallen man. Red-headed Eli Holden would join him; the twins would belay from above. Meanwhile Thompson and Fairlie could begin pitching tents.

The ex-SEAL seemed to blame Fairlie for causing the disaster. Or else he thought it was a good motivational technique to lash him with it. Maybe it was. The pallid, evidently exhausted young man picked himself up and shambled off to work assiduously in the inadequate atmosphere by the light of chemical glow sticks.

The climbers sent to search for Jason wore more chemical sticks looped around their necks like ravers.

Larry and Eli carried flashlights as well. Their beams swept the cliffs and vertical ice sheets as they descended.

But a layer of clouds, deceptively fluffy but looking so dense it seemed as if you ought to be able to walk across them, hung a few hundred feet below. Dead or alive—and Annja, for one, couldn't imagine the cameraman and crew chief could possibly still be alive—Jason Pennigrew lay below those clouds. Loath to leave a man behind, Baron ordered the searchers to keep going down through the cloud layer to search for him or his body.

With visible reluctance, and generally green around the gills, Bostitch countermanded the order. "We can't risk anybody else, Leif. Especially in the dark like this."

Shaking his head in disgust, Baron told the twins to reel Larry and Eli back in. Then he walked off muttering to himself, as far away from the others as the ledge's small area permitted. He and Jason hadn't had much use for each other, and neither had seemed to exert himself too much to hide the fact. But Leif Baron seemed to take his loss personally.

He was reacting in a way, Annja couldn't help notice, that he hadn't done when his own man was killed by somebody Baron had not only hired but also entrusted with his own life, along with everyone else's. Maybe this was his graceless way of overcompensating.

In desolated silence they ate their wood-flavored self-heating rations. They had broken into small groups. Bostitch and Baron sat with Wilfork; the surviving acolytes huddled together against the cliff twenty feet away from Tommy and Trish. Annja ate with Levi. The rabbi kept looking at her and bobbing his head as if wanting to say something soothing to her, but unable to think of what. She found it comforting rather than annoying.

Later she made her way alone among the tents, cautiously, heading back to bed after relieving herself. A dark figure suddenly loomed in the darkness. The stars shining from a mostly cloudless sky were all that enabled her to see anything.

Annja recoiled. She started to form her right hand into a partial fist. At the last moment she caught herself. She made herself relax.

"Why so tense, Ms. Creed?" asked the goofily genial voice of Charlie Bostitch. "Afraid of the abominable snowman?"

"There's no such thing," she said quickly. "And not on this part of the Eurasian landmass in any event. It's just that you startled me. I'm a bit tightly wound up."

He laughed disarmingly. "Aren't we all. Hey, I just wanted to talk to you for a few minutes."

"All right."

He seemed taken off guard by her simple response. "Out here? I mean, we're out in the open right by a sheer drop—"

"Does it make any difference to what you want to talk about?" Annja asked.

He shook his head. It seemed to weigh heavily on his neck. The notion of his own possible smuggled-along stash of alcohol sprang into her mind. She shoved it aside. We're above ten thousand feet here, she reminded herself. And we've had a hell of a day. Don't go multiplying explanations.

"I'm tired, Mr. Bostitch. All respect, can't we please just make this quick?"

To her astonishment he burst into tears. "Please, Annja. Please! You got to help me."

He dropped to his knees in the snow in front of her and

grabbed her gloved hands with his own. "I don't have anywhere else to turn," he sobbed. "I'm at the end of my rope. I'm the worst sinner in the whole world. I *need* this to be the Ark. Don't you see? It's my last hope of redemption."

"No," Annja said. "I don't see." She found herself, totally embarrassed, more dragging the big man to his feet than helping him up.

"You probably think I'm a wealthy man," he blubbered. "And I've been a wealthy man. Very wealthy. But then came the recession, and I made some bad, bad choices... Annja, I tell you, I'm busted. Worse than that. I'm so deep in debt I can never swim out. Not without a miracle.

"I need you to bring me this miracle, Annja. You're the only one who can deliver it. Deliver *me*. You and the rabbi have to help me. I need to redeem myself."

"You think if we find the Ark it'll get you out of debt?" Annja asked.

"It can't hurt, can it? And it'll be a sign of the Lord's favor. And maybe it'll be the sign that's needed, just the missing piece to help Our Lord come back to judge the world in fire before the world's descent into wickedness and sin make Him turn His face away forever in disgust. Maybe it's up to you to open the way so our Lord and Savior can return to walk the Earth once more. Think of it, Annja! Think of it!"

"Wait. Are you talking about financial rescue or Armageddon?" Annja asked, wondering what he was talking about.

"It's all tied up together. Don't you see? This is my shot at forgiveness."

She shook her head. If anything, she saw less than she

had before. She wondered if the altitude really was getting to him.

"All I can do is what you hired me to do, Mr. Bostitch," she said wearily. "Which is to search for whatever's up there, and if we find it, I'll examine it as thoroughly and professionally as possible. And then I'll report the truth. Whatever it turns out to be. Whoever's ox it gores—yours, mine, whoever's. Wouldn't that be what your Lord would want?"

"Oh, sure, sure. He's the Way, the Truth and the Light. He wouldn't hold with lies," Bostitch said feebly.

"Then you and He should be square, whatever. Because no matter what the truth is, doesn't He already know it? It's not as if, whether that's somehow really the Ark or just a rock formation, or even something else entirely, it's going to come as a big surprise to Him, is it?" Annja said.

"You're right. Of course you're right. You're a young woman of really remarkable wisdom, Annja, you know that?" Bostitch said.

He enfolded her in a vast and clumsy bear hug. "You comfort me," he said, disengaging with obvious reluctance. "Could you maybe see your way clear to coming back to my tent with me and talking a little longer? It would give my soul ease, I have to tell you."

"I'm flattered," Annja said, quickly stepping back. "But I'm afraid I have to get back to my own tent and my own sleeping bag before I fall down. My body needs *its* ease. Or I won't be in any shape to make the final push to the Ark tomorrow."

And before he could protest she turned away and slipped into the mouth of the small tent she shared with Levi. The rabbi already lay softly snoring on his back with his mouth open. His hands were outside the bag, clutching his dog-eared paperback like a teddy bear. She smiled at him, climbed into her own bag with every muscle in her body screaming in agony, and was asleep in moments.

THE FINAL ASCENT WAS ON ICE. Whether it was the glacier that crowned much of the vast high cinder cone and held the Anomaly in its slow cold embrace, or just a random stretch of rock sheathed in ice, Annja didn't know. Their path had circled clear around the northern side of the main peak to come up at the Anomaly from almost directly below, on the mountain's northwest face.

How they had settled on the route Annja was unsure. Hamid had obviously had some input into selecting their initial path up the mountain, which she didn't find too reassuring. Still, Baron remained briskly confident and in charge. It wasn't her decision to make. And frankly she was glad. It was painful enough just taking part in this ordeal without bearing the ultimate responsibility for it.

The sun, peeping up over the mountains of Iran and Azerbaijan but hidden from them by Ararat's bulk, filled the world with bloodlike red. Above them the sky was an almost cloudless mauve, shading into peach, that promised metamorphosis into that almost-painful blue the sky sometimes takes on above high mountains. As the party stood staring up the wall to the summit, the ice tinted delicate rose-pink with side-scatter dawn, Levi said, "It's strange, you know."

"What?" asked Wilfork, who stood aside with Annja and Levi, looking somewhat glum, with a cream-colored band around his head and his unruly hair tufting out the top.

"We've had alternating swings of bad fortune with good. We've been both plagued and aided by weird coincidences and freaks of nature. It's as if gods with differing agendas were dueling over our destiny."

"You're a man of God, Rabbi!"

The snarl made their heads turn. Baron was scowling furiously at them past his black sunglasses. "This is not a good time to make blasphemous jokes."

"Okay," Levi said with a shrug. He turned to Annja and gave her a sly, shy grin. He was good at shutting up. Maybe too good, too self-effacing. Yet under the circumstances Annja reluctantly had to admit she was glad. This was not the time for a debate of any sort unless it concerned survival.

Levi's bearded lips moved silently. Annja was no lip-reader. But she was pretty sure he said, But I wasn't joking.

She gave him a thumbs-up. *Eppur si muove,* she replied the same way. She was quoting Galileo's legendary last words to the Inquisition on the question of whether Earth was fixed at the center of creation. She wasn't sure he'd catch it. But he laughed, still silently.

Larry and Josh helped everybody fix crampons to their boots and adjust them to bite forward, into vertical ice. Ice axes were distributed to those who wanted them. Annja accepted; Robyn Wilfork and Rabbi Leibowitz declined. Then Larry led off, planting pitons and camming devices specially designed to protect the ice from shattering around them as he climbed. Josh belayed from below.

Up they climbed by stages, roping themselves in and waiting while Josh and Larry took turns scouting the safest routes. The sun came up without incident in the form of either wind or threatening storm clouds.

On their third such stop, Levi looked down at Annja, hanging over the abyss beneath his boot soles, smiled shyly and said, "I meant it, you know."

Annja had been trying to meditate, keep a lid on her misgivings about what the future held. Not to mention a natural apprehension about hanging like a fly on a wall—or in a spider's web—with nothing beneath her for thousands of feet except the odd ledge just wide enough to give her a good bone-breaking bounce, as a sort of preview of what awaited at the bottom. Now she was confused.

"Meant what, Levi?"

"About the dueling gods. I really feel it could be true." He smiled self-deprecatingly. "Almost, anyway."

"But you're a rabbi!" Uncomfortably she realized she'd just echoed Leif Baron, of all people.

"Yes, but I'm a Qabbalist rabbi. Not the Madonna sort, of course. The more traditional Jewish thing. It's a natural vice for a nerd."

"I've encountered those before," Annja said.

"So I don't necessarily believe the cranky mountain-thunder spirit a lot of the Biblical stories are about was the one true god. He's *a* true god. I believe he exists. So do all others. And they have their little spats."

Annja looked up and then, unhappily, down, to make sure none of the Young Wolves was listening in. Levi was keeping his voice down, thank goodness. Only Wilfork seemed to be close enough to overhear them easily. He seemed to be off in a world of his own. Annja was unconvinced that meant he wasn't eavesdropping. But he seemed unlikely to have the sort of ideological hot buttons most other members of the expedition did.

"The being I and those who are like me worship is the Creator who is the Universe," Levi went on, "and above such petty concerns. But He likes a good show. Some say that's why He made the universe. Or She, or It, or They—the important thing about the Creator is that no one can understand the Creator without *being* the Creator. Coming to fully grasp that is the first step of the dedicated Qabbalist."

"What's the second?" Annja asked.

"Trying our best to divine the Creator's true nature through study of what you call the Old Testament."

"But I thought you said you took for granted you couldn't understand God?" Annja said, trying to understand.

"We're funny that way," he said with a little shrug. It made him twist alarmingly in his ropes. She reached a hand up and grabbed his right boot to stabilize him. Whether the experience unnerved him or not he didn't continue the conversation. That suited Annja fine.

In the early afternoon the storm clouds returned with a suddenness that halfway tempted Annja to believe in Levi's dueling mountain-deities. They slammed together overhead like leaden gates with such abrupt authority she was surprised they didn't produce a tooth-rattling boom like thunder.

And almost the same moment a soft cry was repeated from above by Bostitch and Baron, and Annja looked up to see Larry's head silhouetted against the ominous boiling clouds. Although it was shadowed she could tell he was grinning fit to split his head.

Less than five minutes later Levi and Larry were helping her scramble onto the top of a gently sloping plain of ice, pierced by snow-mounded black juts of rock. A mile and a half ahead of her rose the snow-covered head of Ararat, rising another 1,300 feet above them.

And there, a quarter mile away to the south and west of them, the long, dark mound of the Ararat Anomaly seemed to hang over the edge of the abyss.

21

"It's fantastic," Charlie Bostitch said. He dropped to his knees and began to pray. Too loudly for Annja's taste, although the upward slope inboard of them was gentle enough she doubted there was a great danger of avalanche here. Still, anytime you had big snow and slopes…

"Yes," Robyn Wilfork said, staring with his goggles pushed up on his forehead. "But what *is* it?"

"Noah's Ark, you Godless heathen," Baron growled. And somewhat to Annja's surprise he fell to his knees beside Bostitch and joined him, if more quietly, in prayer. She had known all along that he was a religious fanatic; but to see him demonstrate it in so conventional—and un-martial—a way was still something of a shock.

"It looks like a big rock," Trish Baxter said, coming up beside Annja. Tommy walked a pace behind her, shooting the snow-clad object itself framed by the members of the team and their response. The sound technician seemed un-concerned whether the more pious members of the expedition heard her or not. Annja wondered whether the editors would edit that particular sound bite out of the audio back in New York before airing whatever finally came out of this journey.

Finishing his prayer before his employer did—probably feeling the weight of his sins less keenly, whatever they were—Leif Baron rose up and began in a crisp but not loud voice to direct his crew. That entailed rousing them from their knees as well. He was determined to pitch camp before investigating the Ark, or whatever it was, itself. Snow had begun to fall, ever more heavily.

Levi had pulled his goggles, which he wore over his glasses, up over his forehead. He stood blinking at the Anomaly with snow sticking to the lenses and his long lashes behind them. "It really looks as if it could be something," he said.

"Why don't we go see?" Annja said.

She looked to Bostitch. He was the expedition head and her employer, after all. And he wasn't the first expedition leader she'd known who'd ever engaged in over-the-top displays of emotion on finding the object of an arduous search, either.

"Yes," he said, his eyes shining moistly. "Let's go look."

Even Tommy and Trish seemed perked up by the excitement of the occasion. The whole group seemed to glow with anticipation of discovery. *Of what* remained the question, but it was one Annja was content not to ask aloud. She knew there was no point in aggravating the majority of the party when answers might just be close at hand.

"I have to caution against expecting immediate results, immediate answers," she said, trying to pitch her voice to carry without making it too loud. The clouds had closed in again overhead, causing a sort of slightly echoing cathedral effect. It certainly seemed appropriate enough.

"It can take months for test results to come back, that sort of thing," she said.

"I have faith," Bostitch said. "I think the Lord will make all clear to us very soon."

"Let's hope you're right," Annja replied.

They approached the shape, swinging inland up the gradually sloping glacier so as to come at it from that way. The footing was nowhere near as sketchy as Annja would have thought; the glacier was a pretty stable structure, after all. And while it was going somewhere, it did so very slowly. It wasn't as if it had a deadline.

Still, somewhat to Annja's surprise, she could *hear* it. The glacier moaned and rumbled and grumbled constantly. Its voice was a profound *basso* that straddled the lower ranges of human hearing and reverberated in the marrow of her bones.

The Anomaly itself really was imposing. Several hundred feet long, it rose what Annja guessed was about a hundred feet, although it was sufficiently piled with snow and ice to make it difficult to tell. It was a matte black in the gray light.

"The color isn't inconsistent with basalt extrusion," she said aloud, largely for the benefit of Tommy and Trish, who were focused on her for the moment. The stocky cameraman was walking backward in front of Annja, filming her with the big camera propped on his shoulder. The young blond woman kept the foam-covered end of a microphone aimed at Annja. "Then again, it could be a lot of things. Including an ancient ship."

She thought that only seemed fair, or anyway sporting, to include. Despite its pushing the lower limits of Annja's conception of what it could be. Still, something about it stirred atavistic feelings inside her. It was a sensation as primal as the awe of gazing at the Milky Way through clear night air.

Could it really be the Ark? She couldn't help but wonder.

They had to mount a steep, somewhat slippery bank to reach the object's base. Seen up close it had a texturing Annja had to admit was at least vaguely suggestive of the grain in wood. She took off her glove and touched the black substance.

"So what's the verdict?" Robyn Wilfork asked. "Wood or stone?"

Annja shrugged. "Feels like basalt," she said, "but again, that's not conclusive. It wouldn't be very likely, though, for wood to survive this long."

"Couldn't it be petrified wood?" Larry Taitt asked.

"It'd seem to be pretty fast for that process to take place," Trish said.

"But wood does fossilize," Baron said.

Annja nodded. "That's certainly true. That's why I'm keeping an open mind. Still, under these conditions it usually would not fossilize."

"I see you're not knocking any sample chips off with your ice ax," Wilfork said. "Afraid of defiling a holy relic in spite of your skepticism?"

She pointed up toward the crest. Its white stood out against lead-sullen, lowering clouds. A thin pennon of blown snow trailed away from it.

"More afraid of dropping several thousand tons of ice

and snow on our heads. We need to be careful. Especially at this altitude when, frankly, our judgment is subject to clouding up without our noticing," Annja said.

"I still can't see," Tommy said, one-eyed behind his camera, "how the world could flood so deeply it'd maroon a ship up here, three miles in the air."

"Maybe the mountain rose since then," Baron said. "Maybe they brought the Ark higher."

"Mr. Baron," Annja said, "Ararat is a *volcano*. The way it rose was the same way most volcanoes do—through depositing material during eruption. If the Ark grounded there at some lower level, wouldn't lava have long since buried it thousands of feet under, if the mountain actually were building itself higher?"

She also knew now from her research that the mountain was estimated to have last erupted about ten thousand years before. But the Biblical literalists dismissed geological dating—especially since that would have put the mountain's last eruption before the Creation.

She couldn't see Baron's eyes behind his tinted goggles. But she could see the slight hunch of his brawny shoulders, the deepening lines around his near-lipless mouth. He was not happy with her. How will he respond if I totally rain on his parade and say it's just a giant rock? she thought.

"Hey," a voice called from higher up and to the right, around the northerly end of the great dark snow-cloaked shape. Everybody looked up to see one of the twins waving a mittened hand down at them. "We found an opening!"

Everybody looked at each other. Perhaps it was only Baron grabbing Bostitch by the arm and towing him up to where Zeb was practically hopping up and down with excitement that kept a mad rush up the slick slope from taking place.

Wilfork, nearer to the two expedition leaders, followed them closely. Annja, hauling Levi along the way Baron tugged his boss, got right on their tails. The Young Wolves crowded forward, practically baying with eagerness, and leaving Trish and Tommy to shoot the scene from behind. Annja felt a brief poignant stab of sorrow all over again at Jason's death. He'd have contrived to be right up there shooting over Bostitch's and Baron's shoulder as they saw whatever it was awaiting them within.

It turned out to be a dark passage with Jeb just inside, cheeks round as a chipmunk's with his grin. He turned and led them forward by the thin-milk light streaming in through the entryway, which was two black slabs of stone tipped against each other.

The passage seemed to be rock and ice. Annja felt a twinge of uncertainty verging on fear. What would it take to bring this all down to bury us? she wondered. But her own eagerness overcame her doubts.

We paid lives for this sight, she thought. We might as well at least see it.

Just as the last faint gleam of light from behind played out, attenuated by the twist of the short passageway and the bodies occluding it, Baron and Bostitch vanished from sight. Annja stifled a gasp of alarm. Then she realized they'd stepped to the side. At the same time she sensed a larger space opening before them.

Greenish light exploded outward to illuminate great dark ribs arching overhead. Baron had cracked a chemical light stick and held it high as if it were a torch.

"It's like a bloody cathedral," Wilfork whispered.

The journalist's comparison was certainly apt. Heavy

dark expressions from the wall arced up over their heads like curved beams. Around their feet lay a tremendous jumble of rocks. Some of which, though, looked suggestively as if they might have been posts or beams.

Or is my imagination running away with me? Annja wondered.

In awestruck silence they made their way forward. As Baron swung his light stick left and right Annja saw a fugitive pale gleam from ahead. "What's that light?" she asked.

Baron swung back. Although the glow of the stick was anything but bright it briefly dazzled his eyes enough that he missed it initially. Then he said, "It's coming from the other side of that doorway."

With Levi crowding like an eager puppy right behind Annja followed Baron and Bostitch through the opening toward the faint light. They stepped into an open space vastly larger than the first. The vaulted walls curved over their heads to meet a flat wall tilted about thirty degrees toward them from the vertical. Sunlight—cloud-filtered to gray but almost blinding to eyes accustomed to the dark—slanted down from openings above.

"Oh," Trish said in a tiny voice, stepping through the entry behind the acolytes, who had spread out to either side of the opening, stepping carefully to avoid irregular shapes, probably stone, mostly hidden beneath mounded snow and ice from overhead.

The others came in to stand looking up and turning slowly around, awestruck.

"Dude," Tommy said, sweeping the great chamber with his camera eye. "It sure *looks* like a great big boat tipped on its side."

"So what is your scientific opinion, Ms. Creed?" Bostitch asked, not trying to hide the triumphant note in his voice. "Have we found the Ark, or not?"

"It's still too early to make any kind of definitive assessment, Mr. Bostitch," she said. "But there appears to be a definite possibility this is a man-made structure, as opposed to a natural one."

But a voice in her head was saying, "Definite possibility"? All right, Ms. Smarty, how many natural processes can you name that could account for these formations? Location and circumstance precluded this being any kind of natural cavern. Nor had she ever seen accretion formations—stalactites and stalagmites—that looked anything like what confronted them here.

What natural process or succession of accidents could possibly create what we're seeing, which looks like the beams and compartments—some busted up, most out of place—of an ancient shipwreck?

To her shame she couldn't bring herself to speak the thoughts out loud. It felt too much like…capitulation to superstition and bigotry of which she, at core, was no more tolerant than the New Yorkers were. It felt like betraying science. It felt like betraying *skepticism.*

From the corner of her eye she saw Levi assiduously digging at the juncture between two apparent beams with a pocketknife. He had shucked off his gloves. A shaft of sunlight fell on his back.

"Whoa! Rabbi, I wish you wouldn't do that. It's not, uh, not really considered best archaeological practice any more," Annja said with alarm.

"Sorry, Annja. So sorry," he said. He looked anything but sorry. His thin cheeks were flushed and his eyes bright behind his glasses. "But look at this! Look at what I've found!"

He'd pulled his gloves off. They lay discarded by his boots. In his palm he held out crumbs of some black material.

"Pitch," he said.

The others had begun to cluster around. "What?" Annja said.

"Pitch," Levi said, voice rising in excitement. "It's pitch. You know—made from coal tar, distilled out of bituminous coal. The ancients used it to seal and waterproof joins."

He waved a hand around at the canted cathedral setting. Motes of snow now drifted through the brightening sunlight slanting from above, as if a single rent in the clouds allowed the light to stream down unimpeded by the gathering storm.

"This could be wood impregnated by pitch! The curving walls, the beams. That might account for how wood could survive so long on a glacier."

Annja felt acutely aware of the pressure of eyes on her. She saw the red light of Tommy's camera peeping over Larry Taitt's shoulder.

She shook her head. Not in denial of what he said, but in confession of her own inability to judge so soon. "It may be plausible," she said. "I have to admit I'm no expert on the taphonomy of wood."

"Taphonomy?" Charlie asked.

"The study of how things fossilize," Robyn Wilfork said. "Goodness me. I think I need a drink!"

"We need to remain scientific and systematic," Annja said, raising her voice to try to burst the bubble of excited comments flooding the cavernous space. "We can't jump to conclusions—"

She became aware of Baron's vindicated smirk. Charlie Bostitch had tears running down his big saggy cheeks.

"We need to set up camp outside," Bostitch said. "I know, I know—we're all excited about this. About finally confronting irrefutable proof of the literal truth of God's Word."

"But—" Annja began. No one paid attention.

"But Ms. Creed's right. We need to go about this in a systematic way. We don't want skeptics picking our story apart, now, do we?"

"No!" the Young Wolves cried in one voice.

"Then haul ass outside," Baron snapped, "and start pitching camp."

They hustled out, with Trish and Tommy following behind, locked onto the expedition leaders like sighthounds following the prey. In a moment Annja and Levi found themselves alone in the chamber, seemingly forgotten in the general exhilaration.

"Are we already just footnotes to this story?" she said softly.

"No," Levi said. "Not the story to come."

He put his face up to the slanting sunbeams, turned slowly around and around through them. "It really does seem as if the gods are vying here, both to hinder and help us," he said.

"Levi!" she said, more sharply than she intended. "I really expected something better of you. You seem to be playing right to their expectations and prejudices."

He shrugged. He seemed nearly as transported as the born-again contingent from Rehoboam Academy. "Not to their straight-arrow monotheism, surely?" he asked puckishly, face still uplifted to the sun. "We've found something here. Something fantastic. What it really is remains to be seen, that I admit."

He looked at her. "Don't forget that, while I'm a rationalist, I am also a religious scholar." His eyes and voice were gentle, as they always were. "Unlike some I see no difficulty reconciling the two. I am, after all, dedicated to discovering the truth. Whether or not it accords with any dogma, including my own."

Annja stood flatfooted. I should be as elated as everybody else, she thought. I'm all about finding truth, too. Instead she felt deflated. Defeated.

Am I that invested in my own dogma? Do my beliefs, which I thought served the truth, help to blind me to it?

"What if this really is the Ark?" she asked, in something like panic.

Levi laughed. "Annja, I'd be as astonished as you if that turned out to be the case. For one thing, while I make no pretensions of being versed in geology, I confess to serious reservations about the Creator's flooding the entire planet to a depth of three miles. Where would the water go afterward? And I'm as doubtful as you about the concept of a wooden vessel, however holy, being floated ever higher up the cinder cone on successive surges of lava. There's *something* fantastic here, obviously. It's a huge, remarkable structure. We're standing in it, and I accept the evidence of my senses, at least to that degree. And part of it at least I think we can definitely say is artificial. It's still a long way from that to demonstrating that it's old Noah's boat, though."

"I'm relieved to hear you say that," Annja said in a quiet voice. She became aware of a strange hush in the chamber. It was eerily quiet. "Actually finding out the Anomaly's not just a big rock, much less a discovery as amazing as this, it just—"

She shook her head, feeling helpless still. "It overwhelms me. I don't know what to believe."

"I'm with you on that," said Levi, who'd begun to work his way cautiously through the treacherous tumble of fallen masses, most encrusted with ages of snow and ice. He peered down intently as he did so. Annja didn't think he was just worried about twisting an ankle. "As far as that goes, my own belief is that the whole Flood story, like the whole of Genesis, is an extended metaphor. So let's play at not believing anything at all, until we have some basis to *know*."

Annja laughed. "So I, the trained scientist and dedicated rationalist, get schooled in Science 101 by a Qabbalist rabbi? I don't know whether to be annoyed or grateful, Levi."

"Well, I'd certainly lobby for the latter, if those were the choices," he said waggishly. "Don't underestimate us scholarly rabbis. You can never tell—hey, what's this? Wait, now."

He stooped down and scooped at some snow with his bare hands. His long pale fingers were turning blue, a fact he disregarded, in the cold. It occurred to her to remind him to retrieve his gloves from where he'd ditched them earlier.

Suddenly he grabbed at something in the snow. His joyous whoop echoed through the vaulted, tilted space. Dislodged snow and dust filtered down from above.

"Be careful," Annja cautioned. "We don't want to bring anything heavy down on top of us."

"Sorry, sorry," Levi said. "But just look at this! Look. *Look*."

"It's a clay tablet," Annja said, leaning forward to stare at the object he thrust at her in the uncertain light. "Covered in—is that cuneiform?"

"Yes!" he trilled triumphantly. "Let's see, now. The ancient kingdom of Urartu, of which this area was part, used cuneiform writing. But…no. That's not it. This is written in Akkadian. From the seventh century BC, I'd say. That makes it Neo-Assyrian."

"I recognize the names from school," she said, "but they don't mean much to me. That's far away from my time and place of study."

"Ah, but not from mine, as you're aware." Levi had straightened and held the tablet right up against his nose, squinting to read the little narrow wedge-shaped marks in the light from above. "Probably from the reign of the last of the Neo-Assyrian kings."

"The Assyrians were notably nasty characters, weren't they?" Annja asked. "Even by ancient standards?"

"Oh, yes. Nasty customers indeed. Made no bones about it. Rejoiced in it. Their kings boasted about their atrocities all over their monuments. Complete with very detailed pictures. Not, I've always thought, for the reasons the Mongol and Turkic nomads used epic atrocity, as a deliberate weapon of psychological warfare—the way our enlightened modern governments use genocide bombings of civilian populations. The Assyrians did it, I think, just because they thought it was good fun."

"So you can read it?" she asked.

He glanced at her, then went back to squinting at the dull red tablet. "Oh, yes. Crucial part of my studies. The mystic writings of the ancient Near East form a sort of web, you see—it's impossible to study Hebrew myths and religion from the period without taking them in context."

"But what would an Assyrian cuneiform tablet of any sort, religious or otherwise, be doing way up the mountain here in Noah's Ark?" Annja said.

"What we tend to think of as Noah's Ark," he corrected.

"But things are not that simple. And that ties up with the only reason I can think of."

He shifted his glasses up to his forehead, so they were stacked below his goggles, giving him an alarming six-eyed look. He brought the tablet up almost to one eyeball and then the other. "And that's—yes. Yes! 'Dedicated to…immortal Utnapishtim…saved mankind from the wrath of the gods.'"

He lowered the tablet from his face to turn and stare at Annja in wonder. "Don't you see what this means? If this is—against all odds—an Ark we've found, what we've established isn't the literal truth of the book of Genesis at all."

"It's not?"

"No," he said. And he began to laugh. He laughed so hard the tears sprang from his eyes and coursed down his cheeks into his curly mouse-brown beard. He laughed so hard he had to sit down on an ice-rounded beam and clutch at his thighs.

Annja gaped at him, not understanding a bit of this. "Levi, are you all right?"

"No," he said, struggling to control his laughter. "Yes. Don't you see it yet?

"If anything, this would prove the literal truth of Babylonian myth. And Sumerian, of which it's a straight translation. In other words *not* the existence of Jahweh. Not my people's cantankerous deity. But rather it would confirm the existence of what they taught were false gods—Enki and Anu and Enlil and all the rest.

"That's the wonderful joke. The cosmic joke. If this discovery confirms any theology at all, it's *pagan* theology!"

Over his renewed laughter Annja heard a noise. She turned quickly to face the entryway to the great tilted chamber.

Her eyes met the blue eyes of Larry Taitt. They were saucer-wide and rounded with horror. His face was the color of the snow that lay upon the glacier outside.

Tears welled in his eyes. He turned and stumbled away out of sight.

"I have a bad feeling about this," Annja said.

22

Larry Taitt could barely see through his tears to walk. If it was a miracle he didn't step on anything that would twist beneath his boot and sprain his ankle, or into a concealed opening that would capture his foot and snap his leg neatly as any deliberate trap…it was a dark sort of miracle indeed.

Somehow he made his way outside. He found the sky more full of clouds than he could have guessed from the sun shining through the top of the Anomaly. Snow fell in fat flakes like slow albino moths.

He found his leader and Leif Baron inland of the Anomaly, overseeing as his comrades pitched tents, partially protected by the object's mass against a rising storm. They were getting set up for a full-scale excavation of the site. Robyn Wilfork stood watching nearby. The two remaining unbelievers from the New York television crew were somewhere out of sight, presumably photographing the Anomaly from the outside.

A sob escaped Larry's mouth as he stumbled toward the

older men. Baron whipped around and scowled. Mr. Bostitch turned more slowly.

"Why, Larry," his employer said, "what's the matter with you?"

Hesitantly, stumbling over words he hated the taste of, he told them what he had overheard.

For a moment everyone stood shocked into horrified silence. Baron looked to Mr. Bostitch.

"There's only one thing to do, you know," the former SEAL told his superior.

"You're right," Mr. Bostitch said. "We can't let any of this get out. Instead of proving the Bible's truth, we'll destroy the faith of billions! Then our Lord will be unable to return to sit in judgment over the Earth."

Larry's comrades had stopped working on the tents, which were mostly erected anyway, when he began his story. They all seemed to understand. It was more than Larry, in his current distraught state, could say for himself.

From beneath their bulky jackets the young men produced handguns.

He knew about the weapons. He carried one himself, as ordered by Mr. Bostitch and advised by Mr. Baron, in a shoulder holster beneath his left armpit, inside his parka. It was uncomfortable and the harness bound him in ways that were anything but helpful during the tricky, ultimately demanding business of rock- and ice-climbing. His ribs had turned a rainbow of sullen colors from banging the holstered piece against the rock. Yet he had been ordered to do it, and he believed in discipline, so he obeyed.

But now he was simply appalled.

"What are you doing?" he stammered.

"Our duty to our Lord," Baron said.

Mr. Bostitch clapped a hand on Larry's shoulder. "You've done your part, son," he said. "And thank you. I know it wasn't easy to tell us this. You just sit out here in a tent and leave the rest to us."

"You can't be talking about *killing* them! Ms. Creed and the others?"

"You can't make an omelet without breaking eggs," Baron said. "Didn't you learn that at the academy? It's Leadership 101. To do any less than the Lord demands is to do the Devil's work."

Larry spun to face him. He'd always been afraid of the security-contracting mogul. But he knew right from wrong.

"I won't let you—"

He never heard it coming. The bullet. He merely felt it hit like a sledgehammer between the shoulder blades. His chest seemed to explode in blackness.

He found himself on his knees without knowing how he got there. The glacial ice was very cold and very hard but didn't hurt. Nothing hurt. He felt numb. Detached.

Craning his head over his shoulder he saw the big cold-mottled, pink-and-blue-white face of Charles Bostitch, his slab cheeks shiny with tears, his blue eyes puffy above the sights of a gun.

"Lord forgive you, boy," his employer whispered.

He saw a flash, bright as a thousand suns, and then he died.

"OH, GOD," CHARLIE BOSTITCH said over and over, gazing down at the body of his factotum, in a graceless sprawl with his head haloed in scarlet. Bostitch held his black handgun as if uncertain how such an evil article had come into his hand.

He felt a pressure, comforting, on his other arm. It was Baron. His muscular face was calm. Purposeful.

"You did what you had to do, sir," Baron said quietly. "Think of it as saving the boy from the Devil's clutches. It was an act of sheer mercy to strike him down before he could betray his faith."

Charlie nodded. His stomach rebelled. He turned and vomited into a snowbank.

As he did he heard Leif Baron snapping, "You know what to do. Go. Go!"

SITTING ON WHAT MIGHT HAVE been a curved beam fallen from above, beneath its coating of ice, Levi looked up from peering at the innocuous-looking clay tablet in his palm.

"What was that?" he asked.

Annja came out of freeze. "Levi, stand up," she said, speaking low and struggling to keep her voice calm. "Right now. We have to get out of here. Now."

He blinked myopically at her. "But why, Annja? There's so much yet to look for. We haven't even started!"

"Not now," she said. "That was a gunshot."

As she spoke another hard rap echoed from outside the ruin.

STANDING BY THE TENTS Bostitch saw the two unbelievers from New York, Trish Baxter and Tommy Wynock, run out of the entry where they had, against his wishes, wandered back inside the Ark without the rest of the party to get some footage.

Although it was not without regret, he watched with pride as the leading elements of his fine young men, Josh Fairlie and Zeb Miller, opened fire without hesitation. The two television crewpeople collapsed in the snow. Despite the dimming light their blood glared shocking red against the new bright snow.

"What a pity," he said, shaking his head.

"They couldn't be trusted," Baron said grimly. "It's the only way."

Bostitch shrugged. "Our fine young men can learn to work their audiovisual equipment. With God's help they can do anything, bless them. That's how you teach them in my academy, after all. And Mr. Wilfork can make sure they know what's important to shoot. Film, I should say."

Looking around he added, "Where's that white-haired scamp gotten off to? He was here a second ago."

"Probably hiding somewhere, shaking in terror," Baron said. "After all, he's nothing but a half-reformed old commie. And as my daddy always used to say, you can't trust people who don't believe in God."

Despite the sorrow in his ample belly Bostitch smiled. "Oh, but I do trust him, Leif," he said. "I trust him to be true to a steady paycheck. You can always rely on communists for that. They surely know the value of a buck."

DEEPER AND DEEPER INTO THE RUIN Annja dragged Levi, as fast as she dared. And then a bit faster. She had cracked a light stick of her own. He followed compliantly.

"Why are we going this way?" he asked mildly, stumbling over rubble.

"If we go out the front door we'll run straight into the guys with the guns," she said. "I'm hoping there's another way out."

"And if there's not?"

Her cheeks drew back toward her ears, baring teeth in an expression that was nothing like a smile. "We find a place to hide and try to ambush them. Play it by ear. Unless you can think of something better on real short notice."

"Oh, no, Annja. You'll find the best way. You always do. I have faith in you."

He glanced back to the great chamber. "Look, the light's fading again in there. Maybe the gods really are arm-wrestling over our fate." He grinned dreamily at the thought.

"Whatever," she said. "I prefer to think my fate's in my own hands."

"Couldn't find better ones," Levi said with complacent confidence that half annoyed her and half made her despair.

His belief in me is like a child's in its parent, she thought. *How can I let him down? But—how will I not?*

She heard voices calling from behind, echoing with deceptive gentleness through the cathedral spaces of the Anomaly. The Young Wolves were on their trail. The pack was giving chase.

The way narrowed around them. Annja grimaced. Their enemies had guns; they had no need to close in and face the final surprise of her sword. *I might've just robbed us of room to dodge,* she realized.

But the passage, illuminated by her light stick's eerie green glow, turned abruptly left. That was, to the landward side, toward the unseen summit of Ararat. Bending low and turning sideways was the only way to follow. Annja had to let go of Levi's wrist to do so. But he was moving on his own quite well now.

And then she stopped. Before her was a curve of dark wall. Whether stone, or wood somehow fossilized, or simply preserved somehow, improbably, by pitch, didn't matter. It was solid. Impassable.

Then Levi said, "Wait. There's a cleft here. See?"

He stepped out of view. "I'm out, Annja," she heard him call softly. "This way. It's clear."

"Hey!" A triumphant shout came from too close behind. "This way!"

She spun. "Annja," Levi whispered from outside. "Come on."

But she couldn't just follow him. Their pursuit would follow them quickly enough. And they couldn't outrun bullets. She had to teach the Young Wolves caution.

She had to teach them to fear what they thought was their helpless prey.

As quickly as she dared for fear of turning an ankle, which would be quickly fatal, she moved back toward the bend in the narrowing passage. She heard boots crunch and heavy breathing.

And then suddenly a pursuer appeared. It was one of the twins. His hood had fallen back and he'd lost his goggles. His fair, clean-cut face was flushed, the blue eyes wide with pure predatory lust. Only the red band around his forehead identified him as Zeb.

The delight on those handsome youthful features when he saw her struck her as almost demonic. "Well, what have we got here?" he said, his condensed breath wreathing his face like smoke.

His eyes widened as he saw the slender tongue of steel dart toward his chest. He tried to aim his pistol. But he'd gotten sloppy, forgotten the lessons Leif Baron had almost certainly taught him. Instead of holding the weapon muzzle up, ready to snap down onto target at a millisecond's notice, he'd let it fall by his side as he used both hands to help keep himself clear of the narrowing walls.

The sword hit him in the sternum and bit deep. The blade slipped effortlessly between ribs to skewer his heart. His blue eyes went wide, more from final surprise than fear.

The force of her side kick drove him literally off the blade. As soon as it slipped clear in a sudden spray of blood she opened her hand. The sword returned to the otherwhere, where it awaited her will.

Zeb Higgins bounced off the wall behind him. With a loud groan he toppled sideways out of sight. His companions cried out in surprise and alarm.

Damn, Annja thought. I wanted that pistol. It was lost to her now. She bolted for the open air. For a moment she stuck in the gap. It felt as if cold, hard jaws had closed to trap her. She fought the panic that yammered in her brain, emptied her lungs and slid out into the blessed icy air and milky light of freedom.

Levi caught her arm to help her as she emerged. Then he pointed. "Look!"

As she suspected they were near the end of the Anomaly, away from where they had come up onto the glacier—the southwest, she remembered. From the ice sheet below them Robyn Wilfork stood beckoning them urgently with his arm.

23

"Come on, then," Wilfork insisted. "We've precious little time."

Annja looked at Levi, who stood placidly in the snow to his boot tops, waiting for her. He shrugged.

"Hurry," Wilfork urged. He turned and lumbered away through the fat, swirling flakes.

Through narrowed eyes, Annja watched him go.

"Do we have any other options?" Levi asked.

They didn't so they followed the journalist around the end of the Anomaly to the cliff. The wind had picked up and the temperature had dropped. The cold stabbed at Annja's cheeks like knives. The snowfall thickened. Wind spiraled the dense flakes around them. They reminded Annja uncomfortably of water swirling down a drain.

Next to a sheer drop Wilfork stopped. A rope hung over the edge, belayed with special anchors called pickets designed for use in ice—basically long, thin pieces of aluminum angled lengthwise at ninety degrees with one side drilled with holes. Another line lay in a blue-and-white coil beside the picket.

"It's all I could do," Wilfork said. "They've all gone totally berserkers. Like a hornet's nest somebody tried to use for a bloody football."

Annja gritted her teeth and frowned. Without their packs they'd be limited to what they carried on their persons. It could be a fatal mistake. What other choice do we have? she thought.

"What's going on?" Levi asked.

"Isn't it obvious?" Wilfork said. "They're going to kill you to keep their secret. Your only hope of escape is to get down the mountain. There's no more time. No time to secure yourselves en route. You have to rappel as far down as you can before the secured line plays out."

"Okay," Annja said. "Levi, do you know how to rappel?"

"Oh, yes. It's easy enough even I can do it. Mr. Baron taught me after Mr. Bostitch hired me. 'Bringing me onboard,' they called it."

"Good. You go first. I'll follow. Move as fast as you can. Find a good place to stand before the rope plays out and wait for me to join you," Annja said.

Levi swallowed hard, but he pulled his goggles down and his hood up and grabbed the rope with pale bare hands. Annja felt a pang. He'd left his gloves inside the Anomaly.

But he disappeared rapidly over the edge. The snow seemed to swallow him.

Hoisting the rope coil over her shoulder Annja seized the anchored line and swung herself over the edge. She hoped the bulky journalist would have sense to go somewhere else in a hurry now that she and the rabbi had taken advantage of the literal lifeline he'd given them. Standing there by the sheer ice-faced drop he was conspicuous; he might as well have been a sign announcing that something was happening here.

"Don't worry about me, Levi," she said over her shoulder. She was relieved to see the lanky form of the rabbi swinging away from the cliff face and sliding down, using his descenders properly. He may not have been the most coordinated man on Earth, but rappelling isn't really all that demanding, either. Annja thought maybe he really could do it.

"I won't kick you in the head," she assured him. "I—"

A *tink* sound suddenly came from above. The sheer ice wall vibrated against the gloved hand holding the rope as she attempted to snap a carabiner attached to her own harness by a quickdraw onto the line.

She frowned, totally failing to comprehend what caused the noise. Then a second ringing note of metal on something hard sent a spear as cold as the heart of the glacier right through her belly.

She looked up. She could see part of Robyn Wilfork's face, beet-red beneath his headband. His right hand was upraised with an ice ax clutched in it.

"Robyn!" she said. "What are you doing?"

He slammed the ice ax down. This time the rope vibrated alarmingly in her grip.

"It should be obvious," he grunted. "I'm cutting the bloody rope."

"Why?" Annja exclaimed.

"To earn a hearty reward, I hope." He swung again. By the way he cursed he missed the rope cleanly, although Annja felt it vibrate again anyway. He was clumsy to start with. With the wind, its whistle turning to a moaning roar, coming up, the snow attacked his eyes like cold soft bees. Bulky mittens made his hands even less dexterous than usual. Chill and fatigue seemed to be combining with weight and age to drag on him.

And none of it could buy Annja and the rabbi more than a few seconds of additional life....

"Levi," Annja called down desperately. "Grab rock and hang on!" She knew it wasn't much of a chance. If Wilfork severed the rope her weight would peel him off the wall anyway.

Scrambling frantically upward, she called, "How can you do this to us?"

"I've lost my faith," he said. "In everything except money, anyway. Ah." The last was a sound of satisfaction. The rope jerked violently. Evidently he'd managed to cut partway through it.

"But you're a rationalist!" she said.

"I found the bloody boat, didn't I?" he screamed, bringing the ax down in fury.

A mighty clang rang out, dulled oddly by the closing clouds, but still potent. As Annja began her fall she saw the chopped-off rope end slither over the edge after her.

Hearing her despairing scream, Wilfork turned away and vanished from her view. Apparently he couldn't bear to see his handiwork. He didn't want to watch as a helpless woman and man fell a thousand sheer feet to be smashed on the volcanic rocks of Ararat.

But Annja wasn't falling. The rope hung limp from her harness. Beneath her Levi hung like a terrified baby lemur to its mother's white-furred belly.

Both her hands were clamped hard on the hilt of the

sword. The instant she felt the rope start to go she'd summoned it and jammed it to half the three-foot length of its blade in ice and rock. Once again the mysterious blade had saved her.

She had screamed purely for effect. To deceive their treacherous foe.

It worked—at least partially. Wilfork suddenly reappeared on the rim. Ever-cautious, the lapsed communist had decided to make sure of his prey—and of his reward from the master of the wolf pack, which Annja could now hear baying closer in the storm. In trembling mittened hands Wilfork held a large rock over his own head, apparently to make sure of Rabbi Leibowitz's death if he'd somehow avoided being taken to his doom by Annja's fall.

Finding a foothold Annja released the sword's hilt. It vanished instantly. Like an angry monkey she swarmed up the ice wall. A natural athlete who kept herself fit with the fanatical intensity of the Young Wolves, her hands and feet found holds in imperfections in the frozen-over rock without her consciously looking.

As the journalist held his rock up for maximum velocity he overbalanced slightly backward. It was deadly easy for Annja to reach up, hook his heavily booted ankle and pull.

Bellowing like a bee-stung bull, Wilfork sat down with an impact that clacked his teeth audibly in his head. The heavy rock fell from his clumsy hands. It glanced off his own unprotected head. But the blow was not hard enough to crack his skull.

However, it was hard enough to stun him momentarily. Annja, who'd relinquished her initial grip, seized him by the leg of his insulated blue pants and pulled, twisting her hips outward both for added pull and to clear herself out of the way as his bulky body slipped over the edge and fell free.

Robyn Wilfork's buffalo bellows turned to wounded-horse shrieks. Glancing down, Annja saw Levi looking up, eyes huge behind goggles and glasses. The rabbi quickly hugged ice. Barely missing him, the traitorous journalist plummeted by, arms and legs windmilling futilely. He vanished quickly in the snow.

His screams went on and on.

Once she knew Levi was still safe Annja stopped paying attention to Wilfork's fall from grace. Instead she unlimbered the ice ax hung from her own harness and quickly hammered a piton through thick ice into rock and tied the cut rope to it. Then she called down, as softly as she could, so as not to attract bullets or avalanches they had somehow miraculously avoided so far.

"Levi, do you hear me? Go ahead and rappel down. When you've gone as far as you can—safely!—tug the rope and I'll come down."

He nodded. At once he pushed away from the precarious safety of his grips and vanished in the milky churn of snow.

He has such naive faith in me, Annja thought. I hope I don't let him down.

Yet just now she couldn't imagine—clinging for her life, exposed on a cliff waiting for their pursuers to come and shoot her, or just drop the same rock on her that Wilfork had failed to—what possible chance she had of not letting him down.

But it was not in Annja Creed to just give up. That was the opposite of who and what she was. Also, she knew, purposeful activity was emotionally more comfortable than giving in to terror or despair. If she was going to die, she'd die busy and surprised, rather than squirming helplessly in futile self-inflicted mental agony....

So she got busy. Trying to make as little noise as possible, aided by the sound-deadening effects of the blizzard, she pounded home a rappel anchor. She fed the spare rope through it and made ready to climb down herself when Levi signaled that he had found new purchase.

From above she heard voices in the booming belly of the wind. Though she could make out no words there was no mistaking the high-pitched excitement of the Young Wolves, who sounded like the scarcely postadolescents most of them were. Then came a harder bark, assured and authoritative. *Baron*. The master killer.

Why haven't they looked down and spotted me? she wondered. The closest of her pursuers must be barely feet from her. Then she realized the falling snow was making it difficult for the pack to spot the secured line.

She clamped her teeth shut hard. Her heart seemed to be trying to escape right out her mouth. It beat so hard that, weakened as she was from extreme altitude and worse exertion, she started feeling dizzy.

Must maintain, she commanded herself.

"Hey!" It was Josh Fairlie's voice. "There's a rope here."

She felt Levi's security rope jump against her chest and hip. Once, twice, three times. The rabbi's signal. He was waiting for her.

A pink squarish face appeared, right above her. Josh Fairlie's blue eyes shot wide in surprise.

He shouted something. She couldn't spare the attention to make it out. Cutting loose the rope that held her against the cliff face with a stroke of her ice ax—no point in losing it—she kicked off from the wall and let herself fall free as Fairlie swung a black object into sight toward her.

The snow shut like a curtain above her. Orange flashes backlit it as Josh opened fire on her. The shots sounded oddly muted in the storm.

Bullets cracked past her. None hit.

Annja looked down. She refocused all her attention on her fast-roping descent. Found a place to brake her fall, flex her legs, push off again. There wasn't anything she could do about the bullets, anyway.

It seemed one or two other handguns joined the fusillade, to equal lack of effect. Then they went silent. Baron, no doubt, concerned too much gunplay could break loose unstable snow and ice on the glacier upslope of them. The pack didn't lie at much of an angle, but it was an angle. It probably wouldn't take much more noise to start a slide that would sweep the rest of the expedition right over the edge.

Of course, that would likely finish off Annja and Levi, too. It seems Leif Baron—or Good Time Charlie—isn't willing to sacrifice himself and his band of zealots just to stop us, Annja thought, bouncing again, whizzing downward into churning white blankness.

Then she thought, or maybe it's only that Baron's confident enough not to think they have to make a sacrifice that desperate.

24

So began the descent through nightmare.

Through snow and keening wind and rapidly failing light, Annja rappelled down the merciless mountain. Her legs worked mechanically as pistons, flexing as she came in contact with the sheer face of ice and rock, driving her away again to plummet breathtakingly through the white vortex and the gathering darkness. She used her descenders sparingly to brake her speed, though it made her gut clench painfully at every push off, never knowing where she might hit. Or what might hit her. A broken leg or even a badly twisted ankle would doom them both.

But so would getting caught by moving too slowly. Caution was not survival positive. It was a pure example of a choice between bad options.

She left Levi at the top of each stage, allowing him to believe he was belaying her, although that was hardly necessary. She worried about leaving him closer to their pursuers.

But they couldn't have it both ways. She was by far the

better equipped to find a place to anchor for a new stage before the rope ran out. So it was Annja who launched herself again and again into deepening darkness at frightening speed.

She took them through three breakneck descents, each to around the one-hundred-foot capacity of the doubled rope. It would be easy enough for the pursuit to follow, since she didn't move laterally away from their original line of descent. But she knew that it would take some time for the Young Wolves, fit and eager as they were, to get organized to safely start after her and Levi.

Baron was far too professional to let his pack just swarm howling down the cliff after the fugitives. That could lead to disaster as readily as it might yield success. Too-reckless hunters could be ambushed by their prey; marooned on the cliff face in a blizzard with no way to move in any direction; or get racked up by accident, dead or disabled, for simple failure to respect the mountain. At the very least, they'd quickly spread out and become scattered beyond hope of recall or tactical direction. Annja wanted to take advantage of that organizing interval to produce some separation.

Also they had to do something with Charlie Bostitch. They couldn't very well leave him on top of the damn mountain by himself; he'd never consent to stay alone, and their own numbers were too few to spare anybody to babysit him. Despite the fact he'd gone through the Rehoboam mountaineering program, and held up surprisingly well on the climb, he was overweight and middle-aged and had to be feeling the effects of effort and altitude more than his keen young followers. Baron would probably send two of his bully boys down fast to scout for their quarry. But he wouldn't let them get too far from the rest, either. So Bostitch was going to act as a boat anchor for his crew.

After her third drop it was almost pitch-black. Not even the faintest glow came from the sun at her back. But she found the tiniest of rock ledges running more or less horizontally around the mountain to her right. South.

"We need to shift sideways so they can't just drop blindly in on top of us, Levi," she said when he joined her, faithful and uncomplaining. "Can you follow me?"

"Sure, Annja." He gazed at her with a look that reminded her disconcertingly of a Labrador puppy.

She studied him for a long moment in the gloom, the faint crepuscular glow that lingered on the mountain. The wind had subsided but the snow continued to fall. She could barely make out anything but his eyes, long-lashed and shining at her through goggles and thick glasses.

If he falls, he'll take me with him, she thought grimly. No matter where they moved laterally across the ice wall she didn't dare set an anchor to fast rope down and rapidly increase the distance between them and those who sought their lives. The anchor would give away their new line of descent, and defeat the whole purpose of moving sideways in the first place.

From above Annja heard voices. So she thought. It might have been a trick of what was now a breeze, questing curiously around the sheer mountain face.

"Okay," she told the rabbi. "Stick close."

She started moving crabwise to her left. Levi did as she said. Fortunately he had sense enough not to crowd her; if he bumped her he could send them both hurtling to destruction.

But perhaps his very otherworldliness was their salvation. He understood intellectually quite well what an awful fix they were in. But he didn't seem to feel the threat viscerally; it wasn't as real to him as his books. Or the weird little narrow-arrowhead markings pressed into the ancient clay tablet that now rode in a plastic bag in a pocket of his pants, as safe as he was, anyway. So while Levi still wasn't very coordinated he tended to keep his presence of mind, as she had noticed before, in even the most extreme circumstances. She thought he was quite a remarkable man.

And as her self-defense instructors had always emphasized to her, the biggest single predictor of survival in lethal danger was *presence of mind.* It had been her own personal, private edge long before she came into possession of the sword.

It turned out the sun hadn't yet completely been swallowed by the Urartu badlands behind them. As the snow thinned a faint crimson glow found its way to them, like the light of some alien red-dwarf star. As she edged sideways Annja saw by the dim forge glow how purple—blue in more normal light—the knobbly, skinny fingers of Levi's hands were. The cold must be agonizing for him.

But she needed her own gloves. Her own climbing skill—such as it was—augmented by natural athleticism and rigorous training, offered their sole hope of survival. To give him her gloves would be to increase his comfort at the seriously increased risk to both their lives.

He has to do what he can to keep frostbite from setting in, she thought. But even fingers were a small price to pay for life. She only hoped he saw it the same way—and more, that it wouldn't come to that.

Painstakingly, checking frequently on her companion, Annja moved what she judged to be about seventy-five feet to the north around the mountainside. There some dark rock projected through the ice sheet, looking deceptively bare. She knew they concealed patches and pockets of ice that would shed a hand or booted foot as a duck's back did water, if she weren't cautious. But they offered at least the thin hope she'd be able to climb down.

And thin hope was all the hope they were liable to get.

Working as quietly as she could Annja planted some purely temporary protection devices to hold Levi in place and belay her. He assured her he'd be able to recover the pitons and camming devices and follow her down, using a rappel descender to brake him if needed. He even promised to retrieve the protection she sank on her climb down. That mattered less than making sure they left nothing here on this ledge, which though it was little more than a hint would be glaringly obvious to climbers as seasoned as Baron and his crew seemed to be. Even with night settling in to stay for a while, the Young Wolves wouldn't feel constrained about using powerful lights to aid them.

For that matter Annja and her companion didn't have any powerful lanterns. Allowing herself a morale-boosting moment of self-congratulation at having crammed the cargo pockets of her pants, jacket and even climbing harness with everything she thought she might need in a pinch, she dug out a small chemical light stick, cracked it into a gentle orange glow and hung it around her neck.

The odds of its faint light being seen from above were real but small. The odds of her falling if she tried climbing totally blind approached dead certainty. With definite emphasis on *dead*.

Thinking of the gear bulging out her pockets and hanging tinkling like chimes from her harness, she realized as she worked her way down the rock protrusion that they were running short on rappel anchors, which they couldn't recover the way they did pitons.

It was just one more thing to worry about. On the other hand, if their sideways shift had thrown off the pack, they could afford to descend at a more deliberate pace. And maybe even snatch a few minutes' desperately needed rest. After all, we'd just barely finished climbing up the damn mountain, she thought.

She returned her attention wholly to the task at hand, and foot. She concentrated on picking her way down the rock by the inadequate gleam of the light stick, forcing herself to move deliberately in the face of the need for speed whose urgency threatened to vibrate her clean off the cliff by itself. She made herself pause at intervals to drive in protection. It was as imperative for them to remember always to respect the mountain, and gravity, as it was for their enemies.

After what seemed only a couple of eternities, Annja's boots found another ledge beneath them. By that time her light stick had died to little more than a ghost of luminance past. She could still see that the ledge ran down and to the right. It wasn't much to e-mail the bunch back home about. But it seemed solid, and was close enough to level to afford some relatively easy lateral motion.

She secured herself to belay Levi as he picked his way down. He didn't have a light to help him. But evidently he'd watched carefully as she picked out her route, as well as having the rope as a rough guide. He was moving with more surety although she was certain his hands were stiff and painful. Somehow he dutifully recovered each and every safety anchor as he passed by.

Annja felt an explosive impulse to shout at him, "Hurry! Hurry! They'll catch us!" She bit her tongue to hold it inside.

After another few eternities he settled on the little ledge next to her. He gave her a goofy grin by the last few lumens from her stick. She gripped his shoulder.

"Great job, Levi. Now follow me."

She roped him to her and led them along the ledge by pure feel. After another fifty or sixty feet it both widened and ended. For the first time Annja allowed them to sit, rest, sip water from bottles and chew ration bars with the consistency of asphalt and the taste of wallboard.

By the narrow blue beam of the LCD pin light she always carried in a pocket she checked her companion's hands. She didn't dare use its tiny intense illumination to help climb for fear it would be spotted from above. If a light like that was pointed just right you could see it from ten miles away or more. As it was she dared only use the flash in quick pulses to confirm Levi's fingers weren't going white. Thankfully they seemed free of frostbite. But she winced to see how raw and bloody they'd become from being rasped by rope and rock.

"Do you have some kind of cloth, handkerchiefs, anything you can wrap around them?" she asked.

"How about my spare socks? I always carry a pair."

"If you can still grip the rope with them on."

"Oh, yes." He dug in his pants pockets and came out with a pair of insulated socks. He unrolled them and pulled them on his hands. Then he held them up and flexed them, peering at them. "I wish I'd thought of that sooner," he said, sounding relieved nonetheless.

After a few quiet moments he spoke again. "It's pretty

dark, Annja," he said, sitting and gazing out into what was now lightly falling snow. "Are we going to stop here for the night?"

"No," Annja said reluctantly. "We're not going to stop at all."

"Really? Because we'll freeze to death if we go to sleep?"

"That's a myth. Some explorer with an Icelandic name I can never remember debunked it back in the early twentieth century. You actually radiate a lot of heat when you're moving. Sleeping helps conserve body heat.

"Of course, if you just lie down out in the wind you're liable to freeze to death whether you're awake or not, if it gets cold enough. The bad news for us is that we can't really huddle up out here on this cliff to reduce the surface area we have to radiate heat from. The good news is the wind seems to have died to a not-too-terrible level and the cloud cover's causing an inversion. That keeps the air temperature from dropping too far and fast."

Levi took a bite of energy bar and worked his jaws patiently at it. "So why not try to sleep here?" he asked.

"Two reasons. First, the people who are chasing us have way more options than we do. If they choose to keep hunting for us in the dark, they've got more manpower. Plus they have flashlights and equipment, both to help them climb and to look for us. Although if they use those we've got a good chance to see them coming. For all the good that might do. Anyway, they can also hang themselves out in bivouac bags and get a good night's sleep, plan on making up the distance on us in daylight. We have to be ready for either eventuality."

"All right," Levi said mildly.

"Second…we don't have bivy bags. I don't know about

you, but I don't think I could sleep out here on this ledge no matter how well I tie myself down. And even though exercising causes us to lose heat faster, it makes us *feel* warmer. It's pretty chilly for sleep. So I want to keep descending as well as we can."

It hurt her to say the words. Her body ached from cold, oxygen starvation to the muscles, fatigue poisons and the aftereffects of fear-induced adrenaline overload. Her head felt so heavy her neck could barely support it, and the lids of her eyes felt like leaden shutters.

But her companion's simple response was "Anything you say, Annja."

Wearily she grinned at him. "Surely you could argue a little," she said. "Oh, well. We're burning darkness. Let's see how well we can climb by braille."

ROPED TOGETHER JUST BEYOND arm's length apart, so as not to interfere with each other, Annja and the rabbi groped their blind way down the mountain.

Their rate of progress, either sideways or down, ranged from snaillike to glacial to nonexistent, as Annja found herself forced to rest for a few moments, or had to halt to try to figure out a survivable strategy for negotiating some particularly impassable stretch. Go back and try a different route? Keep looking—feeling—for the finger- and toeholds, the crevices in ice and stone that would securely accept anchors to allow her to move on? All with a mind that seemed to be sagging into a sort of dark, soggy useless mass like gelatin left on a refrigerator shelf for way too long.

The night passed like eons. Even with the inversion and without the wind the air stayed frigid at this altitude. The cold seeped through her muscles like venom from a hornet's sting, and made her very bones ache.

Annja tried to keep her mind focused purely on task. She worked on finding some way, some path, to put still more distance between them and the hunters. It was a salvation of sorts. She had to concentrate, focus her attention like a laser beam, because the slightest mistake could drop her off the sheer face of the Mountain of Pain.

At one point they were able to chimney down a narrow chute, and that gave them sixty more feet. Fortunately it wasn't a difficult technique to learn. Annja coached Levi down even as she descended a few feet below him. It helped keep her mind from the fact that inside the space between icy rock masses was even darker than outside, like a blind descent into freezing Hell.

They rested for a while in the cleft at the base. Annja massaged blood back into her fingers and stuck her hands inside her bulky jacket, squeezing them under her armpits to restore a scrap of warmth and circulation. Unable to feel handholds well enough through her gloves she'd had to take them off.

Annja wondered if, should she lose fingers from her right hand, she'd still be able to summon the Sword. Maybe that's not a huge loss if I can't, she decided. Considering what kind of things it seems to get me into.

Three times she peeled. Once rock broke off simultaneously beneath her right foot and left hand. Once it was what she thought was solid ice that crumbled to her weight. And once she just slipped off for no reason she could immediately perceive.

That last time she took Levi with her. Fortunately the cams they'd emplaced held, although she could hear them creak alarmingly as the pair swung side by side, banging ungently off naked rock. For a moment they stared at each other through the darkness. Annja was just able to make out the rabbi's goggled face. Then she stabilized herself with a boot against the rock face, and began feeling around for more holds to continue the descent from there.

That had to be some kind of microsleep incident, she realized with a little shock of dismay. Mind, body and emotions were all reaching the breakdown point. If I don't rest soon worse is going to happen.

"Are you all right, Annja?" Levi asked anxiously as she helped him back to his own perch. She noted that the ends of the socks on his hands had grown much darker. He was bleeding into them.

"Yeah," she said. "I'm fine."

Lying to him was like twisting a knife in her own guts. But what purpose would the truth serve? Adding to his own stress burden would only make him less able to continue.

"Let's go on," she said, in what she hoped was an encouraging tone. It didn't sound too encouraging to her. The phrase *death warmed over* kept creeping into her mind.

But not long thereafter, moving as if through congealing gelatin, she fetched up against a wide crack in the rock. It was a good fifteen feet wide and even in the slight starlight filtering through the cloud she could see the gleam of ice sheathing its walls. Above them overhangs jutted, more ominous than all the cathedral gargoyles of Europe. She had just clambered over one, swinging herself into a bare rock face that offered plenty of purchase.

I can't go back up over that, though, she thought, looking upward. I just don't have the strength.

"Annja," the rabbi said quietly, "I don't know if I can go on."

She checked her watch. To her surprise less than two hours remained until dawn. She'd feared to see they'd been on the run for an hour and a half or something. That was an unexpected blessing of the pinpoint focus the near-blind groping descent had required of her—time passed quickly.

The fact she wore a watch struck Annja with sudden, sinister significance. Usually she didn't wear one. She almost always carried a cell phone, which served the same function, if not a PDA or other device that could as easily tell her what time it was. There seemed no point in weighing her arm down with something that did nothing but tell time. But on a climb like this Baron had insisted that they all wear wrist chronometers they could check easily without digging in a pocket.

He was right again. That's what bothered her now. He was right way too often. He may have inherited a fortune, just like his boss Charlie, but it was clear he had neither survived as a SEAL nor expanded the private military contractor business—even in the terrific boom associated with the War on Terror—without knowing his job awfully well. And it was he who guided the pack of young, fit, eager raptors who chased them.

She shook her head as if to jar those thoughts loose. "Me, either," she admitted. "All we can do is all we can do. If exhaustion makes us mess up, the crazies on our tail won't have to finish us. We need to rest."

And so she cocooned them as best she could in ropes, facing each other, clinging like opossums to share their meager warmth. So utterly spent was she that despite the discomfort and uncertainty and looming danger she fell at once into a deep sleep.

A FAINT RED GLOW THROUGH her eyelids roused her. She forced gummy eyes open. Off over Azerbaijan, somewhere beyond the vastness of Ararat, the sun was rising. Bands of red light stretched far west over the tormented terrain of eastern Turkey to either side of them. If little light made it around the mountain's bulk to where Annja and the rabbi huddled, even less warmth did. Still, she imagined she felt warmer.

The sun did a surprising amount for her energy and morale. Meaning she felt as if she'd been dead for less than a week now.

She had a vague sense of movements large and menacing on the dawnlit ground beneath them, like Sam and Frodo surrounded by orc armies on the slopes of Mount Doom. Another volcano, she recalled, if a much more vigorous one. Also much warmer.

She shrugged the sensation off. It was only hyperactive imagination. They hung still well around ten thousand feet. There was no way she could see anything down there anyway, if something actually was happening. Still an added sense of unease continued to smolder within.

Great. That's totally what I need. More to worry about.

She looked to Levi and found herself gazing into his wide eyes. They watched her steadily through goggles and glasses. The young rabbi seemed perfectly calm and at peace.

On sudden impulse she kissed him on the tip of his cold nose. He blinked.

"What was that for?" he asked. His voice had a rusty-hinge creak to it. If he was like her it was raw from breathing the thin, icy air.

"For trusting me." She hoped that hadn't been cruel. She felt no romantic or physical attraction to him and she wasn't going to. But she felt a great surge of something like love for him. As if he were a younger brother.

He's ten years older than you, she reminded herself. But in real-world experience, she knew, she was far his senior.

Feels like centuries, she thought, as she began to disentangle them.

She checked their anchors and replaced a couple she didn't trust. Then she expanded the length of safety rope tethering them to one another to twenty feet. It should give her some room to explore for a route down. Although last night, anyway, the only route she'd been able to detect dead-ended pretty decisively against that wide icy crack in the mountain rock.

"What a difference a day makes," she muttered. "Or a little daylight." Being able to see where she was going struck her as an almost decadent luxury.

But shortly she began to frown in dismay. The ugly realization slowly suffused her mind that the only possible paths were back up over the overhang, whose underside she now saw was slick with ice, or across the yawning gap, too far to leap with any degree of safety, to a surface that looked as hard and slippery as glass. Have I trapped us here? she wondered.

Instantly her mind rebelled. There's always a way, she told herself fiercely. And I always find it.

Yet was that mere childish bravado? Her resourcefulness had always served her in tight situations. Otherwise she'd never have lived to be doing her fly imitation up here

on a sheer cliff with several thousand feet to anything resembling a decent-sized nonvertical surface below the
thick soles of her boots.

Everything has limits, she thought glumly. Had her resourcefulness at last done a fatal face-plant against its own
boundaries?

From not far enough above her a shout pealed out like
a morning bell. "There she is! There's the filthy apostate
who killed my brother!"

25

Annja Creed looked up. Fifty feet above their precarious perch she saw three figures peering over another black rock shelf. Despite their hoods and goggles she recognized Leif Baron, Josh Fairlie and Jeb Higgins. Jeb was clearly the one who had alerted the others by screaming at them. Each wore a distinctive colored jacket, but by this time Annja could have distinguished the Young Wolves from each other anyway, by little more than the way they moved and carried themselves.

"So they did keep searching throughout the night," she said. "Levi, we have to go."

"Where?" The question was neither a challenge nor a cry of desperation. It was simply a good question.

She shook her head and sighed. She wanted to cry in desperation. There was only one way.

Thunder cracked. It reverberated between the walls of the ice chasm before them and made the whole great mountain seem to tremble. Amid the colossal racket the lesser *crack* of something passing them by faster than the speed of sound was scarcely perceptible. But Annja, who knew the sound too well, didn't miss it.

"What's that?" Levi shouted, grimacing at the sharp noise hurting his ears.

"They're shooting at us!" Annja said.

Another pistol shot crashed. She never heard that bullet pass. As the echoes died she heard Baron shouting, "Accursed fool, you'll bring the whole mountain down on our heads!"

She risked another look up. Jeb was leaning way out from his perch, clutching a safety rope with one gloved hand while firing his pistol at her with the other. His face was red with rage.

"Oh, no," Annja said.

"What do we do?" Levi asked.

"Hold on," she said. She launched herself into space.

Thunder roared a third time as she flew, feeling weightless. She tried to relax so that she wouldn't break any bones as she hit. She couldn't keep her shoulder blades from pinching toward each other with anticipation of a bullet biting between them.

But Jeb's aim, already wild from passion, was thrown off even farther by the utter unexpectedness of her flying-squirrel jump.

To a wall of sheer, slick ice.

In her brief mad flight Annja dropped several feet. Screaming, she visualized and summoned her sword. She gave herself just enough time to reverse it and grasp it with both hands. Then she thrust, forward and down.

Through thick ice the blade bit. So great was Annja's momentum that all but a foot of the steel vanished into the translucent sheet of ice and snow.

She heard shouting. No words penetrated her consciousness; she had no awareness to spare as, clinging like a drowning woman with her right hand to the sword, she let go with the other to pull her ice ax from its loop in her belt and slam the spiked side of its head into the ice. Her forward-faced crampons bit home then, and she was almost secured.

She held her breath and let the sword go. She sagged alarmingly but with three points of contact kept her grip like a fly on the slippery wall. Groping at her harness, she fumbled an ice picket free and rammed it home. Then she snapped one carabiner off a quickdraw from her harness onto the picket. She was safe.

As safe as she could be dangling over a thousand-foot drop. With a group of murderous religious fanatics hanging over her head. One of whom was shooting at her.

She turned her head. "Levi," she said, trying not to scream. "Jump!"

"Jump where?"

"Across! Just unsnap and push off as hard as you can. Brake yourself with arms and legs when you hit. I've got you. I won't let you fall!"

I hope.

Shots roared again. Their head-bursting noise echoed across the whole face of Ararat. This time bullets pitted the sheer face in minieruptions of powdered ice and stone not ten feet from her.

Goaded by the fresh fusillade of gunfire, Levi unhooked from the piton that secured him to the ledge and flung himself across the abyss.

Unfortunately in his excitement the rabbi forgot to put out his hands and feet to arrest his momentum. Instead he did a face-plant six feet to Annja's right with a pronounced *splat*. Limply he slid down to the end of his twenty-foot slack.

Already wincing in sympathy and dread, Annja barely remembered to brace for the shock.

Fortunately it didn't peel her.

She heard a scream like an angry eagle. She looked up. Eluding Baron's hand, outstretched to drag him back, Jeb Higgins jumped outward from the outcrop to fall with his auto-pistol extended toward Annja. Yellow fire flashed from the muzzle as he triggered more shots.

It did not make for a stable firing platform. Jeb wasn't aiming well. Or at all. Still, Annja plastered herself to the wall and thought flat thoughts.

Jeb reached his tether's end. Annja winced as she heard ribs crack. Nonetheless, he did remember to hit the wall feet-first. His legs flexed and he pushed himself away to close the range. His rage-contorted face was barely a dozen feet from hers as he raised the gun to point at her.

She got ready to die.

Suddenly a sheet of ice, ten feet by twelve and probably weighing upward of a ton, broken loose by vibration somewhere overhead from the gunshots, fell like a guillotine blade on the small of Jeb Higgins's back.

Its leading edge was like a shard of broken glass—sharper than any razor.

Just missing his safety rope, the ice mass sliced his body clean in half. Jeb's eyes went wide as his hips and legs went pinwheeling away below him. Their greater air resistance made them fall at a slower rate than the ice-blade, separating from it. A vast final gush of red hit the cliff behind him like a thrown bucket of blood as his heart made one last spastic pulse.

The light went out of his furious blue eyes. He slumped to hang by his harness from the safety line. The weapon dropped from limp fingers to vanish down the mountainside.

Annja bit down on the sour vomit, stinging with acid, that tried to burst from her lips. She swallowed the vileness, spat to clear her mouth. Even as she did so she was planting an anchor and hastily changing her hookup. Clamping a descender onto the secured line she fast-roped down.

As she approached the rabbi, who hung limply and spun slowly at the end of his rope, she risked an upward glance. She saw Baron and Fairlie still on hands and knees on the overhang. They seemed to be holding a furious debate, but she couldn't hear them, though their mouths moved animatedly. They seemed to be communicating as much with frenetic gestures as words anyway.

She understood. They dare not speak aloud, much less fire any more shots at their quarry. Where one lethal chunk of ice had been loosened enough to break free, another might be on the verge of following. Hanging, literally, by a whisper.

Levi stirred even as Annja reached him. He had blood streaming from his nose, turning his beard to a red mess. His goggles were askew on his face.

"Anything broken?" she asked quietly.

"Gee," he said, "I was supposed to stop myself, wasn't I?"

"Next time. Did you break any bones?"

"Only my nose I think. But it doesn't hurt now as much as it did. I think I blacked out momentarily from the pain."

Annja hoped that was true, and that he hadn't blacked out from concussion. That could be bad. Especially if he'd hit hard enough to make his brain bleed. The slow buildup of hydraulic pressure from a subdural hematoma would inexorably crush his brain inside the skull. Well, she thought as detachedly as she could, we'll know soon enough.

"As long as your legs and hands work, we're good," she reassured him.

"Oh. I'm fine, Annja."

"I doubt that. But we have to move," she replied.

She secured him to the wall of ice. Then as the red dawn light turned tawny and the land around them brightened she began to work her way north around the mountainside, out of sight of Baron and Fairlie.

SOME BREATHLESS INTERVAL LATER they rested together on a shelf of black rock with their legs dangling in space.

"So, you've got some kind of sword, then, I take it?" Levi said. He took a mouthful of water from a plastic bottle. He was showing no signs of slow brain implosion, so that was one less worry.

Annja looked away from him. She shrugged. "I guess so. No point trying to hide it now, is there?"

His face split in a big happy grin. "Cool!"

She looked at him seriously. "If we make it out of here, Levi, please keep it a deep dark secret. For me. For my sake."

"Well, of course, Annja. Whatever you say." He seemed hurt she'd even suggest he'd blab. But he brightened quickly.

"Anyway, who am I going to tell? I'm already regarded as a total fringie in Biblical scholarship and ancient archaeology circles. So if I said I'd hung out with a woman who possessed a magic sword, it'd be a total feeding frenzy. Right?"

"I guess so."

"What about them, though?" He bobbed his head and wagged his eyebrows up and left, in the general direction of their pursuers. "They had to see you pull that sword out of nowhere."

"Either they catch us and kill us. Or we get down off the mountain alive. Which almost by definition means we've by some totally unlikely means managed to kill all of them. Either way, we're not in much danger from them telling people about the sword, are we?"

"Oh. That's true."

"Better take it easy on that water," she said, rousting herself to her feet. "I'm going to have to ask you to take some risks if we're going to have any chance of staying clear of our friends up there. Can you do that for me?"

"Sure, Annja. How could I help but trust someone the Creator has chosen to carry one of his gifts?"

He grinned as if to show he was half joking. With a sinking feeling she suspected it was no more than half.

"Would it make any difference to you if I told you the last possessor of the sword was Joan of Arc?" Annja asked.

"I'd say maybe this time the Creator has decided to trust it to more sophisticated hands."

Annja shook her head. "You're incorrigible, Levi."

From somewhere above once more they heard voices. Annja could make out no words but the sounds came sharp and angry. Jeb's death had slowed the pursuit. But only for a while.

"Time to go," she said.

"Annja?"

"Yes?"

"Do we have any chance? I mean, seriously?" Levi asked.

She frowned. Then she shrugged and laughed.

"We're not dead yet," she said.

"You're right," he said.

ANNJA WAS AS GOOD AS HER WORD. When she could she had them rappel down long casts, a hundred feet at a time. Even if it did eat up her dwindling necklace of anchors. They were coming at last down to less precipitous terrain where they wouldn't need anchors much anyway. And if Bostitch's bad boys caught them they'd have no more need for them at all.

Levi proved as good as his word, too. When Annja leapt from perch to doubtful perch he followed her unhesitatingly, flinging himself through space with abandon. She wanted to warn him not to take the notion that some god or gods were looking out for him too literally. On the other hand she didn't want him to start doubting, either.

The day was mercifully clear. It was afternoon; the sun shone brightly on the west face, where Annja and Levi made their tortuous way down. It was at best a mixed blessing for Annja. Sunshine did lift the spirits—at least alleviate the sense of leaden doom that had been pressing down on her, acknowledged or not, since she'd first heard the muffled sound of gunshots inside the Anomaly.

But the sun's arrival over the top of the peak made it harder to exert herself without overheating, muffled as she was against the high-altitude cold. And it brought increased risk that ice melting or rock expanding in its heat would make the purchase treacherous, even for pitons or camming devices.

They made rapid progress down. Reaching slopes that were anything other than sheer walls would make descent enormously less stressful, if not so quick as fast-roping. It was the same for their opponents, too, of course. But Annja and the rabbi still seemed to maintain a substantial lead over the pursuers.

Then as Annja waited at the top of what looked like the last sheer face they had to negotiate before the slope grew gentler, belaying for Levi as he climbed down to her, shots started cracking out from above. If the bullets came anywhere close Annja saw no evidence.

But the sudden terrifying noise startled the young scholar and made him lose his grip. He fell fifteen feet to the sloping, iced-over ledge like a sack of meal.

The sound of his ankle breaking was like a handgun going off.

26

Annja crouched over him. Another rock overhang ten feet above shielded them both momentarily from gunfire from above. It was a tiny blessing. "Levi?"

He smiled weakly. "Are you going to ask me if I'm all right?"

Though a good six feet wide—which felt broad as an aircraft carrier's flight deck after some of the hair-thin purchases they'd used—the ledge slanted perilously outward. Feeling herself begin to slide down the surface, slippery with a thin film of meltwater from the sunshine despite the fact the air remained below freezing, Annja yanked her ice ax from her belt and drove its pointy end through the ice to anchor her.

"Of course you're not all right. Your ankle's broken. Here, let me—"

Boots thumped on the ice behind her.

She heard the man grunt as he landed, then the beginnings of a triumphant intake of breath. He had obviously jumped down from the overhang directly above them.

Annja was already in motion, rising and turning in a single fluid motion. The ice ax made a soft squealing sound as she yanked it free of the ice.

She didn't know exactly who it was behind her. It didn't matter anymore. There were no friends above them on this mountain of death. Nor neutrals. Only enemies, thirsting for innocent blood.

"All, right, Annja," she heard Josh Fairlie's voice say as she spun. "I have you—"

She aimed the pointy end of her ax at his temple. Despite his own grinding exertions he was young and wired, with reflexes like steel springs. He swerved away from her stroke.

Unfortunately for him, if he jumped back far enough to completely avoid the vicious backhand blow he'd have hopped right off the edge. Annja saw he wasn't tied to a safety line, so eager had he been to score the kill.

Annja spun clockwise and blasted a spinning back-kick into his gut.

Air blasted from his lungs. Doubling over the kick he flew backward into emptiness. Then he dropped, trailing a scream that still seemed more of fury than despair.

On the treacherous slick slope Annja's planted foot shot right out from under her. She didn't quite smash her own face on the ice but the ensuing belly flop knocked the breath from her as surely as her pistonlike boot heel had from the doomed Josh Fairlie. With the last of her strength she drove the her ax's spike down through the ice to keep her from slip-sliding away.

Then, completely drained, she rested and breathed.

For a whole minute.

Then she started to move. "Up," she growled to herself. "Up…you…go." With the last word she summoned whatever strength she had and forced herself up off the ice and onto her feet.

Levi lay huddled against the cliff holding his ankle with one hand. "Annja?" he called to her.

"I'm fine, fine." She waved him off. "We need to move again. If we can get a little breathing room I'll bind the ankle. But we can't afford the time right now."

"You need to rest," Levi said with concern.

"I'll rest later," she wheezed. "Plenty of time. Alive or dead."

SHE USED HER LAST ICE PICKET to secure them for a final rappel down the ice face. She went first, descending among lava rocks and big black boulders onto a steep but manageable slope. Then she held the end of the line as Levi came down.

She didn't look at Josh Fairlie, sprawled faceup on a slab of black rock nearby.

Levi had no trouble bouncing himself away from the mountain face with his one good leg. When he hit bottom, though, his leg buckled.

Annja was there, catching him with an arm around him, keeping him from going all the way to the ground, strewn with sharp black pebbles. She eased him to a seated position. Then and only then she turned and gazed down at the broken corpse.

Josh's face was bone-white. The hazel eyes stared sightlessly back the way he'd come to this sorry state. His head was about half the normal depth; glistening red surrounded his dead face like a halo and ran down the side of the rock like wild long hair. She shook her head.

"You don't go easy on yourself, do you?" Levi asked. "You don't want it to become too easy."

"No. That's the fast track to becoming a monster worse than the ones I fight against. I don't lose sleep over the men I kill—they're always trying to kill either me or somebody I've chosen to protect. But I don't ever let myself take it lightly," she said.

She knelt by the body and gingerly opened the thick yellow-and-blue jacket. Fortunately it wasn't soaked. She reached inside.

"He was somebody's beautiful baby boy once. Some mother will probably cry her heart out when she finds out he died broken on this godforsaken mountain. What I did was right and necessary. He probably deserved it—as punishment, I mean, not just as an act of self-defense. But it's a terrible responsibility. And it has to be."

Levi was staring at her wide-eyed. "What on Earth are you doing?"

"Looking for this." She held up his Josh's black pistol. It was a SIG Sauer P226, very popular among government types, Annja knew from too much experience. Especially the U.S. Navy SEALs, one of whom Baron had been. She gripped the top rear of the slide with her left palm, pushed forward with her right enough to crack the chamber and glimpse the yellow gleam of a shell casing. Then she locked it up again, stuffed the pistol in her harness and quickly searched the body for extra magazines. She came up with two. She would have liked to count cartridges in the magazine in the well but there wasn't time.

"Right," she said, rising and turning back to her companion. "Let me help you up. Time to go."

The rabbi looked at her with pain in his eyes. "Annja, you've got to leave me," he said.

"No." She knelt, slung one of his arms over her shoulder. His usual schoolboy gallantry forced him to get to his feet—foot—as best he could.

"Come on, now," she said, "we need to keep moving." She started walking him downslope at an angle, both to make their three-legged descent easier and to head for the cover of a huge outcrop fifty feet away.

"You're the rationalist, Annja. Be rational now. One of us has a chance to get away—you, alone. The two of us— one and a half…" He shook his head. "We have no chance. It's simple mathematics."

"That's not how I do things," she said. "Now keep that foot away from the rocks or you'll regret it."

"What will we do, then?" Levi asked.

"You hop as long as you can. Then I carry you," she said.

"But—"

"Shut it and hop, please."

He stared at her a moment. Then he did as she said. He was helped by the fact that she continued to move at an angle downslope. He had to hop or get dragged.

Shots blasted after them. Annja set her jaw. Levi looked back once, then turned his face forward.

A bullet cracked off stone and tumbled whining past them. The sound set Annja's nerves on edge. She kept moving. Levi hopped with redoubled vigor.

They reached the outcrop, its black lava covered in razor-edged pockmarks. Annja dragged Levi hastily behind it. She heard the remaining Young Wolves baying to each other in angry frustration.

"Wait one," she said, easing Levi down and propping his back against the boulder. She drew the gun and leaned out around the rock. She lined up the sights on the first face she saw, which she guessed from the dark goggles was Baron's, so that it seemed perched like an apple atop the white-dotted front sight. Then she squeezed off a shot. Followed quickly by another.

She missed both times. On the second shot she actually saw black chips fly from the ledge three feet below where Baron's head had so abruptly vanished. She ducked back no less quickly.

Missing didn't bother her…much. One of the trickier feats in marksmanship is shooting at somebody at a significantly different level than you are. And after all the difficulty in hitting a target down a sheer slope, with the added challenge of keeping one's own perch, was probably all that had kept them alive so far.

Annja's main intent in opening fire was to show their pursuers that the prey could now reach out and touch them back. Chasing somebody armed with a gun is always a tough move because it's so easy for them to hole up somewhere and shoot you from cover or at least concealment, and a nice, stable firing platform. No matter how fanatical they were—and these boys did seem to be extreme in their devotion—they had to face the cold truth that if they all got picked off they'd fail their angry deity, rob Him of His chance to come back and scour the Earth in fire to show His love. They wouldn't be martyrs, they'd be failures. So like it or not they had to move more cautiously.

It still sucks I didn't take out Baron, though, she

thought. The security man really did seem to be that good. Given his battle savvy and his command skills she judged he made up half the effective strength of their opponents. Or more, given that it was down to him, Charlie, Eli Holden and ex-marine Zack Thompson. The ex-SEAL was equal to the rest easy, even if you didn't count Charlie Bostitch as a liability rather than an asset.

"That should keep their heads down," she said, turning back to Levi and tucking the handgun away. "All right, up you come."

His face was pale with the pain of his broken ankle. To her great relief he didn't give her any brave go-on-without-me guff this time. "Maybe I can hop along okay if I hang on to the back of your harness."

"Try that," she said. "If you can't keep up I'll damned well carry you."

"You wouldn't?" After a moment he shook his head. "What am I saying? Of course you would."

"In a New York minute," she said as he latched on and she began to make her way down the rock-strewn slope.

"You're insane, Annja Creed," she heard him say. "But I think now I know what they mean by divine madness. Truly, you are touched by the Creator's hand."

"Whatever," she said. "Right now it's the Angels of Death up there I'm more worried about."

IT WASN'T EASY CLIMBING DOWN ARARAT. Especially with Levi left with only one working leg. Apparently Annja's new ability to shoot back was making the pursuers more cautious. She spotted them following a good five hundred yards back. Clearly they were waiting for better terrain to close in and finish their prey.

She took advantage of their wariness to tend to Levi's left ankle. It was swelling ferociously. They had nothing that would serve adequately as a bandage; there wasn't any time to go pulling off harnesses and jackets to try cutting up a shirt to wrap the ankle. She knew none of those things would work very well anyway. Annja had Levi clamp his teeth on the nylon web tether of a quickdraw while she untied his boot and relaced it around his injured ankle as tightly as she could. He thrashed like a gaffed fish but managed not to pull away.

Going down Ararat was still lots easier than going up the mountain. The fugitives weren't following anything close to the path they'd taken on the ascent. As far as the expedition was concerned they were in unknown territory. Because they couldn't reconnoiter, but had to take pretty much whatever route they could find on the fly, they couldn't avoid technical climbing.

Oddly, that was easier on Levi than trying to pick his way down on his good leg. When they had to resort to pitons to keep descending she roped him close to her, and in daylight mostly unobscured by the clouds that began to reassemble in late morning they managed to find routes that offered pretty good handholds. The mountain's igneous rock was good for that, although it quickly sliced the socks Levi was using as improvised mittens to useless tatters. Then again, it was getting warmer as they continued their descent. The wind was only an occasional gust instead of a constant warmth-draining river of cold. And while they still had to navigate plenty of packed snow and ice they weren't on ice all the time.

The day ground past in a haze of black rock and panting breath; of cloud shadows alternating with bright sun.

Annja's body and limbs turned to lead somehow shot through with dull red pain. She ignored it and pushed on.

As Annja expected the pursuit remained circumspect. The Rehoboam Academy types closed the distance again, but never that she could see to less than about fifty yards. Cover was abundant here, with big jagged boulders and black rock outcroppings. She didn't have too much trouble keeping something between them and their pursuers, although with avalanche damage steadily diminishing more than a few bullets came their way.

For her part, any time Annja glimpsed a face above them she shot at it. It didn't bother her that she never tagged anyone. She didn't worry about conserving ammunition; three-high cap magazines were enough for lots of cautionary shots, and she didn't expect to win a firefight against four trained men. Anyway, busting caps at them periodically helped keep their minds right.

"Good thing we're in a restricted military zone," she muttered as they made their way and she got ready to lower Levi down a narrow chute. She could chimney down like a monkey; but there was no way he was going to, with a busted or even sprained ankle.

"Why so, Annja?" Levi asked.

"Anybody on the mountain who isn't you or me," she said, "is the enemy. Down you go."

Though she secured herself well to the top, and used figure eights to brake the rope as she played it out and let him down by degrees, she still had to let him down fast. It was rough. His wounded foot banged at least twice against the unforgiving black stone walls, eliciting choked-off yips of pain. The sheltered scholar was not strong, quick, or tough. But he was showing incredible fortitude.

At last she got him to the bottom, if in a little more limp a heap than she would have liked. Feeling a rising sense of urgency she unroped, recovered her protection and, putting her back to one wall of the crevice and her boot soles to the other, free-chimneyed rapidly down to join Levi.

"Let's move," she said, hoisting him up and slinging his arm around her neck. "I've got a bad feeling—"

With a scream of rage a large male body flew at her from the rocks to her left.

27

With no choice Annja let go of Levi. He went down like a sack of grain. But she managed to turn to face their attacker.

He had sprung out of a fissure between two large rocks, reaching with both hands for her throat. She grabbed his forearms and hung on. They felt like blocks of wood.

No trick could have enabled Annja to keep her feet against the impact of the mass of such a large and muscular young male body. Without conscious intent she allowed herself to be thrown over backward. In combat it was always better to go down under your own terms than get knocked down. She knew—she thought—no rock waited immediately behind her to snap her spine or implode her rib cage.

As she fell Annja got the cleated sole of her right snow boot into her assailant's midriff. Pain shot through her back as she landed hard on lumpy but mostly level rock. She ignored it, concentrating on her technique, such as it was. Pulling her opponent's arms over her head, urging his flying mass past, she thrust hard with her right leg.

It wasn't pretty, but it was effective. The Young Wolf flew right over her to smack against a big rock.

It was a crude circle throw. Ideally you finished the technique by pulling your opponent's head in toward you, helping him tuck it so as to land safely on his shoulder and roll out unharmed. Annja would've been fine if Zach Thompson had come down face-first and busted his neck. He didn't, but her move got him away from her.

Not bad, given that she'd only done the throw a few times.

As she sprang to her feet the careful, ever-meticulous part of her mind filed a quick note to herself—not the first such—to practice grappling combat more. She pirouetted to face the man who'd jumped her.

He was already up and starting toward her again. She'd recognized the sturdy, blond ex-marine immediately. His clean-cut face was white with adrenal rage and twisted like a rag. His out-of-control landing against hard stone must have at least painfully jolted him, if not cracked some ribs or worse. But in his current state he felt no pain.

He also moved much too quickly for Annja to summon the sword. She launched a front kick for his groin or lower belly, hoping to jolt him enough to increase engagement distance. Closing fast, he batted her leg away with his left hand and punched her in the face with his right.

The blow missed breaking her nose but filled her vision with a yellow-white flash of pain anyway. Still, it had been clumsily delivered. Had he gotten a full running-start strike in it could have broken her neck. Ears ringing, she staggered back, bringing up her hands to push-block a follow-up blow.

She deflected a straight left from her face. It was a feint. His right fist caught her in the belly. She bent over, the air smashed out of her lungs. He tried to follow it with an elbow smash to the face, stunning her or breaking her neck. Either would've been fatal; the first would simply have taken more time. Far too much time, if he let his friends catch up and got creative....

But Annja still had her presence of mind, battered and half-blinded as she was. And she had the reflexes of a cat. She just managed to turn her body in so the rising elbow caught her in the left shoulder.

The blow straightened her up and knocked her back. She slammed against a rock wall. Her head snapped back and cracked into the rock. Lightning shot through her brain and her stomach lurched.

She didn't lose consciousness. But for a moment she lost control over her limbs and mind. Her body sagged against the cold, merciless rock as her thoughts spun, fraying like tissue paper in a washing machine.

I'm going to die, she knew. He's going to beat me to death. Her wits were too scattered to focus her will enough to summon the sword before he was all over her.

But somehow he wasn't.

Annja forced herself to concentrate. Forced her vision to narrow to a field where her eyes could make sense of what they saw. She forced her brain to process the inputs of her eyes.

She saw Zach Thompson looking away from her, down and back at Levi. The skinny rabbi was clinging to Thompson's leg with both arms. His lips had peeled back into his beard, which had grown out over the last few days into a curly brown tangle. His teeth were clenched. His legs trailed back after him over the dark rock.

Thompson cursed and backhanded Levi in the face. Levi grimaced. His goggles came off, his glasses went askew on his nose. He screwed his eyes shut tight and still hung on.

Growling inarticulately the Young Wolf knotted his hand into a fist and drew it up to his ear to smash the rabbi in the face.

Sheer outrage did for Annja what all the power of her own will couldn't. Snapping herself together she launched herself from the rock. Her right hand formed a half fist. The sword filled it.

"Ahhhh!" Annja screamed, partly to distract him from beating down the helpless Levi, partly to vent the white-hot rage that filled her and drove out all traces of pain and fatigue. She held the sword back over her shoulder two-handed, as if it were a baseball bat.

The cry snapped Thompson's face around. The beginning of a triumphant leer died on his face as the muscles of his mouth went slack with total overpowering surprise. His eyes went round. The pupils expanded to crowd the pale blue irises to tiny halos.

With all the force of her righteous wrath Annja swung the sword. It took Zach Thompson at an angle across his face.

Feeling no impact she thought she'd missed. He still stared at her. She managed to stop herself short of piling into him. She drew back the sword for another strike.

The color red began to bloom on Zach Thompson's white-and-blue stocking cap. A line of red appeared, running from his left brow, right beneath the knit cap, across his nose to the edge of his right jaw. His eyes, still wide and staring into Annja's, dulled. She had the quick impression of Zach's face turned into a horrible caricature of a Picasso portrait. His body slumped to the black rock beneath his boots.

She lowered the sword to the rock and leaned on it, panting. She felt sick and utterly spent.

"Thanks, Levi," she said.

"Least I could do." He had settled his glasses back on his nose. One arm had snapped off. He started casting about for his goggles. "You're, ah—you're sinking!" he exclaimed.

"What? Oh, holy—" The tip of the sword's blade had already sunk four inches into the hard volcanic rock. She had just kept leaning on it, leaning farther forward without being aware of the fact as her weight drove it in. She pushed herself back upright, letting go of the hilt. The sword vanished.

"Once again, thanks," she said. "I probably would have fallen over if it had continued to sink like that."

Levi found his goggles and pulled them on over his knit cap, pulled them well away from his face so as not to dislodge the one-winged glasses perched precariously on the bridge of his nose. Then he let them settle onto his face. It was rapidly puffing up and going pink from the effects of Zach's backhand.

"There," he said. "I hope that holds them in place."

He turned to look at her with a silly smile.

"Zach!" Leif Baron's voice ricocheted down to them from above. He was obviously not close; but he wasn't high enough or far enough away for any kind of comfort. "Zach, you idiot, where are you?" they heard him calling out.

"Can you keep going?" Annja asked the rabbi urgently.

"As well as I could before. I don't walk on my face. Although it sure feels as if I have."

She reached a hand to him. They gripped each other, forearm to forearm. She hauled him to his one good foot.

He swayed against her, then, pushing off with an apologetic smile, straightened himself.

"Let's get going," Annja said. "Only a few thousand feet left."

"Piece of cake," Levi said, without much conviction. She had to give him an A for effort, though.

They were getting near enough the bottom that they could get a good detailed look at the terrain awaiting them below. A fairly substantial stream seemed to wind around the base of the mountain, sporadically visible as they picked their way from cover to cover. Beyond it stretched a mile or so of flats, tan with dry bunch grass and dotted with dark scrub. Shiny patches of white showed where snow remained. It seemed the recent fall had concentrated on the peak. Annja frowned slightly, remembering Levi's half-joking assertions that gods were battling each other over their destinies. West of the flats the land rumbled up into sinuous black ridges separated by narrow gullies.

Annja kept getting bad vibes from the landscape below. She couldn't see anything that looked more dangerous than a thorn bush. Not consciously, anyway. But she couldn't shake a nagging sensation she was missing something potentially major. And possibly deadly.

She said nothing about any of that to Levi. They had too many clear and present dangers to worry about possibly phantom misgivings.

As she looked down to pick their dubious way through the scree and obstructions Annja felt a cool touch on her face. Her vision seemed to dim slightly. Raising her head to look out she saw shadows swiftly coming over the panoramic landscape of Ağri Province.

She looked up. Between the two struggling human

specks and the sun the clouds were gathering. Though the light from above turned their edges to incandescent silver, their bellies were an ominous slate-gray. They seemed to be moving with unnatural speed. Where they came together they visibly churned.

"Wow," Levi said. "Looks like a movie."

"Do me a favor, rabbi," Annja said. "No editorial comments on the meteorological phenomena. Please."

"Anything you say, Annja." But his eyes twinkled behind his one-winged glasses.

In breathtakingly short order Annja and her companion found themselves hobbling through premature twilight. They descended by steep slopes covered with black gravel that had a dangerous tendency to slip out from under foot. Their progress was a halting three-legged dance, with Levi right behind Annja clutching onto the back of her harness for dear life.

At least here if they slipped on loose gravel and fell, there was much less risk of shooting off over a precipice to certain death. But an uncontrolled tumble down a rocky slope wasn't fun, nor safe, either. Especially when you were being hunted by religious fanatics fanatically intent on letting out your blood.

They entered a fantastic-looking landscape of violent juts and frowning looms of rock, rough granite, smooth-textured basalt and sharp-edged lava, pitted and matte-black. Annja picked her way between the great outcrops, using her hands to support her on the surrounding rock when she could to counteract the chancy footing.

"It's like being in some kind of old black-and-white movie," Levi said.

"It is, isn't it?" The rock looming around them was predominantly black to begin with, as was the gravel and soil underfoot. The granite did muster shades of dark gray; the crisp bunch grass that sprouted from the gravelly slope and niches among the outcrops was leached of color and moisture by premature winter. In better light it might've been at least a wan tan.

But the oddly sudden overcast's half-light leached even the much brighter colors of Annja's and Levi's jackets to the point they only suggested hues. The grass came out looking a vaguely silvery-gray.

The land leveled. It was temporary; they were still several hundred feet at least above the base of the cinder cone. It was a relief all the same.

Annja was becoming acutely aware of how loud the black gravel was crunching under their boots, when Levi said, "I wonder why they haven't attacked us for so long?"

She almost laughed. She'd started wondering the same thing.

"I think they probably decided there was no point either in wasting bullets or attacking us where there was a real lively chance they'd wind up splattered on some rock without us even having to do anything. We still have a long way to go. Maybe they even thought we'd figure we were about out of the woods and get careless," she said.

"What do you think they'll do now?" Levi asked.

She shrugged. They mounted a low rise to get between rounded house-sized protrusions. Annja winced as the dry branches and gray leaves of a bush rattled at their passage. Hearing her own words had led her to decide to take a route offering better cover in preference to following the path of least resistance.

"Baron's the professional tactical guy. Which sucks

from our standpoint. I'm not a professional. But if it were me running the circus I'd split the group up."

"Divide your forces? I thought that was a major no-no," Levi said.

"Okay, I'm not a big military historian, either, and there's a limit to how much my knowledge of, like, the Battle of Pavia in 1525 is going to be applicable to this happy twenty-first century of ours. But I've, uh, I've been in some fights. *Battles,* you might even call some of them. Small ones. Mostly," Annja said.

"Somehow, I rather figured that."

"So anyway, if you're going to try a pincers movement, a very basic tactic to catch your enemies on the flanks, what you have to do split up."

As she spoke she began to swivel her head more constantly left and right. They came out into a shallow bowl covered with dead grass, that stretched maybe twenty-five yards between big outcrops.

"Hitting flanks are important for all kinds of reasons. One is if you get your enemies looking left, your pals coming from the right get free shots at their backs. See?" she explained.

"All too clearly, I'm afraid."

"Yeah. Well, stay alert. Also, the better trained your troops are, the more leeway you have to do things like split them up."

She sighed through briefly gritted teeth. "And I'm afraid Baron and Eli Holden are both really good at this sort of thing. I bet they run the students through all kinds of tactical field exercises at the academy. If they didn't before Baron signed on, they sure do—"

She actually *felt* the bullet pass her face to strike the basalt boulder ten feet to her right.

28

The wind of the projectile's passage brushed the bridge of her nose and her cheeks with a dainty touch creepily reminiscent of the television show's makeup people dusting her with a powder puff to take the shine off freshly applied makeup. The hard flat rap of the handgun shot overlapped the noise of the slug striking rock. The bullet whined upward and away.

"Down!" she said in warning.

Figuring Levi would either have the presence of mind to follow her lead or, failing that, simply lose his balance and fall on top of her, Annja threw herself facedown on the gravel. The rabbi landed not on her, as expected, but beside her, promptly enough that she figured he had gone down on his own instead of toppling when his support went suddenly missing.

"Oww." Levi managed to keep his voice low. His face was pale behind his grown-out beard, thin mobile features twisted in pain.

Annja bit down on her impulse to ask if he was all right. Clearly he wasn't. He had a broken ankle. Falling down, even though not *on* it, must have hurt like hell.

She looked around. Past the outcrop to their left a black promontory rose a story or so higher. The shot had come from that direction, right enough. But the higher projection was also one hundred and fifty or so yards away. For the shooter to hit that close to her head with a handgun at that range, firing at a downward angle, he had to be either way better or way luckier than he could possibly deserve to be. She knew, or anyway suspected strongly, that among the Christian leadership skills Rehoboam Academy taught its pupils was the gentle art of combat handgunning. That type of training concentrated strongly on the short ranges at which handgun fights almost inevitably took place, not long-range shooting. She suspected the shot had actually come from a closer, lower height now masked by the nearby black boulder.

A muzzle flash caught her eye from a pile of rusty-tinged black rock topped with wind-gnarled brush just past the end of the boulder that screened them. She grabbed Levi and rolled over with him, toward the loom of rock to their left. She tried to ignore the groan of anguish he wasn't able to stifle.

Another bullet kicked up gravel a couple of feet away from where they'd lain. Annja's move hadn't come quickly enough to save them if it had been going to hit them anyway. The missile had come from about fifty yards away. It was still an uncomfortably good shot with a handgun, even if the shooter were prone and had the piece well braced.

They were out of sight of the spot where she'd seen the muzzle-flare bloom like a lethal yellow-light flower. For the moment. "Get on my back, Levi," she ordered.

"What?"

"On my back. Quickly."

He hesitated a split second, which was long enough for her to fight and at least temporarily win against an impulse to grab him and give him a good shake. Then she felt his weight sprawl on top of her.

With a reverberating groan of effort she pushed herself up to all fours. I knew someday I'd be grateful for doing all those push-ups in my daily routine, she thought. She hated push-ups. She did her best speed crawl—more of a vigorous slow-motion crawl with the doubled weight reminding the muscles in her shoulders and forearms of the abuse they'd been through in the last day and a half—right up to the side of the big basalt jut to their left. There she collapsed, panting, her arms and shoulders feeling as if they were on fire.

Levi's breath was loud in her ear. That's why it's hard to catch your breath, she told herself.

"You can get off now," she said in a strained voice.

"What—oh. Sorry, sorry. Ouch." The last came out as an involuntary exclamation as he rolled off too fast and jarred his damaged ankle again.

"No need to apologize," she said. She looked around. Ten or twelve feet behind them a smaller rock outcrop maybe three feet high stood near the boulder. There was at least a shoulder-width distance between them. Some bunch grass sprouting around it offered some additional concealment. Anything helped, she thought.

"Levi, can you get yourself back in between those rocks there?"

He drew a deep, shaky breath. "Yeah, I think so," he said.

"Okay. Hide as well as you can and keep your head down."

"What's going on?" he asked.

She paused, sucking her lower lip. "I think the shooter is trying to drive us. Like a beater for wild game. Chasing us toward the hunters to get shot."

"What're we going to do?" he asked, finally sounding alarmed.

"You're going to make yourself scarce like I told you. I'm going to try to even the odds."

It took a massive act of will to wrench herself out of the gravel's embrace, sharp and cold and as comfortable as the finest bed she'd ever slept in. Her every joint creaked and every muscle screamed protest. Leaving behind her companion and any objections he might care to voice to her plan, she started running bent over, back the way they had come.

At first she moved like a none-too-spry octogenarian who'd lost her walker. But movement quickly made her feel better. Just as she knew it would. Even if it was entirely in her mind, she felt no more than a rusty forty by the time she'd passed the little clump of rock she'd told Levi to dig in behind and started climbing up the steep bank that would lead her up and over the protective cover of the boulder.

Possibilities flashed through her mind. Were there two shooters off to her left, which was south? Was it just one, cunning enough to hurriedly shift positions so he could fire on the fugitives where they'd dropped into what they thought was cover after his first shot? Was that even their plan, what she had suggested to Levi? What if instead of waiting the other half of the pincers was closing in even now as she scrambled over the sliding, rustling black surface upslope of the boulder, ducking from lesser rock to rock cluster? With Levi left behind, unarmed, injured, helpless? Was she focused too much on Baron and his youthful red-haired acolyte, and underestimating the threat of fat, middle-aged Charlie Bostitch?

As quickly as she could she moved back down the far side of the boulder that hid Levi from the shooter she was sure about. Ahead of her two squat pillars of dark stone rose a couple of stories in the air. Slim as she was there was just room to slip between them.

She clambered up six or eight feet to the crack. It was a tricky climb; she had to stuff the handgun she'd taken off Josh Fairlie's body into her belt to make it. Then, turning sideways, she forced herself between the columns. It was tighter than she'd thought.

She emerged onto flat ground at just under the level of the cleft. Thirty feet away Eli Holden stood on top of another basalt outcrop about four yards high. He held his SIG Sauer muzzle up and shifted weight from the front of one booted foot to the other, as he craned to try to spot the quarry he was trying to creep up on and surprise in their hiding place. His jacket hung open and his close-cropped red-haired head was bare.

He and Annja locked eyes. For what seemed a very long time they simply held that tableau, staring at each other.

"It doesn't have to be this way, Eli," she at last managed to say in a low voice jagged as an ancient lava tube.

His cheeks drew back, tightening his mouth into an almost sweet smile. "Yeah," he said, so quietly the word was almost lost on a rising breeze. "Yeah. It does. I wish it didn't, too."

He sounded entirely reasonable. It was odd; she had

sized him up as a stone-dumb fanatic who let others do the talking as well as the thinking. Instead he sounded wistful, and his voice was that of a man who was thinking, and was pained by his thoughts.

He moved first. For all Annja's lightning reflexes he would have had her cold had she not expected it.

But all he had to do was lower his P226, get a flash sight impression, shoot her. She had to draw from her belt. Which put her fatally behind the curve.

She threw her left hand straight up over her head, cupping the fingers as if gripping something.

The sword appeared, glinting dully in the twilight.

She saw Eli's head jerk back in surprise at the impossible appearance of such an utterly unlikely weapon out of thin air. Then her right hand was up, the front sight of her weapon at the level of the center of his mass. She fired twice, trying not to yank the trigger and jerk the weapon offline. Shooting one-handed she had to fight hard against the bite of rifling grooves into the fast-moving projectiles that tried to torque her sight off-target and pluck the piece from her hand.

Her first shot missed. She saw or thought she saw the second pluck the inner right hem of his jacket. He flinched. His arm, which had just come straight and level, jerked upwards a fraction. His gun roared, firing over her head.

Releasing the sword Annja dropped her left hand to cover her right and the front of the gun's trigger guard, locking her arms into the steady triangle of a classic isosceles stance. She pulled the fore-sight back down to the center of Eli's blue flannel-check shirt, which looked darker than it had a second ago. She fired a quick double tap.

He staggered and fell. His body rolled back out of sight

behind the rock jut he was standing on. His gun clattered down into a tangle of sharp-toothed rocks and thorny brush where Annja knew with sick certainty she'd never have time to find it.

Instead she turned around and scrambled quickly up the slope again, to pass above the two basalt columns she'd pressed between.

Trying to move quickly from rock to rock she ran back to the north. She went past where Levi lay thankfully hidden from her sight. She was sure the danger now was advancing from that direction. Leif Baron either thought she was dead or thought Eli was. In either case he'd be moving in, whether to finish off just the rabbi or both of them.

She didn't know where Bostitch was. She hoped he had the sense to just stay out of things and keep his head down. He'd hired an elite thug with a body like a cartridge with his head for the bullet. The wise thing was to let Baron do a bullet's job.

Freed from the necessity of propping up poor half-crippled Levi, and the too-long present risk that a single misstep would plunge her a thousand feet to take a long nap on a hard-rock mattress, Annja sprang across the rocks and gravel with relative ease. She no longer felt stiff or sore. The turbocharge the gunfight with Eli had given her didn't hurt, either.

She made no effort to stay quiet or unseen. She wanted Baron to home in on her, and not the defenseless Levi. What she was trying to do was attract attention while making herself a terrible target.

She succeeded. As she anticipated, Baron spotted her first. She was jumping from one level to another four feet down when the first shot, snap-fired from about thirty yards away, passed through the space she'd occupied a heartbeat before. The second round of the double tap cracked somewhere high over her head.

Loose chunks of rocks slid out from under her feet. Annja let herself sit down hard and slid down another dozen feet to the bottom of a narrow dry streambed in a crunching slide. She scrambled up a pile of granite rocks on the far side and peeked over.

This time she saw Baron first. He was moving between boulders not twenty yards from her. Either he was lucky or his peripheral vision caught the quick purposeful motion as she thrust her captured handgun toward him. He vanished from sight even as the weapon bellowed and bucked her hand.

She was down to her last half magazine. She thought she had about six shots left. She'd never quite got the hang of counting shots fired in the stress of combat. Nobody she'd ever talked to had, either.

They played hide-and-seek with guns among outcrops six and ten feet tall. Annja ran a few paces, then bent between two rocks and fired two quick shots toward where she guessed her enemy was. He popped up over a rock seven feet to the left of that and fired two quick shots in return. She had ducked back already and was on the move to another spot.

She heard Baron curse. She scrambled up an eight-foot chunk of granite and snapped a quick shot over the top toward the sound.

He fired back. She had already turned and slid back down the rock.

Been fighting a desk a little too long, haven't you, Jocko? she thought. You may keep your hand-eye skills sharp-shooting off your hundred rounds a day or whatever. But you've forgotten that you can't miss fast enough to catch up.

Being well drilled in that philosophy herself, what Annja was doing—busting caps while scarcely aiming—ran totally against her grain. But she had a plan.

If she hit him, bonus. But what she was mainly trying to do was get him to do what he'd just done—waste cartridges. She was well aware there were limits to how much ammunition the pursuers could have brought down the mountain with them.

It wasn't that Annja was really counting on getting Baron to exhaust his reloads. She was just doing whatever she could think of to tilt the odds her way. She figured it was worth a try.

And in any event, she knew with certainty that if she actually traded deadly shots with him, she'd die. She wasn't expecting to settle this with a firearm.

She spent the next two shots sparingly. She kept moving fast among the field of big rocks and outcroppings. She doubted her opponent had any kind of hearing protection, any more than she did; all she could hear was the ringing in her ears, particularly loud crunches. And if Baron did have earplugs in he definitely wouldn't hear her moving.

They kept closing the range between them, even if it was three steps closer and two steps back. Sensing she was getting near the former SEAL Annja scrambled up a big rounded granite boulder. She hoped to surprise him with a short-range shot from above.

As she reached the top Baron's head popped up like a bald prairie dog, facing her not eight feet away. He had shed his jacket and wore only a black T-shirt despite the cold. Both off balance, they each snapped off a one-handed shot. Hers sent rock dust clattering against the dark amber lense of his goggles. His just missed the left side of her face.

She turned at once and slid down the rock. The slide of her gun was locked back over an empty magazine.

But as her boots thumped onto the gritty ground at the base of the boulder her mind burned with a single image, branded on it in an instant. She'd seen Baron's identical black P226. It was identically slide-locked.

"Can you hear me, Annja?" she heard him call from the far side of the boulder.

She started moving up the slope. I know where you are, she thought. You know where I was.

"I'm empty," Baron said. "All out of cartridges. You are, too, I bet. I saw your slide locked back."

He was moving now, too. The weird acoustics in this Devil's rock garden made it hard to tell where.

"You're going to die, Annja. You and the rabbi. You know that, don't you? You know I don't need a gun to kill you both."

She stopped with her left shoulder almost touching the side of a granite rock ten feet high. It ended just a foot or two ahead of her.

"You've got the Devil in you, Annja Creed," Leif Baron called. "You must be full of the Devil himself to get the kind of power you've showed. That's it, isn't it? You're full of the Devil."

She ground her teeth and waited. He was getting close. She could feel him.

"But I've got the cure for that, Annja. My knife. A good, sharp knife. It'll end your suffering, Annja. It'll cut the Devil right out of your black heart."

The voice seemed to be coming from everywhere at once. The rocks were casting it back at her from every direction. The echoes seemed to mock her.

"You'll love having that steel cleanse you, Annja. It'll feel better than the Devil's will. And the best part of it is—"

She heard a crunch of gravel. He was right in front of her. He held a SEAL combat knife low by his right hip. Ready to plunge deep in her flesh and *slice*.

"The pain will be over...."

His voice faltered.

Then he looked down to see the gleaming broadsword pressed right up against his six-pack. Two strong female hands clutched the hilt, with bones and veins standing in bold relief.

"Mine's *bigger*," Annja hissed.

She plunged the blade into him. Hard.

29

"Come on, Levi," Annja said.

She heard the brush stir. Levi's head appeared between the rock clump and the boulder.

"You killed both of them? Baron, too?" the rabbi asked.

"Eli and Baron. Yes."

"I knew you could do it."

"That makes one of us. But to my surprise, I did. Come on, take my hand. We're not off the mountain yet."

"What about Mr. Bostitch?" the rabbi asked as he got gingerly up on his one good leg. He swayed and had to grab her shoulder to steady him.

She got them headed downward. Away from the crest. And toward bidding a none-too-fond farewell at last to the Mountain of Pain.

"I didn't see him," she said. "Let's just hope he decides that what all the king's horses and all the king's men couldn't do, the king's better off not even trying. Or something. Losing all his acolytes and his superhuman killing machine must've shaken his morale. A little bit, anyway."

Levi shook his head. "I don't know, Annja. He seemed pretty desperate. Men who don't think they've got anything left to lose strike me as good martyrdom candidates."

"Oh, well," she said. "All I can think of to do then is stay frosty. And if he catches up with us we'll do our level best to make sure he gets to be a martyr."

"I'm down with that," the rabbi said.

"SO WHO ARE *THEY*?" Levi asked in a whisper. While Annja had zipped her goggles in a pocket he still wore his. They were sort of holding his one-winged glasses in front of his eyes.

The two of them lay side by side on their bellies, screened by brush and rocks at the top of a forty-foot bluff. Below them lay the stream, the base of the mountain and freedom.

Across the stream from them a couple of hundred bearded men in long coats sat and smoked on the flats. The clouds still made a mean lead ceiling that seemed low enough to brush the hidden tip of the great mountain. The sun, a hard white disk of blindness, had just rolled behind the clouds. It had already shifted far enough south that it didn't shine directly in Annja's and Levi's eyes as they gazed west from the bluffs. But the late-afternoon light, mellow and yellow, unreeled long shadows along the ground toward them from the seated men.

The waiting men all had Kalashnikovs and rocket-propelled grenades near at hand. They appeared to be watching the cliff intently. If they were conversing Annja was too far away to hear. They weren't being boisterous about it. In fact they looked deadly serious, these bearded, smoking, well-armed men.

"Kurdish militia," she said, sick to her stomach. *"Peshmerga."*

"Is it just me, or do they not look too friendly?" Levi asked.

"They don't look friendly. Something tells me they're our late guide Hamid's pals. Waiting here to make sure no infidels get down off their Fiery Mountain alive."

"How'd they know we'd be coming down around here?"

"Binoculars," Annja said. "Ears. Gunshots carry."

"Oh. Yeah."

She studied the situation. It didn't look good. There were some arroyos eroded deep into the reddish face of the bluff, steep but not sheer, that they could probably use to get down all right. If there weren't a hundred guns shooting at them.

A hundred yards or so to the north the stream widened into a green pond where a rockfall had blocked its original course. After another hundred and fifty yards or so the bluffs petered out and gave way to a slope strewn with furniture-sized rocks that ran all the way down to the stream. The same thing happened maybe four hundred yards south, but with bigger and fewer rocks.

"They'll be keeping an eye out to see if we try going down there where it gets less steep," Levi said.

"That's about how I've got it sized up. How're you feeling?" Annja asked.

"I hurt. I'm running on empty."

"Me, too. But we may need to hike for a few more miles. Work our way around the base of the mountain until we get out of sight of the reception committee. We could try to slip past the inevitable patrols under cover of night. That kind of thing."

He sighed. When he looked at her his eyes seemed to gleam moistly behind his thick glasses.

"This isn't going to end, is it, Annja?"

"Oh," she said, "it'll end."

"It won't end well, I mean."

"Probably not. You weren't planning to live forever, were you?"

"I was sort of hoping."

She laughed quietly. Then she clamped down hard when it threatened to run away with her. "Me, too. Well, we can go on hoping for a while yet. Let's get rolling before our poor overworked muscles set up like freshly poured concrete."

She started to slither back away from the edge. Gunfire erupted behind them. The shock and sheer cataclysmic noise took her breath away. A line of earth geysers zipped by them on the other side of Levi, outbound toward the patiently sitting men.

She caught a glimpse of those men throwing away their smokes and jumping to their feet, snatching up their weapons. Then she twisted her body to stare back at the mountain.

A rumpled figure stood on a granite knob a hundred yards away with Ararat's black cone rising behind him. It was Charlie Bostitch. He had his jacket hanging open, his gut hanging out and lank hair hanging almost in his eyes.

In his hands he held an object maybe two feet long. With a sinking heart Annja made it out through the gloom as a folding-stock AKSU short assault rifle. Unlikely as it seemed, it almost had to be the weapon that had gone over the cliff with Hamid. Evidently the Young Wolves had found it. That legendary Kalashnikov toughness meant it was actually still in working order. That had to be more than you could say for its former owner.

"I can't let you slip away from me, Annja," Bostitch shouted. By the throb of his voice she could tell he was crying. "Not alive."

"Get ready to run for it," she said quietly to Levi.

"Run?" He looked at her incredulously.

"Hop," she said. Then, pitching her voice to carry to the man on the boulder pulpit, she shouted, "Sure you can, Charlie. It's over. You lost. Give it up. Anyway, all the *peshmerga* in this part of Turkey are waiting at the foot of this cliff to carve us like Christmas turkeys."

Bostitch shook his head. "That doesn't matter to me. It makes no difference whether I live or die. My Lord's waiting on me, Ms. Creed. I just have to make sure you can't pour your poison in the world's ear."

He started down the side of the rock. As he did he loosed another burst of gunfire. It didn't come close to striking her. Annja winced anyway; that abbreviated barrel made the AKSU loud.

"You're Jezebel," Bostitch shouted. "You're the Whore of Babylon. I should have known you were wicked when you introduced lust into my heart. When you tempted me. You brought this on yourself. Now you have to pay the price," he ranted.

"Now would be good," she told Levi.

Clutching his hand she set off at a trot, though she ached to sprint. But Levi could never keep up with her trying to run on one leg; and she wouldn't be setting any records trying to carry him, either. Bostitch had started off down the south side of his boulder. She took them north.

A whole Fourth of July's worth of gunfire broke out

from the Kurds on the ground. What they thought they were shooting at Annja had no clue. The angles were wrong for any of them to see them or Bostitch.

It sure didn't help the situation. Bostitch paid no attention. Maybe he didn't notice the fireworks. He sprayed another burst after his fleeing prey.

Somebody at the back of the pack must have tried a long lob shot with an RPG, which could fly for over a kilometer. The rocket motor burned itself out while the projectile was still climbing toward those sinister clouds. Annja never saw it coming.

The rocket-propelled grenade didn't hit close enough to hurt them with fragments or blast effect. But suddenly the earth just erupted in a twenty-foot column of dirt and smoke with a yellow jet of flame at its core, ahead and to the right of Annja as she and Levi ran their three-legged race to the north. The noise was terrific, laced with harmonics too high to actually hear but that seemed to shoot through Annja's brain. She shied away.

The sudden shift in direction caused her to put a foot wrong. A chunk of rock the size of a cantaloupe turned beneath her right boot. Pain stabbed through her ankle and then her hip as she fell, headlong and twisting.

She cracked her head on a somewhat larger rock, half-buried in the ground.

She didn't lose consciousness. Not quite. But for a while her world was a hell of bright flashing lights and vertigo and a sense that her stomach had turned into a washing machine gone berserk.

When her senses cleared she lay on her back with her head cradled on Levi's right leg, which was cocked back toward his body as if he were trying to sit half-lotus. His left leg with its injured ankle was stretched out straight across the black ground.

She blinked her eyes reluctantly back into focus. She realized the rushing, screaming roar that filled her head wasn't actually *in* it. Instead it passed overhead, seemingly across the sky.

Levi had his head uplifted. "It's a jet, Annja. Looks like a fighter."

"Great," she muttered. "That's all we need. It probably hates us, too."

He slid his leg out from under her. "You should probably get up now," he said. "We've got a lot more immediate problems."

The world erupted in shattering noise. For a moment Annja imagined the ancient volcano had decided to wake up and spoil everybody's day at once. Then dirt thrown up by bullets striking too close for comfort rained down onto her face.

She snapped upright. Bostitch was stalking them. Tears gleamed on his puffy cheeks, shining like gold in the near-horizontal radiance of the sun. He pushed the stubby Kalashnikov out in front of him and ripped out another burst. Dirt spurted up between him and his prey.

Seeing Annja respond he raised the stock to his shoulder. From fifty feet away the hole in the muzzle looked her in the eye. She caught her breath and braced for a last desperate dive to the side.

It wouldn't work. But she was damned if she was going to die frozen like a terrified rabbit.

The muzzle bounced up and down. Up and down. She realized Bostitch was jerking the trigger. Bad form, that. Worse, from his viewpoint anyway, the weapon wasn't making any noise. No fire. No nasty little bullets moving at several times the speed of sound.

"Empty," he said. She could barely make him out through the ringing in her ears. It sounded as if Quasimodo had set up shop in her skull. "It won't save you. The Lord provides…I've got more…" he babbled.

She scrambled up. Pain stabbed through the joint of her hip. Her right ankle wobbled. She found herself tipped against Levi. She wasn't sure how he'd gotten to his feet unaided.

"Down to two legs between us," she said out of the side of her mouth.

She looked over her shoulder. Her tiny hope of possible escape died. The ground fell away not ten feet behind them as if severed by God's paper cutter. Down on the flats the Kurds were still firing enthusiastically. Through the grass at the brink she saw a little arc of green below.

They had nowhere to go. She took Levi's hand.

Bostitch had dropped the empty magazine from his weapon. He brought another orange plastic banana mag from a pocket of his jacket. He fumbled to stuff it into the rifle's well. His hands didn't seem to be cooperating with his eyes too well.

"I got you now," he said. "You can't escape."

Leaving his big unsteady hands to sort out the reload as best they could he lifted his face to show the victims waiting for his sacrifice a wide, gloating smile.

"It's the end. The end for you sinners. I'll be washed in the blood of the Lamb."

Over the madman's right shoulder Annja saw a speck appear against the sky. It was a small darkness above the great dark mountain. Setting sunlight glinted off a wing as it dipped forward and rapidly began to grow in appearance.

The magazine finally went home with a click. A screaming came across the sky.

Bostitch ignored it. He racked the charging handle to chamber a fresh round.

Something dropped from the sleek belly of the slender winged shape. It was a long, thin egg that twinkled in the slanting sunlight as it tumbled, end over end.

"You are weighed in the balance," Bostitch crowed in triumph, raising his short rifle.

Yellow light bloomed brilliantly behind him. A dark shape, the ruptured canister, tumbled at the front of what quickly became a rolling wave of flame.

"And you are found wanting!" Annja screamed.

At last some presentiment of the wrath to come made Bostitch turn. He dropped his rifle and threw up his arms in a futile attempt to shield his flesh from the tsunami.

It wasn't the water, but the fire this time.

Annja had turned, too. She dragged Levi over the cliff with her.

As they dropped toward the pond she heard Bostitch's maniacal shrieking as liquid hellfire consumed him.

She'd known from glimpsing a sliver of it that the pond lay below. Whether they could reach it by jumping she didn't know. Nor did she know if it was deep enough to safely break their fall.

It didn't much matter, she thought, oddly calm as they fell, still hand in hand. It's a quicker way to check out than Charlie's got. She pulled in the deepest abdominal breath she could.

Not really wanting to watch, Annja flicked her gaze

upward as her feet reached the water. To her horror she saw that a glowing cascade of flame had rolled right out over the cliff into the air. It was falling right on top of them.

The water swallowed her. Somehow she still held on to Levi's hand as they went down through the cold liquid. Her feet hit silty bottom. Her right ankle panged. Her left leg flexed and absorbed the last of her momentum.

She'd shut her eyes when they hit. She opened them again. She clearly saw Levi next to her, looking astonished; the rounded mud bottom of the pool, the water weeds growing from it; the tail-flick of a startled fish fleeing the commotion. All lit by a weird yellow glow whose brilliance defeated the water's murkiness.

She looked up. A ceiling of fire hung a few feet above their heads. It was literally that—napalm burning on the surface of the pool. And they were beginning to bob right back up into the floating inferno.

Getting a fresh death grip on Levi's hand Annja went horizontal and began to kick for all she was worth. She gestured for Levi to swim with her. Or she hoped she did. And hoped he could see her signal at all. His goggles and glasses were gone.

For a moment he fought her, wide-eyed, bubbles streaming out his nose and open mouth. She squeezed his hand hard. Cognizance came into his eyes. He nodded.

She let go to free their arms. Side by side they swam beneath the lethal glow. The need for fresh air tore at Annja's lungs. But she willed herself to keep going until they were out from under that hideous glare.

They came up against the accidental rock dam that had formed the pond. Annja braked with a hand and let herself shoot to the surface. She broke through.

The air was hot and stank of petroleum fractions. The fire had already started to die off into little patches of yellow flame, rocking on the water and giving off greasy black smoke. Levi came up splashing at her side. He thrashed his arms and shook his head wildly.

"Annja! I can't swim!" he shouted.

"I'm glad you didn't remember that when you were doing it a moment ago. Just put your feet down. Foot. You'll touch bottom," she said.

"Oh." He calmed down. A moment later, once more leaning together for mutual support, the two hobbled up the west bank of the pond, with the little waterfall outflow burbling right beside them.

They found themselves face-to-face with a line of bearded men with long coats, stalking toward them through the scrub beyond the streambed. Their shadows were grim decisive lines before them. They were fifty yards off; evidently they had withdrawn a healthy distance when the napalm-fall spilled over the cliff.

Now they were back, with weapons at their hips. Catching sight of the sodden pair they shouted in triumph. The Kalashnikovs came up.

Again the sky screamed. This time a strange snarling joined the jet engine's banshee cry.

The men in front of Annja started coming apart in quick sprays of red. It was as if they were strange puppets stuffed with firecrackers, not real living, breathing men. They weren't being cut down. They *exploded*.

A slim shape swept low overhead from right to left, passing above the smoking remnants of the men it had destroyed. If there were any survivors they had had the sense to go down fast and try their damnedest to become one

with the planet. Annja whipped her head counterclockwise
to see a fighter aircraft, its delta wings and a slim, tubular
fuselage orange in the light of the setting sun, pull up from
its strafing run. She could see the single yellow flame of
its exhaust.

More snarling broke out overhead. Annja and Levi
ducked as big noisy explosions started going off on the
flats to the west of the stream. Clouds of dirt and smoke
flew everywhere. Things flew through the air—rocks, shattered weapons, tubular objects shoddily wrapped in flapping cloth. Those last bits didn't bear too much thinking
about. Especially when a detached arm bounced not fifteen
feet away from Annja and rolled to a stop. The carnage was
everywhere.

Annja realized that a pair of shapes like gigantic mutant
dragonflies were hovering a hundred feet in the air, turning
and dipping this way and that. They were behind all the
racket. Machine cannons mounted beneath their domed
bulging snouts and rocket pods beneath their stub wings
were ripping holy Hell out of the *peshmerga*.

"Oh, my God, they're Hinds!" Annja exclaimed.

She glanced at Levi. He was staring slack-jawed up at
the flying monsters. She wasn't sure how much he could
see without his glasses, but whatever it was he saw, he
wasn't making any sense at all out of it.

"You know," she said. "Russian helicopters. Like, from
Soviet times."

She realized she was babbling. She also realized he
almost certainly couldn't hear her. If the earlier outburst
of fire from the Kurds had sounded like the Fourth of July,
this sounded as if they'd decided to move the pyrotechnic
display into the drained-out hold of an oil tanker.

Still, she felt relief. She was pretty sure. She didn't actually understand what was going on any better than Levi seemed to. But the horrible deadly aircraft weren't shooting at *them*. In fact they were shooting at the guys who were going to shoot at them.

"That has to be good, right?" she said it aloud, as if she'd spoken the thoughts preceding. Which was all good, since just now her thoughts were as audible as her words were.

What was going on around them didn't seem to be a battle as much as it was a massacre. Annja realized that if you had to be in a battle, that was definitely the kind of battle to be in. Provided you weren't on the side getting slaughtered.

She was pretty sure she'd feel horrible later for thinking that.

A sudden blast of wind beat down upon them. Annja looked up, almost overbalancing and toppling back into the pond as she saw another huge shape dropping toward them below a flashing circle of rotor.

It settled down to land on retractable wheels not thirty yards from them. Annja and Levi just stood and gaped despite the bits of dirt and dried vegetable stuff getting blown in their faces. It wasn't as if they were going to run from a helicopter. Even if they had all their legs in working order.

This was a different model chopper, looking even bigger than the huge, grotesque gunships, more resembling a pregnant guppy than an armed dragonfly.

A hatch opened in the side closest to them. Out spilled a bunch of guys in *salwar kameez* and Chitrali caps, serious beard shadows and angry moustaches, all of them carrying Kalashnikov rifles and one or two light machine guns with drum magazines. As the helicopter's twin turbine engines throttled down with a whine the Afghan-looking men fanned out to set up a defensive perimeter. In case anybody still cared.

Down from the chopper stepped a tall pale-skinned man, inexpressibly natty in a fedora and a tan London Fog coat.

"Ms. Creed," he said politely, above the *shoop-shoop* of the big slowing rotors. "Rabbi Leibowitz."

"Are we rescued or being taken prisoner?" Annja asked feebly.

"Yes," the man said.

"All right," Annja said. "This is officially too much."

And she passed out from exhaustion.

30

Annja opened her eyes.

There was a nurse doing something next to her bed by a cheery yellow light. Or Annja thought she was a nurse, from her crisp white-and-green uniform and the little white old-timey cap perched atop her head.

Apparently sensing the patient had awakened she turned to smile at Annja. She was a young woman, pretty, dark, with raven-black hair bobbed short beneath her paper cap.

She left the room without saying anything. A spray of cheerful yellow flowers stuck up out of a pearlescent ceramic vase on a table beside Annja's bed. Annja didn't know what they were. Maybe some kind of daisies? An ethnobotanist she wasn't.

Beyond the flowers stood another bed. In it Rabbi Levi Leibowitz, dressed in white pajamas with gray pinstripes, lay propped up against a pile of pillows. He had a bandage plastered right across the bridge of his nose. He blinked at her through what she dimly understood must be new glasses perched on the bandage and smiled shyly.

"Levi," she croaked. "You made it."

"Hi, Annja," he said. "You, too. I guess our gods won out after all."

"What's with the bandage?" she asked.

"Zach Thompson broke my nose, remember? They fixed it. Cosmetic surgery. They seem pretty good at it."

"Who?"

"The doctors here."

"Where is here?" she asked.

"Welcome to Yerevan," a masculine voice said from behind her. She had only heard that dry tone and clipped intonation once before. Even so, she knew there was no way she would ever forget it.

"Who are you?" she said, fairly certain she had a good idea. She turned to look at the man who sat in a wooden chair beside the window. The bright morning sun rushing in obscured him in its glare.

She decided to test her theory. "So the United States is currently friends with Armenia?" she asked.

"Armenia is friendly to us. And that's what really matters, isn't it?" the man said.

"I suppose. Yeah," she replied, not sure she really wanted to know what was going on. It was never a good thing when government agents showed up out of nowhere. Even if they did save your life. She had the sinking feeling there might be people out there who knew more about her than she wanted them to.

The man crossed long slim legs and leaned forward slightly to clasp his knee with pale spidery hands.

"I have to thank you both for the show you put on. It made for highly entertaining viewing," he said.

"What are you talking about?" Levi asked.

"You didn't have a satellite tasked to watch us?" Annja asked.

"Oh, no." He shook his narrow head. "You did, however, occupy the undivided attention of your own personal Global Hawk remotely piloted aircraft."

Feeling suddenly weary Annja shook her head. "We never had a clue."

"That's kind of the point of a spy drone, isn't it?"

"So what about those aircraft that…rescued us, I guess?" she said.

"Rescued you, indeed."

"The Hinds and the fighter plane, whatever it was—"

"Sukhoi Su-17. Fitter-C. Ground attack plane, actually. Rather elderly but gets the job done. We can all aspire to that, can't we?"

"Were they Armenian?"

"Oh, yes."

"But…we were in Turkey."

She sensed as much as saw his thin smile.

"Hot pursuit of Muslim terrorists covers a multitude of sins, in these years of the Long War, " the man said.

"I see. And those dudes with you in the helicopter?"

"Baluchi mercenaries. Don't waste your breath asking," he said politely.

"'Course not," Annja replied wearily.

He leaned back and draped an arm over the back of his wooden chair.

"I'd like to offer you both, on what we might call an official unofficial basis, the profound thanks of the United States of America."

"What for?" Levi asked.

"You've helped to tie up a number of ends, which, if left loose, posed major threats to national security."

"Like what?" Levi blurted.

"Leif Baron, for one. He'd become a loose cannon. He spent so much time working among and with Islamic crazies that some people were starting to say he'd forgotten which side he was really on."

Annja frowned. She couldn't quite buy that. Baron was a psychopath and a fanatic, but treason would violate his self-image. And he was unlikely to join Muslims waging war against Christianity.

Or am I wrong about that? she found herself wondering. It wasn't as if she'd actually known him well. Maybe Baron the religious zealot had found not a new faith, but rather alliance, with spirits far more akin to his than those of the West's decadent materialists, who seemed bent on abandoning all religion. She'd read right-wing American fundamentalist tracts in praise of Islamic fervor.

She said nothing. Arguing with government mystery men was not a fruitful pastime.

But Levi didn't know that yet.

"That doesn't make any sense," he said flatly. "I can't believe the government would carry out such a convoluted scheme, just on, what? The off-chance of eliminating a single suspected rogue? It's just too…too Rube Goldberg. There's got to be more to it."

"Of course there is," Annja said. "And we'll never find out what it is. Our expedition might have served to cover any number of different ends or operations," she explained.

"Thank you for talking sense, Ms. Creed," the man said.

"Say," Levi said. "What about the Assyrian tablet? It

was in the pocket of my pants. What happened to it? It must be extremely valuable."

"I'm sorry, Rabbi Leibowitz," the man said. "Anything other than personal effects you might've brought down the mountain have been confiscated in the interests of national security. For reasons that should be obvious, they cannot be returned."

"But it's a priceless artifact! Its historical significance is beyond question—"

"What its significance is," the man said, "is moot. Please understand, Rabbi. Ms. Creed certainly does. What you think you recall happening up on Ararat never really happened."

Levi sent Annja a pleading look. She shook her head sadly.

"What *really* happened," the government agent said, "as will shortly be made public, is that your expedition proved the Ararat Anomaly was simply a basalt formation. It's geological, not any kind of human artifact."

"What?" Annja said. "I saw it. It was definitely human-built. It was—" She stopped, frowning. *Not a ship,* she realized with sudden shock. That quickly turned to chagrin at not seeing it earlier.

"It's a temple, Annja," Levi said. "Constructed partially out of wood, hauled painstakingly up that terrible peak for obscure but obviously powerful religious reasons."

He shrugged. "I suppose it's not any weirder than Stonehenge or the Terra-cotta Army, is it, really? And don't feel bad that we didn't figure it out earlier. We were sort of busy."

The government agent smiled. "The Anomaly is just a rock," he repeated. "Sadly, unexpectedly savage weather caused an avalanche that tragically wiped out the rest of your expedition. The world is very fortunate that Ms.

Creed and Rabbi Leibowitz survived to tell the truth about the fate of the expedition and what they found. You're both heroes."

Annja did not miss the fact that he emphasized the word *truth*.

"And that truth is what you're scheduled to tell the eager global media in a press conference tomorrow," he said. "Should anyone suggest otherwise, that will constitute an extreme breach of national security. There will be no trial. The matter will be settled covertly."

Levi shook his head in disbelief. "So the ancient Assyrian relic we brought back—excuse me, *didn't* bring back—goes where? To that warehouse where they put the Ark of the Covenant in the first Indiana Jones movie?"

The government agent swung his cocked leg back and forth. "You have a highly active imagination, Rabbi."

"But what interest could the U.S. government possibly have in keeping something like this secret?" Annja asked. "The Ark—Noah's Ark—hasn't got anything to do with national security."

"It does when the country's run by born-agains!" Levi said.

"Should that circumstance ever have pertained, Rabbi Leibowitz," the man said, calm as ever, "it no longer does, I can assure you. The inmates proved inadequate to the task of running the asylum.

"As to how such arcana impacts the nation's security, Ms. Creed, you might be surprised. Be aware that, above all, the U.S. government, in common with the other governments of the Earth, has a vested interest in maintaining order. That includes the accepted order of things. Including the public understanding of the world and how it works. That in turn encompasses large areas of scientific and, we might even say, esoteric knowledge."

"What?" Levi said. "You mean flying saucers? Cold fusion? Antigravity? This is ridiculous. You can't be serious!"

"I'll leave you now," the man said, rising. "You need to rest up for your big press conference tomorrow. In a couple of hours some of our media specialists will meet with you to help you prepare."

He left the room quietly.

When the door shut behind him Levi turned to Annja. "What are we going to say?" he pleaded.

"Whatever they want us to say," she replied dully.

"Why won't you resist them? I thought you were a fighter."

"I am when there's something worth fighting for," she said quietly.

"But the *truth*—we can get the truth out! If not at the press conference, then over the Internet!"

"No, Levi," Annja said. "Believe me. We can't."

He sank back. "You know what you're talking about, don't you?" he said weakly. "You've done this sort of thing before."

"Yes, unfortunately I have," she said.

Tears welled up in his eyes and rolled down cheeks peeling with sun and wind burn, into a beard neatly trimmed by Armenian nurses.

"So it was all in vain. Those poor deluded young men. Mr. Atabeg. Even…even the Kurds, who died for something they thought was worthwhile. All the pain. All the blood."

"No, Levi. It wasn't in vain," Annja said.

"But we failed."

"No."

Blinking away tears, he looked at her, confused.

"We went up the mountain to find something, remember?" she asked gently.

"The truth about the Anomaly." He spoke haltingly, as if he suspected some kind of verbal trap.

"Yes. And that's what we did, isn't? We learned the truth, you and I. We found it and we brought it back alive. And if we can never share it with the rest of the world—*we* know. They can never take that away from us, can they?"

He looked at her for a long moment. Then, slowly, he smiled.

"No," he said. "No, I guess they can't."

He lay back. He seemed exhausted. He probably was, given what he'd been through. For that matter, so was she. Even though she felt only a little residual pain in her right hip and ankle, suggesting those injuries had been minor, it would take time to get her strength back. She'd been right up to the edge. And as far beyond it as she ever had been before.

"Annja?" Levi said in a small voice.

"Yes, Levi?"

"If this is what victory feels like, may the Lord preserve me from ever knowing defeat."

"Amen," she said.